COCKTAILS ON THE BEACH

A CONTEMPORARY ROMANCE ANTHOLOGY

HELEN HARDT LEAH MARIE BROWN
EMKAY CONNOR LYZ KELLEY

Cocktails on the Beach
A Contemporary Romance Anthology

Helen Hardt
Leah Marie Brown
EmKay Connor
Lyz Kelley

HARDT & SONS ♥

This book is an original publication of Hardt & Sons

This is a work of fiction. Names, characters, places, and incidents either are the product of the author's imagination or are used fictitiously, and any resemblance to actual persons, living or dead, business establishments, events, or locales is entirely coincidental. The publisher does not assume any responsibility for third-party websites or their content.

Escape Copyright © 2021 Helen Hardt, LLC dba Hardt & Sons
Exes and Ohs! © Copyright 2021 Leah Marie Brown
Next Rock on the Right © Copyright 2021 EmKay Connor
Her Perfect Guy © Copyright 2021 Lyz Kelley, Belvitri LLC
Edited by Helen Hardt
Cover Design: Marci Clark, Nerdy Kat Media

All Rights Reserved
No part of this book may be reproduced, scanned, or distributed in any printed or electronic format without permission. Please do not participate in or encourage piracy of copyrighted materials in violation of the author's rights. Purchase only authorized editions.

Paperback ISBN: 978-1-952841-05-7

PRINTED IN THE UNITED STATES OF AMERICA

Created with Vellum

ESCAPE
A WOLFE ISLAND NOVELLA

Helen Hardt

To all the Wolfes of Manhattan fans... Welcome to Wolfe Island!

1

EMILY

I stop looking over my shoulder on the fourth day.

I don't notice this until the evening, when I sit down by myself at the bar. I've been at the Wolfe Island Art Colony less than a week, but until today, I've been watching my back.

When you're hiding from the devil himself, you don't let your guard down.

A second after sitting down on the wooden stool at the beachfront bar, I look behind me.

That's when I realize it's the first time I've done it today.

Whether that's good or bad, I can't say. I shouldn't be getting too comfortable.

"What'll it be, pretty girl?"

I shift my gaze toward the bartender's deep voice—

And nearly drop my jaw onto the counter. His eyes are such a gorgeous mixture of emerald and cognac. Most would simply call them hazel. I see a swirl of Prussian green and olive green with hints of Renaissance gold.

And believe it or not, those amazing eyes pale in comparison to the rest of him.

I smile shyly. I've kept to myself since I arrived on the island, spending most of my time painting the scenes outside my hut. This is the first time I've ventured to the beach.

"You going to answer me?" Hunky bartender raises his dark brown eyebrows.

"Yeah. Sorry." My cheeks burn. "Just some water, I guess."

"You guess? You can do better than that, pretty girl."

Pretty girl. The second time he's called me that in the span of two minutes. I don't feel pretty. On the outside, I suppose I'm okay. On the inside, a disaster.

"Cat still got your tongue?" He smiles a lazy smile that makes him even better looking. "Trust me?"

I part my lips and lick them. Trust him? I trust no one. *No one.* He has no idea what kind of can of worms he's opened.

"I'll take that as a yes." He reaches under the bar and pulls out a martini glass.

I hate martinis, but still I say nothing.

"Try my specialty. Virgin?"

My jaw drops. "Of course not!"

He laughs. "I mean do you want the virgin version of my specialty?"

"Oh." God, my cheeks can't get any hotter. I can only imagine what they look like in the light of the setting sun. "That's what I meant. I don't want the virgin one."

"Got it." He smiles.

Yeah, he doesn't buy it, but I give him credit for letting me try to weasel out of my embarrassment.

He turns toward the back of the bar and pulls three different bottles from the myriad options.

Three bottles? Maybe I should have gone with the virgin.

He fills a stainless steel shaker with crushed ice and adds a stream of the golden, the yellow, and the hot pink. I eye the bottle closest to me—the pink one. Crème de Noyaux. Never heard of it.

Next he adds what appears to be orange juice and then pineapple. A Mai Tai maybe? No, he said it was his specialty. Surely he didn't invent the Mai Tai. Or maybe he invented this particular version.

He adjusts the lid and shakes several times. Once he's done, he slides a slice of lime around the rim of the martini glass, dips it in sugar, and then strains the contents of the shaker into the glass.

I notice the color first. It's a lovely pinkish-orange, the shade of last night's sunset that I tried to capture on canvas but couldn't.

He pushes the drink toward me and sets a cocktail napkin next to it. "Tell me what you think."

Good enough. I inhale and pick the martini glass up by its stem. I sniff. Nice fragrance. Orangey and almondy. Very tropical.

"Well?" he says. "Are you waiting for a little umbrella?"

I can't help myself. I laugh. I laugh like I haven't in a long time, and it feels good. Really good.

"You got one?" I ask.

"Your wish is my command." He reaches under the counter and then pops a tiny pink umbrella into my drink.

If I had my phone, I'd shoot a pic and post this on Instagram.

I don't have my phone, though, and I deleted all my social media accounts.

In fact, the only person who has a clue where I am is my brother, Buck, and he's sworn to secrecy. He helped me get the invitation to the colony when I needed to leave town in a hurry. The person I'm running from can't touch Buck.

No one can.

"I'm out of dry ice. Otherwise, I'd put a tiny chunk in the drink and fog would swirl out of it."

The bartender's deep voice jolts me out of my thoughts. Just as well. I hate thinking about what brought me here. I prefer to think about why anyone else comes here—to learn, to grow, to create.

And probably to meet a gorgeous bartender with a bronze tan, broad shoulders, dark hair that falls below his ears, and eyes that seem to pierce a woman's soul. Even in the bright blue island shirt with palm trees and flamingos—this guy pulls it off as if it's this season's Armani.

"I ordered a bunch for Halloween next month," he continues. "I'm working on some great new concoctions." He eyes the drink I still haven't tasted. "What are you waiting for, pretty girl?"

I grab the stem of the glass once more and bring the drink to my lips.

Flavor explodes across my tongue. Pineapple, orange, banana, almond. And rum. A *lot* of rum. I swallow.

"Well...?" he says.

"It's delicious." I swallow again, this time against the sharpness of the alcohol.

He smiles. "Too much?"

I return his smile this time. "Nope. Just enough."

2
SCOTTY

"What's your name, pretty girl?"

I admit it. I call them all "pretty girl." This one, though, gives new meaning to the phrase. "Pretty girl" isn't nearly descriptive enough for her long dark hair, deep brown eyes, rosy cheeks, and dark pink lips. And that body...

She's tall and slim with breasts that are spilling out of her halter top.

"Emily. What's yours?"

"Keanu."

She smiles. "No shit?"

"My mom's a big fan. Plus, I'm half Hawaiian. Everyone around here calls me Scotty."

"Why?"

"That's my last name. Scott. Not Reeves."

"Ah. Got it."

"What's your last name, pretty Emily?"

She falters a moment. Then, "Smith."

Smith. Nice try. I'm more likely to believe it's Hornswoggle than Smith, especially after she stumbled.

"Okay, Emily Smith. Nice to meet you."

She clears her throat softly. "You too."

"What brings you here? Are you an artist?"

"I'm trying to be."

"This is the place for you, then. Roy and Charlie Wolfe are great. Both really talented too."

She nods. "I haven't met them yet. I just got here a few days ago."

"A few days ago? And I'm just now seeing you? Where've you been?"

"In my room, mostly."

"Emily, you've got this gorgeous island at your disposal and you've been in your room?"

"Not the whole time," she says. "But the view from my lanai is breathtaking. I've been painting it every day."

"Look around you, pretty girl. This whole *place* is breathtaking. I consider myself lucky every day that I landed this gig."

She takes another sip of the drink and winces. Yeah, it *is* pretty strong, but I've never had anyone not love it.

"What's this called?" she asks.

"It doesn't really have a name. It's just my special drink."

"Seriously? It doesn't have a name?"

"No. Why should it?"

"Because it's delicious. It should be in that book. What's it called? *The Boston Bartender*?"

"You mean *Mr. Boston Official Bartender's Guide*."

"Yeah. That one."

I laugh. "That'll be the day."

"Why not? It's wonderful."

"I'm sure it's been done before."

"I've never heard of anything called Keanu Scotty Scott's special drink."

She's got me there. "Tell you what," I say. "*You* can name the drink."

She swallows her latest sip. "Me?"

"Sure. Why not? You're the one who thinks it's supposed to have a name."

"I'll have to think on it." She takes another sip and then sets the drink down on the coaster I provided. "What's Crème de Noyaux?"

"It's a liqueur made from apricot kernels or peach and cherry pits. Which is weird, because it tastes like almonds."

"What makes it pink?"

"It's a chemical reaction from the acid in the pits when the sugars ferment into alcohol."

"Really?" She widens her eyes. "Interesting."

I smile. I've given that bogus explanation to many a female since I created the drink during my first bartending gig in Honolulu, and every single one of them has bought it. For some reason, women always want to know why the liqueur is pink.

Take that back. A chemical engineer—who was hot as hell, by the way—called me out. Other than her, though, everyone has bought it—and I still got her between the sheets.

For some reason, though, lying to Emily unnerves me. I have no idea why. Certainly not her looks. I've put one over on my share of beautiful women.

"I'm kidding," I say. "It's artificially colored."

She looks. "I suppose I might know that if I were more worldly."

"Trust me. A lot of really intelligent women have fallen for it. Doesn't mean you're not worldly."

"I'm not," she says. "At least, I don't want to be."

"Oh? What do you want to be, then?"

She sighs. "Right now? I just want to be invisible."

I shake my head and grin. "You're way too beautiful to ever be invisible."

Her cheeks redden. So do the tops of her breasts.

Damn.

"Thank you," she says finally.

"No thanks needed. You want another?" I point to her nearly empty cocktail glass.

She shakes her head. "I should probably quit while I'm ahead. I haven't eaten anything since breakfast."

"Oh? I'm just about off the clock. Want to grab dinner with me?"

The words tumbled out of my mouth before I could stop them. I've been working here for a couple months—since the colony opened. It's a dream gig, and getting involved with the colonists is probably not the best way to keep it. What am I thinking?

Easy answer. I'm thinking I might die a little if she says no.

"I should get back," she says.

"Oh. Sure. I understand."

"It's just..."

"Hey, you don't owe me any explanation, p— Emily."

She smiles then, and it's like a holiday carol. Bright and beautiful and joyous. God, what's the matter with me?

"You know what, Keanu?"

"Scotty."

"Okay." Her smile brightens further. "Scotty. I think I'd like to get some dinner. When are you off?"

I glance at my phone that's sitting on the end of the bar. "Just about...now." I was off ten minutes ago, actually, but Emily took precedence. I shove the phone in my pocket and pull my signature move.

I jump over the bar and land next to her.

"Goofball," Lyle, who's taking the next shift, says under his breath.

I ignore him. He's my pal and makes a mean drink, but he can fuck off at the moment.

I hold out my arm, and Emily pauses a second before she links her own through it.

Yeah, this beautiful woman is definitely hiding something. Maybe I'll get her to open up.

Or at least open her legs.

I wouldn't mind tapping what's between them.

Wouldn't mind that at all.

3
EMILY

"What do you feel like tonight?" Scotty asks me.

"I have no idea."

"It's mostly island food, but if you want something American, we can go to the burger bar."

Truth be told, I haven't been to any of the restaurants here at the colony. I've either ordered room service or had food delivered beachside when I left the room to attend a class. Now, I'm a little freaked.

"A burger's fine."

"A burger it is, then." We step up to the burger bar. It's not a bar so much as a sit-down place with tables. All the eateries here at the colony are outdoor, covered in thatch roofing, of course, in case of rain, which sometimes occurs in the afternoons. Still, it's always so warm that having no walls doesn't matter.

A scantily clad hostess takes us to a table for two. "Your server will be with you in a minute."

"What's your pleasure?" Scotty picks up the menu on the side of the table.

"Just a basic burger."

"Cheese?"

"No. I'm one of those weird people who doesn't like cheese on a burger." True story. It takes away from the flavor of the meat, in my opinion.

"Heathen!" He smiles.

"Hey, Scotty." A nice-looking man in an island print shirt—this one yellow with tropical flowers, and even louder than Scotty's—and surf shorts struts up. "Who's your friend?"

"Hey, Nemo. This is Emily."

"You an artist?" Nemo asks.

I nod. "I try to be."

"Welcome. When did you arrive?"

"Four days ago."

"Really? Most people from the states can't wait to try the burgers here."

I have no idea what to say, so I say nothing.

"I'll have the usual," Scotty says, nodding to me.

"What's the usual?" I ask.

Nemo laughs. "You don't want to know!"

I raise my eyebrows at Scotty.

"The staff makes fun of me. It's a double, medium rare, with horseradish cheddar, green chili sauce, and a fried egg."

"Ugh." I twist my lips into a grimace.

"Don't knock it till you've tried it," Scotty laughs.

"I don't do eggs," I tell him. "They're gross."

"That's it." Scotty shakes his head with another smile. "It's over between us."

It's a joke, I know, but still warmth creeps to my cheeks. I didn't come here to have a fling. I came here to...

God. So don't want to think about that at the moment.

"I'll have a single, medium, with lettuce, tomato, and pickle."

"One basic American, sans cheese." Nemo scribbles on his pad.

"That's me," I say. "Just a basic American."

"Pretty girl"—Scotty smiles—"there's nothing basic about you that I can see."

Basic. Such an innocuous word. What I wouldn't give to actually be a basic American at the moment. Just another girl no one notices.

Invisible.

Invisibility has its perks.

"So here we are," Scotty says, after Nemo leaves, "one Scotty and one basic American."

"Your burger is called the Scotty?"

"Sure is. No one else orders it."

"Shocking." I take a drink of the water Nemo left for us.

He laughs.

"So the burger you invented has a name, but your special drink doesn't?"

"Yup."

"That makes no sense at all."

"Just never found the right name," he says, "and now I know why. You were meant to name it, pretty girl."

I swallow another drink of water.

Feelings bubble inside me. Feelings I don't want to have. I came here to escape. To be invisible. The last thing I need is to start down this road.

Scotty's probably just being nice. He's a bartender on a tropical island, for God's sake. He probably beds someone new each week. Each day, even.

I clear my throat. "How long have you been tending bar?"

"Here? Just since the colony opened a few months ago. Before that I was at a resort on Fiji."

"And you're from Honolulu?"

He nods. "Born and raised. My mom's a native, and my dad's a fighter pilot from LA."

LA. I don't mean to react, but my facial muscles tighten.

"Where are you from, pretty girl?"

"Portland," I lie. I don't want anyone to know I'm from LA. I've escaped LA, at least for now.

"Portland, Oregon?"

"You know another one?"

He laughs. "No."

"Yes. Portland, Oregon."

"Tell me about the Pacific Northwest. I've only been to California. And to Florida once when I was a kid."

"You didn't travel much outside the islands?"

He shakes his head. "Nope. I'm an island boy through and through. We traveled to Cali once in a blue moon to see my dad's folks, but mostly they came to us. People love to visit Hawaii, for some reason."

"I can't imagine why." Especially if all the men look like him.

"Big tourist trap if you ask me. Once you do Diamond Head and the Pearl Harbor thing, there's not much to do except lounge on the beach."

"I think that's probably the point," I say.

"I suppose. When you grow up there, it's not nearly as exciting."

"Really? If that's the case, why are you working on another beach?"

He laughs. Really laughs this time, like I've just said something hilarious during a standup routine.

"You got me, pretty girl. I'm a beach bum through and through."

"So you can't fault others for wanting just a taste of that life, then."

"I don't. It's just... I don't know. Every once in a while I wonder if there's more out there for me, you know?"

"Why bartending?" I ask.

"Why not?"

I shake my head and swallow another drink of water. "Are you ever serious about anything?"

"Sure I am. I seriously think you're the most beautiful woman I've seen since I got here. And this is a tropical island, pretty girl. I may have only been here for a few months, but gorgeous women are at a premium."

"At an art colony?"

"Sure. Some of the artists. And the women who work here. I swear Roy Wolfe only hired good-looking people."

"I think you just gave yourself a huge compliment," I can't help saying.

"I'm talking about the female population," he says, "but hey, if the shoe fits."

I laugh. Truly laugh.

And I realize Keanu Scotty Scott is the first person who's made me do that in…how long?

A long time.

A long, long time.

4

SCOTTY

Nemo drops off our order.

"Dig in," I say to Em.

Already she's Em to me. Em or pretty girl. Emily is too stuffed-shirt a name for this dark-haired beauty. She's Em, the goddess of art. Is there even a goddess of art? Probably somewhere in Greek or Roman mythology, but I don't have a clue.

Only one goddess in front of me. Em.

She picks up her burger carefully and takes a bite. "Oh!" Grease runs down her chin.

"Forgot to mention. These are the juiciest burgers ever."

She wipes her mouth with her napkin. "I see."

"Burgers are an American thing," I say, "but I swear Diego does them better than anyone in the states. Not that I'd know, since I haven't been there in forever."

"Diego?"

"He's the chef here."

"Of all the food?"

"Just this place. Burgers are his specialty. He's a master."

"I'll say." She swallows and wipes her lips again. "This is delicious."

I take a bite of my Scotty classic. To make Em feel better, I let the juice and egg yolk drip from my lips a little before I clear it away with my napkin. Honestly, the dripping's the best part. Seems to make me enjoy the food even more.

"Tell me your life story," I say.

She flinches a little. Only a little, but I notice. I notice everything about her. The curve of her jawline. The one freckle on her upper lip. The way her left eye squints slightly when she smiles.

"Not much to tell," she finally replies.

"How did you end up here?"

"I'm an artist. This is what I do."

"I get that, but most people pay a lot to be here. You must be a successful artist."

She flinches just a little once more. Then, "I do okay."

"Yeah?"

"But I'm not paying to be here," she says. "A fellowship opened up, and I got it."

"Good for you! You must be uber talented, then."

She takes another bite of her burger and chews. And chews. The meat and bun must be masticated into mash by the time she swallows. "Like I said, I do okay."

I swallow a drink of my water. "What are you hiding, pretty girl?"

"Nothing," she says way too quickly, dropping her gaze.

Nothing my ass. But I won't push it. Not my business. I don't have to know her life story to get her in the sack.

Except that I *want* to know her life story. Already I'm feeling a connection that's new to me. New...and a little frightening. But I've never been one to back down in the face of fear.

"Tell me about your work," I say.

"Modern, mostly. Oils. But since I've been here, I've been concentrating on the beauty of my surroundings. The colors are so vivid and bright. I swear, sunrises and sunsets don't look this way in El— Portland."

"Not with all that smog," I agree, deciding consciously not to comment on her stumble.

"I've started three different projects just from the view of my lanai," she continues. "I love mixing color, and these are some new shades I've never worked with before. Plus all the flora. Tropical flowers are something else. And everything's so green! Even the palm trees are greener than the ones at home."

"Are they?"

"They seem to be. To me, at least."

Her eyes light up when she speaks of color. Not surprising, given she's an artist. But I can't help but notice the light in those gorgeous browns is short-lived.

Yup, definitely hiding something.

"You want to take a walk on the beach after dinner?" I ask.

"Don't you have to go back to the bar?"

"Nope. I work days. Nine to four with a half hour for lunch."

"People drink that early?"

"Some do. We also have an awesome juice bar. You should come by in the morning and I'll make you one of my special blends."

She smiles. "You have a specialty for just about everything, huh?"

"Not going to lie. I do." I polish off the rest of my burger.

Em's sits half-eaten on her plate.

"Not hungry?" I ask.

"I am, and it's delicious. It's just so big."

"I guess I should have warned you. The single is a half-pound of meat."

Her eyes go wide. "You just ate a pound of beef!"

"Nah. The doubles are made with third-pound burgers. Though I could easily put away a pound."

She rakes her gaze over me. "How do you eat like that and stay in such great shape?"

I waggle my eyebrows. "Like what you see?"

She blushes. Adorably. Man, she's fucking hot.

"I'd say yes," she says, "but I'm pretty sure you turn on the charm with every woman who sidles up to your bar."

She's not wrong. "Maybe. They don't all get a dinner invitation, though."

"Dinner's free," she says. "The colony is all inclusive."

"So it is. But, pretty girl, I'd gladly take you out and pay for the finest dinner on the island. We'd have to go across to the resort, though, and it doesn't open for another month."

She blushes even redder. "I don't know what you're after, Scotty, but I'm pretty sure I don't have it."

"Who says I'm after anything?"

"I know the type. I'm from LA, remember? You're a typical beach bum who beds a new woman every week. I'm not gunning to become a notch on your bedpost."

Yeah. I've heard those words before. Many times. And almost every time, I've gotten the woman who uttered them into my bed despite her protestations. But that's not what concerns me at the moment. This wasn't a mere stumble. I raise an eyebrow. "LA? Not Portland?"

Her cheeks turn crimson and she drops her gaze to her unfinished burger.

"Why'd you lie, Em?"

She twists her lips and then finally lifts her head to meet my gaze. "I'm sorry. I..."

"It's okay," I say. "You don't have to explain."

"No. I do, actually. I got too comfortable too quickly. I let my guard down. I shouldn't even be here talking to you." She stands.

I rise as well. "Sit, Em. Please. It's okay. I'm not angry at you for lying. And if you can't let your guard down here, on a beautiful island, I don't know where you can."

"I can't," she says. "Not here. Not anywhere."

She's frightened. The fear rolls off her in waves.

I could walk away. Easy. Walk away from whatever she's carrying around.

Except I don't want to.

Is it the fact that she's hot? No. She's far from the only hot woman available at the colony. No, it runs deeper. She's hiding something, and I find myself caring about it.

About her.

5
EMILY

"About that walk on the beach?" Scotty says.

I shouldn't have lied to him, but I was trying to maintain distance. That didn't work out so well. Already Scotty has me feeling too comfortable. Giddy, even. Like I've had a couple drinks, except it's been over an hour since my Scotty special at the bar.

Maybe Lucifer won't find me here. Maybe I truly am safe.

I shudder without meaning to.

Just his name—Lucifer. He's not actually the devil, of course, but Lucifer *is* his real name. Lucifer Charles Ashton III. Yes, he's the third in his line to actually bear the first name Lucifer.

And boy, has he lived up to the name.

He's known in the LA underground as Lucifer Raven. Ironically, he's blond, but despite his coloring, he's full of darkness.

I was seduced by that darkness. By his power. By his seductive male beauty and his lavish gifts.

I let myself get comfortable, painting in my room. When I went to the bar earlier and met Scotty, I realized I hadn't looked over my shoulder at all today.

Until now.

A walk on the beach...

The gorgeous white sand beach beckoned from the moment I arrived. Artists with easels sat on their portable stools painting all day and even continued after the sun went down.

I've ventured to the beach exactly twice for classes, ordering a quick sandwich and throwing a few strokes on canvas, until that niggling on the back of my neck got unbearable, and I left. I've painted mostly from my lanai. I haven't taken advantage of this beautiful place, but I have my reasons.

One reason, actually.

A reason that wants me back in LA. Either back in LA, at his side...

Or dead.

Damn! Where is that easy relaxation I felt only hours ago sitting at the bar with Scotty?

"You going to answer me?" he finally says.

I inhale. The beach. I'm here, at the colony. Who wouldn't want to walk on the beach? I could feign illness, but he just watched me eat. Besides, I like Scotty. I don't want to tell him a little white lie, especially after my first one blew up in my face.

I don't want to tell him *any* lies, which is why I shouldn't talk to him at all.

"I'm kind of tired," I say. A little white lie after all. So much for that plan.

"It's seven o'clock."

"Yeah, but I'm still on LA time. We're five hours behind here. Plus, jet lag and all."

"Didn't you get here three days ago? Or was it four?"

I let out a huff. "For God's sake, Scotty. I'm not interested. Okay?" Yeah, the lies are just rolling out of my mouth now.

"I call bullshit," he says.

"Call it whatever you want. I didn't come here to hook up. I came here to—"

"To hide," he finishes for me.

"To *paint*. I came here to paint."

"Then why'd you show up at the beach bar?" he asks.

I don't have an answer. At least not one that makes sense.

"Just felt like a drink." I shrug.

"And then you accepted my invitation to dinner."

"A girl's got to eat."

"I see." He sighs. "Okay, I get it."

I nod. "Thanks for dinner. And the drink." Though he didn't pay for either. The art colony is all-inclusive.

"No sweat off my back."

"Yeah. I suppose not. So I'll see you around?"

"I'm sure you will. I work here."

I've upset him. And the truth is, I really do want to go on a walk with him. I like this guy. I wasn't sure I ever wanted to like a guy again, but Scotty wormed his way under my skin in record time.

And boy, is he good-looking. The best-looking guy I've seen in a while, and I'm used to LA beach boys. They don't come hotter than that.

Except here on Wolfe Island, apparently.

"You know what?" I say. "Let's live in the moment."

"Baby, that's what I always do."

"Let's take that walk. It's just a walk, right?"

"It's whatever you want it to be."

I cock my head. "You'll be okay if it's just a walk?"

"Em, listen to me. You're beautiful. If I tell you I'm not attracted to you, you won't believe me. Would I love to watch the sunrise with you? Hell, yeah. I'm human. But I'm also not a damned rapist. Sometimes a cigar is just a cigar. Sometimes a walk is just a walk."

Crap. Now I've pissed him off.

"Freud," I say.

"What about him?"

"Your cigar comment. It's attributed to Sigmund Freud."

He nods. "I majored in psychology."

I stifle my surprise. "You went to college?"

"What? You think a beach bum like me is automatically not educated?"

"No. I didn't mean—"

"That's exactly what you meant."

I sigh. He's right. I can't get out of this. "I'm sorry I misjudged you."

"University of Hawaii," he says. "Magna cum laude, even."

"Did you ever consider…"

"Doing something besides bartending? Of course I did. But I love what I do. I can live on the beach, make some great dough. Plus, I invested in a buddy's tech startup back in school. It gives me a nice little side income."

"Cool." Cool? *Really, Em?* He just told you he's not a beach bum loser, and you say cool?

"How about you? How'd you end up here, pretty girl?"

"I told you. A fellowship."

"I don't want the canned response. I want the truth."

My mouth drops open.

I want to tell him. I want to tell him everything. Dare I?

"Art school," I finally reply. "Art school at UCLA. I've sold a few pieces, but it takes a while to get a name in art, even in LA, where up-and-coming celebrities throw money at art—and new artists—just to look like they're cultured. So I wait tables on the side."

Not a total lie. That was my life *before* Lucifer.

"How old are you?" he asks.

"Twenty-six. You?"

"Twenty-five." He smiles. "That makes me your cub."

I smile despite myself. This man makes me feel good. Really good.

And boy, it's been a while since I've felt good.

"Sometimes a walk is just a walk," I say.

"True enough."

"So let's go." I grab his hand.

It's warm in mine.

And it feels nice. Really nice.

6

SCOTTY

I'm not the kind of guy who wears his heart on his sleeve, or even believes in any of that mushy stuff, but damn... Em's hand in mine shoots a spark through me that I feel all the way to my toes. And specifically in one other place that's become pretty darned attentive at the moment.

"If you love the sunset from your lanai," I say, "you won't believe how gorgeous it is out here when we're walking on the beach."

Em looks to the west, where the sun is just getting ready to meet the horizon. "Tangerine. Sort of. With an element of fuchsia. How can the sun be a different color here?"

"Because there isn't any smog to take away from its beauty."

"I suppose, but I've been to Hawaii before. Sorry, but this is different."

"Parts of Hawaii are pretty industrialized," I tell her. "Honolulu, for example, and Hilo on the Big Island. Sure, you can probably see things a lot better than you can in LA, but this island is in a category of its own."

She sighs. "It sure is. When I see beauty like this..."

"What?"

"Oh, nothing."

"Come on. Tell me. This is a walk on the gorgeous beach at sunset. Almost a prerequisite to share your feelings."

She looks toward the west once more. "I almost feel like this place can absorb all the negativity in the world, you know? Like nothing bad can ever happen here."

I squeeze her hand. Clearly she doesn't know the history of this island. The Wolfe family covered it up as best they could, but some of us still got wind of it when we got here to begin work. I'm not going to be the one to shatter Em's illusions. No reason at all to tell her this island used to be a private resort where men could pay to hunt women as if they were prey. Where women were abducted and held captive and subjected to the sadistic fantasies of sociopathic multi-millionaires.

I say only, "It's a gorgeous place, for sure."

"It almost makes me feel..."

"...safe?" I finish for her.

She turns to me, her eyes troubled. "Yes, safe. But I mean that in a purely hypothetical way."

Sure, she does. I don't want to push, but I desperately want to know what Em's hiding. I want to help her, which is odd, as I barely know her. What is she running from? And why? Who would want to hurt this angel?

"Tell me something about yourself," I say. "Something no one else knows."

She wrinkles her brow. "Like what?"

"I don't know. I'm not asking for any deep, dark secret. Just something no one else knows about you. It can be a freckle on your ass, for all I care."

She rolls her eyes. "My ass is free from freckles, thanks."

"Something else, then."

She nods. "How about this? You go first, since this is your idea."

I inhale. "All right. I once had a threesome."

She laughs. "Only once?"

I stop walking. "Yeah, only once. Not exactly the reaction I expected."

"Most lotharios like you have had a few threesomes. It's the island mentality, right? Island time and all that?"

"First...lothario?"

"It means womanizer."

"I know what it means. Not a dumbass beach bum, remember? I just didn't realize we were in the nineteenth century. Also, it implies that I'm selfish in my seduction of women. I can assure you that isn't the case."

"Oh. I didn't mean to imply—"

"Actually, you did. You absolutely meant to imply that I'm some kind of ruthless seducer of women who cares only for his own pleasure. I guarantee you both the women in my threesome were well taken care of."

She's quiet for a moment, and she releases my hand. "I'm screwing this up, aren't I?"

I grab her hand again. "I think you deserve another chance."

"You're serious, then?"

"About only having one threesome? Of course."

"No, I mean you're serious that no one else knows you had the threesome? Because there are at least two others who know."

I can't help a laugh. "You're right. I did bend the rules. The two women know, but no one else does, at least not from me. I don't kiss and tell, despite what you may think about lotharios like me."

She looks down at the sand. "I shouldn't have said that."

"No, you shouldn't have. Look. I like women. I like sex. I'm not ashamed of that."

"I never said you should be."

"I suppose you didn't. Now, you owe me a response. Tell me

something no one knows about you. Or no more than two people, I guess." I smiled.

She pauses a moment. Then, "No one knows I'm here."

"Here on the beach?"

"Here. On the island."

"Not true," I say. "*I* know you're here. Everyone else on the island knows you're here."

"I mean—"

I touch my finger to her lips. "Shh. I know what you mean. I know you're running, Em."

"I'm not—"

I cup her soft cheek and bring my lips to hers. Yes, I'm shutting her up, because she's lying to me and I don't want her to do that.

But I also desperately want to kiss her.

I slide my lips gently over hers, probing the seam with my tongue. A few seconds pass, but then she sighs and parts her lips.

I dive in, finding her silky tongue, and though I'm aching to kiss her deeply, I take it slowly and gently, melting into her mouth.

Yes, slow and sweet and—

She cups my cheeks harshly. *She* deepens the kiss. *Her*. Em.

I respond with vigor, delving as deeply as I can into her with my lips and tongue. She's warm and inviting, and she tastes like hamburgers and mint, which is suddenly my favorite flavor in the world.

And I realize I'll do anything to get this woman in my bed.

Tonight.

7
EMILY

This kiss...
I knew it would happen. Expected it, even.
But this...

Scotty's kiss is unlike any other kiss I've experienced...and I've been with some expert kissers.

Scotty, though, has made kissing into an art—and I love art.

Not just painting, which is my preferred medium, but all art. Sculpture, poetry, music...and kissing.

His tongue is velvet against mine, his lips full and soft. I scrape my fingers over his dark stubble and then wrap my arms around his neck, pulling him closer to me.

Our bodies are melded together now, and my nipples harden, press into his chest. I kiss him more deeply, until—

He pulls away.

My fingers go absently to my lips. What just happened?

"My place?" he says.

He wants to get me in the sack. Of course he does. He's a beach bum lothario.

What's holding me back? Lucifer and I are over, despite what he thinks. And Scotty...

I want Scotty. If he's this good at kissing, he's got to be amazing at everything else.

My whole body is on fire, but… "I can't."

He nods. "I understand."

Except he doesn't. He thinks I don't want him. The fact is, I don't want to pull him into my drama.

Because Lucifer *will* find me.

It's only a matter of when.

This beautiful island may be off his radar for now, but he'll find it.

You'll never escape me, Emily. You're mine. Mine to do with what I want.

Even now, so close to Scotty, Lucifer's low voice haunts me.

Scotty grabs my hand. "I'll walk you back to your room."

"But…"

"But what?" He turns and meets my gaze.

My God, his eyes are something out of a Renaissance painting. Are they brown? Green? Golden? They change, according to the angle, according to the light.

"You promised me a walk on the beach. Or did you really mean a walk to your bed?" I smile, hoping he can take the joke.

"I'm not going to lie, pretty girl. I want to make love to you. Desperately."

Desperately.

I need you desperately, Emily.

Lucifer was fond of that word.

"I didn't come here for that," I say.

"Why did you come here, then?"

"To paint," I say too quickly. "Why does anyone come here?"

He touches my cheek. Just a flutter of a touch, but I feel it intensely between my legs. A small sigh escapes my throat.

"I think it's more than that," Scotty says softly. "It's written all over your face. Your eyes, especially."

Emily

"Oh? What do you see in my eyes?"

"I see desire, Em. I see passion. But I also see fear."

"You can see all that? From a major in psychology?"

He trails his finger over the shell of my ear, pushing my hair back. "I can see all that because I'm interested in you. In what makes you tick."

"You're interested in getting me on my back," I say.

He chuckles, shaking his head. "You do have a one-track mind."

"*I* have a one-track mind? You already admitted it."

"I did, so why are you the one who keeps bringing it up?"

My cheeks burn. He makes a good point, which pisses me off. Because the truth is, I want nothing more than to get between the sheets with this gold medal kisser. I want to lose myself in his magnificent body, underneath his magnificent tongue.

"Let's just finish our walk," I say, without looking into his eyes again.

Those eyes—they're hypnotic. If I look again, I fear I'll melt into a puddle of honey, and he'll scoop me up and take me to his place.

Which is what I want now more than my next breath of air.

"Good enough." He flips off his slides and picks them up. "Let's try the water."

I look down at my dress. "In this?"

"Just wading in the sand."

"What about jellyfish?"

"You see any?" He gestures.

I don't. Not like the beaches in LA sometimes. I've gotten used to always wearing flip-flops on the sand.

"The beach guys are good about letting us know if we need shoes. We haven't had a jellyfish invasion since I've been here."

I wiggle out of my flip-flops and step into the sand, letting it squish between my toes. I laugh. Actually laugh!

"What?" Scotty asks.

"It just feels good. Sand between my toes, like when I was a little kid. I'd almost forgotten."

"You're from the California coast, and you've forgotten sand between your toes? We need to take care of that!"

I gasp as he swoops me into his arms and carries me toward the water. "What are you doing?"

"Showing you what's important in life."

Scotty carries me to the water's edge, but he keeps going. Soon he's nearly up to his knees in the water.

"You wouldn't," I say.

"Want to bet?"

In the next second, I'm tumbling into the water, splashing.

"That's a risky game," I say, spitting out salt water. "What if I couldn't swim?"

"The water's two feet deep, pretty girl. You aren't in any danger of drowning."

Except I am.

Scotty just doesn't know it.

8

SCOTTY

Em looks far from happy. The dunking was a mistake. A big one.

"Hey," I say, pushing her damp hair behind her ears. "I'm sorry."

"It's okay. You were just having fun."

"Yeah, the operative word being 'you.' I thought it'd be fun for both of us."

"How in the world is a dunking fun for me?" She shakes her head.

"Tell you what." I grin. "I'll dunk myself, and then we're even."

I dash into the water and dive in. Though the water's warm, it's still a welcome respite to the tropical humidity. It douses the perspiration from my body as I swim, the water so clear that I see the wonder of the Aquarian wildlife.

When I finally come up for air, I'm a good hundred feet away from shore.

I wave at Em, who looks gorgeous with her wet halter and skirt clinging to her amazing body.

She smiles.

And I feel like I've won the fucking lottery.

Does this mean she forgives me? I swim freestyle back to the shore.

She's laughing.

Nice.

Very nice.

"Are we even now?" I ask.

"Except you went into the water of your own volition," she says. "I didn't get a choice."

"I'd have let you throw me in, but I'm a little bit heavier than you are."

She shakes her head. "Is there anything you won't do?"

"A few things," I say.

"Like what?"

"Hmm... Here's a good one. I won't eat goat cheese."

"Yuck! Me neither."

"This is so meant to be," I tell her.

"Yeah, that's what I'm looking for in a man. A mutual hatred of goat cheese."

"You found him!"

She shakes her head, smiling again. Trying not to laugh. Her lips are quivering.

"Why, Em?" I ask.

"Why what?"

"Why are you so determined not to succumb to my obvious charms?"

She looks to the sky, smiling, and then she meets my gaze. "If only..."

"If only...what?" I narrow the distance between us, my toes sinking in the wet sand.

"Nothing."

I cup her cheek. Man, her skin is soft. Like freaking silk. "It's not nothing. Tell me."

"I hardly know you."

"You know about as much about me as anyone. More, even. Most people here don't know I went to college."

"Why not?"

"Because I don't talk about myself a lot."

Her eyebrows nearly fly off her forehead. "Really? You? A bartender? You haven't stopped talking since we met."

"It's what bartenders do, Em. We talk to customers about what they want to talk about, not about ourselves."

Her forehead wrinkles when I say Em.

"You don't like Em?" I say.

"I like it, actually," she says. "My brother calls me Em."

"You have a brother, then?"

"Yeah. Just one. No sisters."

"What's his name?"

"Buck. Buck Moreno."

"So he's a half-brother, then?"

"No, why?"

I grin. "I thought your last name was Smith. Don't tell me you're married!"

She reddens. I mean *really* reddens. Like I totally want to see how far down that rosiness goes.

"Not married," she says. "Divorced."

"Ah..." I smile.

I'm not buying that lie either, but I'll let her remain a mystery for a few more minutes.

But only a few more minutes.

Because after those minutes pass, I'm going to kiss her again. Then I'm going to take her to my hut and fuck her silly.

If there was ever a woman who needed a good fuck, it's Emily Smith Moreno.

"Scotty..." she begins.

"Yeah?"

"I'm not divorced."

I drop my jaw in mock surprise.

"And my name is Emily Moreno, not Emily Smith."

"You've been lying to me?" More mock surprise. "Not just about Portland and your last name?"

"Yeah, but I have reasons. Really good reasons."

"Which are...?"

"I can't tell you," she says. "I can only tell you that it has nothing to do with you. I...like you."

"I like you too, Em." I thumb her lower lip. "And you can tell me. You can trust me."

She scoffs softly. "I've been burned by those words before."

"By the person you're hiding from?"

She bites her lower lip then. "I have to go. Back to the hut. I'm... I'm tired."

I should let her go.

She's got baggage, this one, and if there's one thing a beach bum like me doesn't need, it's baggage. I love the carefree life. I love being as free as the soft wind that blows on the island.

I love my life.

Right. Let her go, Scotty. Let. Her. Go.

I grip her shoulders and kiss her again.

9
―――
EMILY

His lips are so firm on mine, and again, I want to give in to the kiss, let him take me away and forget everything I'm dealing with.

His tongue tangles with mine as he deepens the kiss, and a raw growl emanates from his chest into mine.

How easy it would be to allow this... To fully escape the ties that bind me to LA.

To Lucifer Raven.

What if Buck can't stop him?

What if he finds me?

Buck has the Wolfes behind him, But Lucifer...

Lucifer has his father's money—not Wolfe money by a long shot, but still enough to do as he chooses. And Lucifer has something that Buck and the Wolfes don't have.

He's obsessed with me.

He'll do anything to get me back.

All my energy is required to push Scotty away. Our kiss breaks with a pop of suction.

His green-gold eyes are burning. On fire, even. They pierce me, and I swear I can feel the scorch on my flesh.

"Em..." he growls.

"I'm sorry, Scotty. I'm so sorry." I turn and run away from him.

Or attempt to. Running on sand is difficult. I should be used to it, being from LA beach country, but I nearly stumble.

Scotty catches up to me, grabs my shoulders again, and whips me around to face him.

"Em," he says, "you've got to let me help you."

"You can't help me." I wipe what might turn into a tear away from my eye. "No one can."

"You're wrong."

I look to the sky, dragging my fingers through my tangled hair. "God, I wish I were!"

He cups my cheek, rubbing his thumb over my bottom lip again. Just his touch sends me reeling. Such a loving touch—a touch meant to spark desire in me.

It does that and more.

"What if I stop the lothario routine," he says. "What if I take you to my place and we talk. Just talk."

I can't help myself. I roll my eyes. "You've been coming on to me all evening, and you think I'm going to fall for the 'let's just talk' line? I'm not that innocent or gullible, Scotty."

He gazes at me, and his eyes—those gorgeous eyes—narrow slightly. Only slightly, and his lips curve downward.

Is he upset? Upset that he won't be bedding me, most likely.

"Em," he says, "it's not a line. I want to help, but it's clear that you don't want my help. I'll walk you back to your hut."

"It's okay," I say. "Please. I don't want to be any more of a spectacle than I've already made myself." I walk off the beach and onto the boardwalk that leads to the colonists' huts.

I don't expect him to follow me. It's still light out, and this place is safe anyway.

At least until Lucifer finds me.

I get to my hut and unlock the door. As I walk in, I look over my shoulder.

Scotty is ten feet away.

He *did* follow me. He sure was quiet about it. It was sweet, too, for him to make sure I got back safely while honoring my request not to be a spectacle.

Walking with the best-looking man on this island would definitely make me a spectacle.

Being a spectacle is not a good way to stay invisible.

Not a good way at all.

BUCK TAUGHT me how to pick locks when I was sixteen. He's six years older than I am, and he'd just returned from Navy SEAL training. I remember being surprised at how simple it was.

"Practice," Buck said. "Practice a lot until it's second nature to you. You never know when you might need the skill." He gave me a lock-picking wrench before he left for his first assignment.

I no longer had the lock-picking kit. I lost it on the beach one day when I was showing it to a friend. Just as well. If I'd had it when I hooked up with Lucifer, he'd have found it when he confiscated all my stuff. Then he'd have known I could pick locks.

That's how I escaped from Lucifer.

It was simple luck that he forgot to turn the deadbolt that day. I'd stolen a couple paperclips from a pile of documents several weeks earlier, and I'd pretty much given up hope.

Until that day.

That day when he forgot to lock the deadbolt.

I knew as soon as he left.

The soft click of the lock on the doorknob, and then the louder click of the deadbolt.

Only the soft click that day.

The lock I could easily pick.

I waited a few minutes. I had to make sure he was gone. But after twenty minutes passed, I didn't dare wait any longer. I had no idea when he'd come back, and I wanted to be long gone by then.

I straightened the paperclips each into one long wire and began.

I inserted one wire into the bottom of the keyhole and applied a little pressure. The other went in at the top of the keyhole. I scrubbed the top wire back and forth while I applied more pressure. My heart jumped when the first pin clicked into place.

Ten minutes later, I turned the doorknob.

I was familiar with Lucifer's place. It was a beachfront house on a private beach with lots of security.

Security wasn't a problem for me either. I'd spent the last several weeks studying the system. Lucifer never let me watch when he keyed in the code, but each number had a certain sound. I'd memorized the sounds and the position of his hands.

Yeah, that's how badly I wanted out of there.

This man.

This man who, when I met him, I thought could be the one.

He was gorgeous and brilliant and rich.

He was also domineering and arrogant and tyrannical.

He was born into money, but once I got deep into his world, I found out he didn't depend on family money.

Lucifer made his money in drugs.

The underground drug trade on the streets of LA.

Once I knew too much, he started locking me up.

"It's because I love you," he'd say. "I want to keep you safe."

I believed him at first. Actually believed him! I was clouded by lust and by love.

Once he realized he could control me, he became even more autocratic.

Though he denied it, I was essentially his slave.

Now, I was free!

I disarmed the security system and left the house.

I left the house!

The first time I'd left the place without Lucifer since I moved in over a year prior.

I had no phone, no money, and only the clothes on my back.

But I had the will. The will to escape.

I also knew how to get off the property without being seen. I'd studied the video feeds Lucifer kept.

I knew how to get off his property undetected.

Once I was safely off his land, I found a crowded beach where no one would recognize me.

A lovely woman with two kids lounged near the lifeguard.

"Excuse me, ma'am. I'm so sorry, but my purse got stolen, and I need to call my brother to come get me. Could I borrow your phone?"

"Of course." She smiled and handed me her cell phone.

"Thank you. I'll only be a minute." I walked away so I could talk in private.

One call.

To Buck.

That's all it took.

Three hours later, I was on a plane to Wolfe Island.

10

SCOTTY

I followed her.

This island is safe, but still... She's so scared of something or someone, so I wanted to make sure she got to her hut safely.

Damn.

Horny and off the clock. Not such a problem when you're on an island of lovelies.

Except only one woman invades my mind.

Em, with her long dark hair, her searing brown eyes, her milky skin.

Normally I'd hang at the beach or at the bar, people watching, conversing, probably picking up a woman. Usually a staffer. Bedding the art colonists is pretty frowned upon, though I'll admit I've done it a time or two. Or three.

My buddy Lyle is tending bar, so I pony up and take the last available stool next to Nemo, our server from the burger bar. He and Lyle are also my roommates. Well, not roommates so much as suitemates. Staffers share huts, but we each have our own bedroom, which is cool. I'm four years out of college and totally over the "hang a sock on the door if you've got a girl inside" days.

Lyle's a blond surfer boy from LA but Nemo's half Hawaiian like I am. He looks the part more than I do, though—black hair and dark brown eyes, tan skin. I got my dad's hazel eyes and slightly fairer skin. The three of us have kind of become known among the staffers as the Island lotharios, to use Em's word.

"You too, Scotty?" Lyle says, sliding an ice water in front of me. "What are the two most eligible beach bums doing here at the bar when you could be hooking up? What happened to that gorgeous hunkette you were with when you got off duty?"

"She's tired. Went back to her hut."

Lyle erupts into boisterous laughter. "You couldn't seal the deal, huh?"

"You mean the chick you had dinner with?" Nemo asks. "Man, she's a hottie."

A hottie? A hunkette? Words I've used to describe women many times, but coming from the mouths of Lyle and Nemo, they seem immature and patronizing. I vow never to use them again.

"She's got class," I say.

"Too much class to hook up with the likes of you, huh?" Nemo punches my upper arm.

I love these guys, I do, but man, are hookups all they think about?

I can't escape the irony of my thought.

Hookups are all I thought about until this evening. In fact, I was damned determined to get Em between the sheets.

I let her go.

Sure, I can say it was her obvious baggage, and that's probably part of it.

But it's way more than that.

I let her needs take precedence over my own. She wasn't ready to be with me, so I let her go. I didn't press her. Normally, I press a little more. I never force a woman, of course, but I can be very persuasive.

"Her name's—" I stop.

She's hiding. She probably doesn't want her name spread everywhere.

"What?" Nemo asks. "What's her name?"

"She wouldn't tell me."

"Easy enough to find out. I can get the guest list from Manuel. Which hut is she in?"

For God's sake. He's right. Any staffer can find out who she is. "Emily," I say. "Her name's Emily. And the two of you keep your hands to yourselves."

"Why the 'she wouldn't tell me' thing, then?" Nemo asks.

"She's trying to keep to herself," I say. "I don't want you guys bugging her."

"Dude," Lyle says, "if you like her, we'll stay away. Buddies' rule book and all. Bros before hoes."

"Would you stop saying that?" I give him an evil eye. "It's degrading."

"I gotta agree, Lyle," Nemo adds.

"Okay, okay." Lyle straightens his posture. "Buds before chicks. Is that better?"

"Slightly," I say. "Not really."

"You've got it bad," Lyle says, mixing a drink for a colonist. "Friends before women. Does that work for you?"

I take a sip of water. "I do like her. Thanks."

"I'm off in thirty," Lyle says. "Siri and Angel are having a beach party on the staffer beach. Somehow they got their hands on a couple kegs. We should go."

"That's where I'm headed," Nemo agrees.

"A kegger, guys? Really?" I shake my head.

"Since when are you too good for a kegger?"

"I'm not. It's just..."

"It's just your fantasy woman won't be there," Nemo says. "Am I right?"

"So invite her," Lyle says.

"To a staff party? I don't think so. I don't need to get my ass fired for fraternizing."

"You already had dinner with her," Nemo reminds me.

Good point. We're actually supposed to mingle with the guests. It's encouraged. Roy and Charlie Wolfe want this place to seem like a home away from home for the artists. A place where they can study their craft and also have a luxury island experience. Meet people, know the staff members who are helping to make their stay comfortable.

No one brings colonists to the staff parties, though.

"Nah," I say. "I'll bach it with you two tonight."

Siri Campbell and Angel Akina are lifeguards at the beach. Excellent swimmers, both of them, so they have rocking bodies. We call them night and day. Siri was born in Jamaica and has gorgeous dark skin and hair, and Angel, despite her Hawaiian last name, is blond and fair.

And of course they're both knockouts.

Lyle and Nemo have sampled Siri and Angel, respectively.

I haven't yet had the pleasure.

Siri, clad in a white bikini that accentuates her gorgeous brown skin, is the first to welcome me.

"Scotty!" She grabs me in a hug and shoves a red plastic cup containing beer in my hand. "Good to see you!"

"You see me every day, Siri."

"Yeah," she laughs, "and it's always good! Welcome to our kegger!"

"Thanks."

"I can't believe Angel got her hands on these kegs," Siri continues. "Her cousin is a distributor, and he sneaked a few extra into the last shipment."

"Lucky break," I say.

"Isn't it?" She gulps a swallow of beer. "Have a good time!" She flits away and joins another group of staffers.

I watch her. Siri Campbell has the best ass on the beach.

Except maybe for Emily's ass, which I've only seen with a wet skirt clinging to it.

It was *fine*.

Lyle and Nemo are already in party mode and making the rounds. Normally I'd be with them, but something holds me back tonight.

Not something so much as some*one*.

Within two minutes, though, Nemo finds me and drags me into the circle where he and Lyle are holding court with a bevy of female staffers, Lauren Suvac among them. Lauren's another bartender, and she and I hooked up once. Nothing serious. She's a gorgeous blonde with massive tits and a cute spray of freckles across her nose.

"Hey, Scotty." She puts her hand in mine. "How's it hanging tonight?"

"Good, Laur. How about you?"

"Feeling kind of lonely." She squeezes my hand. "And horny."

Yeah. Normally I'd be all over that. Lauren's great, because she was an anthropology major in college. She doesn't believe in monogamy. "There's just no science to support it," she told me once. "Most mammalian species never form monogamous relationships. They have different partners for different times in their lives."

Yeah. I kissed her to get her to shut up.

Funny.

Monogamy doesn't sound quite so bad to me tonight.

"You interested?" She tugs on my hand.

"Maybe later." I kiss her cheek quickly. "Want to take a swim?"

"Sure! Last one in the water's a rotten egg!" She peels off her fire-engine red one piece and runs into the ocean in her birthday suit.

So it's that kind of party, huh? I disrobe quickly as well and follow her into the water. It's warm, and the sun has fallen below the horizon, casting a blue veil over everything. Lauren's huge tits float on the water and draw my gaze.

But…

Been there, done that.

I dive under for a minute, let the water cover my body. When I reappear, Lauren has set her sights on Nemo, who's joined us in the water.

Just as well. Nemo needs to get laid, and Lauren's a sure thing.

I, on the other hand?

I don't *need* to get laid. However, I desperately *want* to get laid. By Emily Moreno.

I get out of the water and grab a towel from the stack Siri and Angel provided. I dry off my hair, wrap the towel around my waist, and go in search of my clothes.

Siri grabs one of my butt cheeks. "Best ass on the beach, Scotty."

"Yours is better."

She laughs. "Lyle took an informal poll at the bar tonight. You won best guy ass and I won best girl ass."

"I can't find any fault with those results."

"You want to roast marshmallows?" Siri asks. "We started a small bonfire. Got everything for s'mores."

"Sure. What the hell?" I hastily get back into my shorts and island shirt and follow Siri to the small fire.

We're allowed to have a bonfire, but only in this one location on the staffers' beach. The Wolfes are great to all of us. Our own private beach, great living quarters, all food and drink included. I guess that makes up for the meager pay. No tips, either. It's forbidden. The artists are here to create, not go broke. Roy Wolfe's words. Of course, a few of them still tip. Lyle and I learned quickly who they were and we give them extra special service.

Still we make enough to get by and put a few bucks each check into savings. With shelter, food, and drink included here, it's an amazing deal. I was lucky I got hired on Wolfe Island. I take a roasting fork and load it with two marshmallows. Angel and Lyle are among the others around the small fire. Siri and I join them.

"You got any dark chocolate?" I ask Siri.

"Sure thing. I remember you don't eat Hershey's."

"Tastes like sour milk to me," I say.

"I got you some Special Dark."

"You're awesome!" I give Siri a kiss on her smooth cheek.

Funny. I've kissed two women's cheeks tonight. Lauren and Siri. And I felt nothing. Not even a slight stir downstairs.

I'm off my game.

Except I know I'm not.

I'm *on* my game. Totally on it.

I just have my sights set on another woman.

Once my marshmallows are brown but not burnt, I move them from the fire and slide them onto a graham cracker along with a square of dark chocolate. I top it with another graham cracker, and just as I'm about to shove it into my mouth—

I shift my gaze toward the other side of the beach.

Darkness has fallen, and a lone woman wanders barefoot,

right at the shoreline. She's dressed all in white—a sundress—dark hair falling down her back.

An angel.

A fucking angel on the beach.

I absently drop my s'more in the sand and begin walking.

11

EMILY

I feel safer in the dark.

Silly, I know.

If Lucifer wants to find me—and he does—he will. Eventually. Buck will do what he can to throw him off my trail, but in the end...

He'll find me.

You're mine, Emily. You'll never escape me.

This is the edge of the colonists' beach. A fire burns in the distance. I inhale. Mmm. Smells like campfire and roasted marshmallows. S'mores.

I haven't had a s'more since I was a little girl. I used to be a Girl Scout. Emily Moreno was a good girl. She was always prepared—the Girl Scout motto. She earned good grades and never got into trouble.

Never.

Until she met Lucifer Raven.

I'm an accessory to myriad crimes, now. Not by my choice, but that won't matter to the people who want to bring down Lucifer and his underground syndicate.

I know too much, as well.

Which is why Lucifer can't let me go.

Security here on the island is top notch, according to Buck. He should know. He's been in the Wolfes' employ since he left the Navy. He and his friend Leif are two of the Wolfes' hired guns, so to speak. They're jacks of all trades with a SEAL background. I don't even want to think about some of the stuff my brother most likely did when the Wolfes were all suspects in their father's murder.

Thankfully, that's all over now. Turned out Derek Wolfe had led a double life. He was a bigamist, a kidnapper, a rapist, and a psychopath.

Nice guy.

The ocean pushes toward me, tickling my bare toes.

I let out a sigh.

I'm in paradise.

Paradise.

And earlier today, I met a man. A nice man who seemed interested in me. Wanted to know why I'm running. Why I'm hiding. Sure, he's a bartending beach bum, but I liked him. I wanted to get to know him.

Wanted...

Wanted to feel his strong arms around me.

But I couldn't. It wouldn't be fair to him, when I belong to someone else.

Except I don't belong to someone else. Damn. Lucifer's words haunt me to the point where I actually believe them sometimes.

No. I do *not* belong to Lucifer Raven.

I belong only to me.

But he will come for me.

And I can't bear the thought of Scotty being in his way. If Scotty got hurt because of me, I'd never forgive myself.

The water meets my toes once more, this time more forceful,

and the water flows up to my ankles, burying the gold anklet. Then just as quickly, the water flows back out to sea, leaving my feet buried in the wet sand.

Buried.

I'm like my feet, in a way. Buried. I so want to climb out of Lucifer's grasp, but I know my time here on Wolfe Island is only a temporary respite.

He's coming.

I can feel it.

"Hey, pretty girl."

I jolt at the words and look up. Scotty's walking toward me carrying two red plastic cups. He hands me one.

"Brought you a drink."

I look into the cup and sniff. "Beer?"

"You too good for beer, pretty girl?"

"No. It's just been…a long time since I've had a beer." I take a drink, letting the cold maltiness coat my mouth and throat. I swallow. "It's good."

"It's basic Bud Light. The stuff of frat parties."

"Still, it's good. Refreshing."

He takes a swallow. "It is that. Nothing like the Scotty special, though, right?"

I smile. "That was in a class by itself."

"You come up with a name yet?"

"Not yet." I take another sip of beer.

"We've got time."

"I suppose." Except he's wrong. There's an invisible timer around my neck. I'm just not sure when it's set to expire.

"You want to come to a party?"

"Your bonfire?"

"Yeah. It's a staff party, but I bet they'll let you in." He points. "That's our beach over there. For staff use only. It's really nice."

"If it's for staff use only, I shouldn't go over there. I don't want to get anyone in trouble."

"You won't, but I get it." He smiles and pushes a lock of hair out of my eye. "Will I see you tomorrow?"

"I don't know. I may not leave my hut."

"Emily," he says.

And I listen. I listen because he's never called me Emily before. Either pretty girl or Em.

Never Emily.

"...you're on a beautiful island. You can paint to your heart's content. That's why you're here. But I'm not going to let you waste your time here by sitting alone in your hut every day until you leave.

"I—"

"Look." He grabs both my hands.

Tingles shoot through me.

"I won't force you to do anything. I don't have that power over you and I don't want it. But whatever you're hiding from, it won't find you here. I promise you."

I can't help it. I shake my head and let out a scoffing laugh. "You just don't know."

"I'll know if you tell me."

I meet his gorgeous gaze. "Nice try."

"You don't have to tell me anything. In fact, we don't have to go back to the staff party. We can walk along the shoreline, as you've been doing. Or I can leave you here. You can walk alone. It's safe."

"I don't want to keep you from your party."

"I'd much rather have your company. May I walk with you?"

I nod. He drops one of my hands and we begin walking, hand in hand, in the opposite direction, away from the staffer beach and his party.

Toward the colony, the bar, the restaurants. We walk past the people who are out painting in the dark, past the couples chatting intimately, past the night lifeguard on duty, past the surf and rent shop.

Past everything, until the shoreline and the moon are our only company.

And my hand is still in his.

And I like the way it feels.

I like it very much.

I almost feel...*safe*.

12

SCOTTY

I'm a bartender, which means I'm a talker. It also means I can recognize when a customer doesn't want to talk. If I talk too much to someone who doesn't want it, I don't get a tip—at least at bars where tipping is allowed. It's all about reading people.

I'm reading Em now. She doesn't want to talk.

That's okay.

Sure, I want to know more about her. Man, I want to know everything about her, but in her time.

I don't know how long she's booked here on the island. I could check with Manual, but does it matter?

I'm a live-for-the-day kind of guy. *Carpe diem* and all that. I always have been, and today's no different.

Perhaps Emily will leave tomorrow. Perhaps she'll stay a couple months.

All that matters is this moment. Right now.

And although I won't deny that I'd love to get her between the sheets, I'm content, in this moment, to walk along the shoreline with her and simply hold her hand.

So I'm surprised when she stops walking and turns to face the ocean.

"It's so vast," she says. "I can see so far just in the moonlight."

"The moon doesn't actually make any light," I say. "It's a reflection from the sun."

She smiles. "You learned that as a psychology major?"

"No, I learned that in seventh-grade earth science."

She laughs. Just a slight laugh, but it's beautiful. It's joyous. It makes a grin split my face.

"You're something, Emily Moreno."

"Am I?" Her tone is slightly flirtatious.

I trail a finger over her soft cheek, down her neck. "You definitely are." I lean in and give her a chaste kiss on the lips.

I pull back, but shock rolls through me as Em wraps her arms around my neck and pulls me into a clench, crushing our mouths together.

Unexpected…and awesome.

Her soft lips slide against mine, her tongue probes mine.

Em is taking charge of this kiss. Very different from our previous kisses, and I'm loving it. Really loving it.

I glide one hand down her shoulder to her breasts, resisting the urge to cup one. Instead, I slide my hand down her waist to her hips and around to one of her ass cheeks. I pull her toward me, let her feel my hard cock against her belly.

Then she unclenches herself from my grasp.

I'm sorry. The words are on the tip of my tongue, but I can't bring myself to say them. I'm not sorry. Not sorry at all.

I want more kisses. I want more than kisses. I want to make love to Em, hard and fast, and then slowly and passionately.

But I won't pressure her.

"I'm sorry." The words I considered saying come from her lips instead of mine.

"Don't be," I say. "Never be sorry. If you're not feeling what I'm feeling—"

She shakes her rapidly. "I am. I'm feeling exactly what you're feeling, Scotty. I swear it."

I inhale. I love the smell of the beach at night. Sand and saltwater and shells, but tonight, I get a waft of Emily's citrusy perfume, her coconutty hair, her...sultry musk.

Yeah, I can smell her need. Her ache. Her want.

It mirrors my own.

Should I ask her if she wants to go to my hut?

No. She stopped the kiss. She wants me and I want her, but she stopped me from going any further.

"You want to walk back?" I ask.

She breathes in and reaches both arms out, as if sizing up her wingspan. She faces the ocean, closes her eyes, inhales again. "This place makes me think anything is possible."

I want so badly to touch her, to kiss her, just to grab her hand even.

But I don't.

I can't.

I can't disturb the picture she makes as she faces the sea, her eyes closed, her arms stretched out, her hair curtaining down her back, and her white dress flowing around her body in the soft evening breeze.

So I watch her. Take in the perfect embodiment of beauty before my eyes.

And I'm not sure I'll ever tire of gazing at her.

13

EMILY

The breeze on my flesh, the oceanic fragrance, the warmth of Scotty's body... We're not touching, but still, his presence invades me even as my eyes are closed. The flimsy fabric of my dress grazes my bare legs, the water tickles my toes.

And if I open my eyes, I'll see the moonlight streaming onto the midnight blue sea.

So lovely.

I expect Scotty to say something. Or to touch me. Kiss me.

But he doesn't.

He lets me be. Simply be.

Which comforts me.

He said I was safe here.

He's wrong, but I am at least safe for this moment.

I open my eyes, turn to face him.

He's gorgeous in the moonlight. It glints off his dark hair, creates a black veil over most of the colors in his clothing, but not his eyes. Not those olive-gold orbs that nearly seduced me the first time I gazed into them.

The darkness doesn't affect them at all.

"You're beautiful," he says, his low voice even lower than normal.

I take a step toward him, my feet sinking in the sand. "So are you."

He smiles. A wide smile that shows his sparkling white teeth against the dark of night.

"Will you do something for me?" I ask.

"Anything."

"Take me somewhere. Take me somewhere on this island where you've never taken another woman."

He widens his eyes, and for a moment, I fear a place like that doesn't exist on the island.

I try to hide my frown.

He grabs hold of my left hand, entwines my fingers through his. "I know just the place. Are you up for a little danger?"

I hold back a scoff. I'm in danger just by existing. "What kind of danger?"

"There's a cliff about a mile up the beach. It's off limits to colonists and staffers. My buddies and I visited it once."

"What's so dangerous about it? Is it high?"

"No. Not at all. But parts of it are covered in coral, which can cut you up pretty badly, and neither of us is wearing shoes. But I'm not suggesting we actually get on the cliff."

"Why are you suggesting it, then?"

"Because right before we get to the cliff is a gorgeous stretch of beach. The sand is snow white, and the sunsets and sunrises are glorious."

"So you've been there with your friends..."

"I have. Nemo and Lyle. My suitemates." He smiles. "But I've never taken a woman there."

"Why not?"

"I've never wanted to."

"Wait, wait, wait. You went there with guys, and you say it's a gorgeous stretch of beach, but you never went back with a woman?"

"I never did."

"Why?" I can't help asking.

"It's too special," he says. "I never wanted to share it with a woman. Until now."

His words melt the last layer of ice around my heart. Lucifer Raven disappears, and for this moment, I'm safe.

Safe with Scotty.

And I want to share this with him.

"Let's go," I say.

We walk another mile or so until I see the cliff he's talking about in the distance. "Beyond the cliff is the other side of the island. There's a retreat center there, and beyond that, the Wolfes are building a huge resort."

I nod. "My brother told me all about it."

"Oh?"

"Yeah. He works for the Wolfes."

Scotty nods. "I may apply for a job at the resort. Resorters are allowed to tip."

I laugh. "You're hardly living in poverty here."

"Not at all. But a guy's got to plan for the future."

I widen my eyes. Scotty is so much more than a beach bum. He's thinking about his future. I like that.

"I'm sorry," I say.

"For what?"

"For thinking you were a beach bum with no goals."

He stops walking. "That's what you thought?"

"Well, if it looks like a duck…"

"Hey." He cups my cheek. "I live day to day. I pull each sliver of happiness I can out of each minute of my day. But that doesn't mean I don't think about the future. In fact…"

"In fact…what?"

"In fact, I've been thinking more about the future during the last twelve hours than I have in a long time."

I don't reply. Does he mean me? Silly to even think that. We hardly know each other.

Still, his words warm me. Soothe me. Comfort me.

And, of course, turn me on.

The night is warm, and the ocean breeze cushions us. This tiny stretch of beach is isolated, pure white sand. What must a sunrise look like from here? A sunset?

I need to come back here with my paints.

But for now...

"Scotty?"

"Hmm?" He plays with my fingers.

"Kiss me. Please."

14

SCOTTY

I press my lips to hers gently. Oh, I'm raring to go. I'll gladly kiss her into tomorrow, but I get the impression she needs slow tonight.

So I gently pry her lips open with my tongue, delve between them, explore her mouth languidly.

She kisses me back, and then, to my surprise, she takes the lead.

She deepens the kiss, exploring my mouth this time, and tiny little groans vibrate from her throat into me, fueling my desire even more.

I grab a fist full of her long glorious hair and give it a sharp tug. She responds by grabbing my ass and pulling me closer to her.

The kiss, the beach, the world... It's all perfect.

I want her so badly. I haven't wanted a woman this badly in a long time, perhaps not ever.

She breaks the kiss and gasps in a breath. I inhale as well, trailing kisses across her cheek to her ear.

"You're so beautiful, Em," I whisper.

She shudders beneath my touch. "I wish..." she says.

"You wish what?"

"I wish we could stay here. Just you and me. Where there aren't any other cares in the world."

"We can." I nip at the outer shell of her soft ear.

"Mmm...we can't. The carriage will turn into a pumpkin eventually."

"But we don't have to think about that right now."

"But..." She sighs, trailing her fingers up my arms. "But...it always happens. It's inevitable."

"Shhhh," I say. "It won't happen tonight."

I ease her onto the soft sand until she's lying on her back, her dark eyes glowing in the moonlight. I've never seen anything lovelier. We're close to the shoreline but still on dry sand.

I kiss her again, deeply, our tongues tangling, our lips sliding, and then I work a strap of her white flowing dress.

She doesn't stop me.

Soon her breasts are bare, and my God, in the moonlight, I swear she's a goddess. Aphrodite herself. So beautiful and perfect, her nipples brown and hard and tight. I brush my fingers over one and then the other.

Then I lean down and take one between my lips.

She moans softly, so I suck harder, gripping the hard nub with my teeth and biting gently.

"Mmmm... Good, Scotty."

Very good from where I am as well. I cup the other breast and lightly thumb the nipple. I could spend hours on these gorgeous tits alone, but there's a certain heaven between her legs that calls me.

I let go of her breasts for a second—she whimpers—and remove my shirt. My dick is aching inside my board shorts, but I don't want to scare her off. I'll leave it encased for now.

But her dress. The top of it is bunched around her slender

waist, while the bottom of it is still covering the gems between her legs.

I ease it over her hips.

And suck in a breath of air.

She's not wearing panties.

Nothing. Not even a tiny lace thong. Her pussy is shaved clean, and her clit is glistening.

Oh. My. God.

I quickly ease the dress off her legs until it's sitting next to us in a puddle of white.

"Commando," I say huskily.

"I'd already showered. Thought I was going to bed, but then something called to me."

"What?"

"The ocean, I think. Or maybe..."

"Maybe what?"

"I think maybe it was you, Scotty."

I smile, glide my finger across her lower lip. "You think?"

"I suppose it sounds silly."

"Not silly to me. I think I made it pretty clear I wanted to spend more time with you."

"You did. But...I have no right to drag you into something I can't finish."

"Baby," I say, "all we need to think about finishing is tonight." I kiss her again. Hard.

She wraps her arms around me, and I roll on top of her, bracing myself so I don't crush her. She's naked beneath me, the sand cushioning us. My dick prods through my board shorts. Her pussy—only the thin fabric of my shorts separates my dick from her honey.

"Em..."

"Hmmm..."

"Tell me to stop now. Please. If you can't go through with this, you have to tell me now."

"Don't stop," she says on a breath. "Please don't stop. Take me, Scotty. Take me away from the cruel world."

"I'm not an escape, Em. But I can take you away for this moment." I move off of her quickly, remove my shorts, grab a condom out of my pocket, and sheath myself.

Then I move on top of her once more. "You sure?" I ask.

"Yes, Scotty. Please."

I thrust into her heat.

A groan begins deep in my soul and flows outward as I cushion myself within Emily's tight pussy.

My God.

It's like she was made for me.

Every other woman I've ever had suddenly disappears from my mind.

There's only Em. My wonderful pretty girl. Em. Emily.

Emily Moreno.

And I vow, as soon as I plunge into her, that I'll keep her safe.

Safe from whatever she's running from.

Safe from whatever she's hiding.

Safe.

Safe and comforted in my arms.

I pull out, thrust back in. Pull out, thrust back in.

"Scotty," she gasps. "Please. Scotty, please."

I thrust again and again, kneeing into the sand. "Em. God, you feel good."

"So long," she breathes. "It's been so long since I've felt so... Felt so... Ah!" She clamps around my dick.

God, a woman's climax never felt so good.

"That's it, baby. Come. Come for me."

She shrieks, but it doesn't matter. No one can hear us all the way out here.

"That's it," I say. "Keep coming. Keep coming."

Thrust.

Thrust.

Thrust.

And—

"Fuck!" I clench my teeth as I release inside her warmth.

Each pulse sends a quiver through my heart, through my soul.

And I wonder...

I wonder...if I'll ever feel this whole again.

15

EMILY

I'm lost.

So lost in a sea of pleasure and happiness.

In the air, the breeze blows around us, and the sea roars in the distance, until—

"Oh!" The ocean rolls toward us, envelops us in the warm Pacific saltwater.

"Wow," Scotty says. "I couldn't have planned that any better."

I laugh, though I'm still quivering from the best orgasm I've ever experienced.

Is it the tropical island? Is it the man above me? Is it the fact that we just acted out a scene in *From Here to Eternity* with perfection?

Is it the fact that I'm running?

Probably a little of each.

Mostly it's Scotty.

Scotty, who gave me comfort. Who let me decide.

Who let me escape, if only for a few timeless moments, into his world of joy and lovemaking and tropical breezes.

"I don't want to move from this place," I say. "Not ever."

"No need to be in any hurry," he says.

"You have to work in the morning."

"That's still a few hours from now."

"What about sleep?"

"Sleep? Who needs it? I'll forgo sleep for the rest of your stay if it means I get to spend every minute with you."

Nice line.

I don't say it.

Because it's not a line. Scotty is sincere. I don't know how I know, but I do.

This man won't harm me.

Sure, it's an island fling.

It's not forever.

But it's now.

And now is all that matters.

WE WATCH the sun rise together. If only I had my palette and a canvas. The blues and oranges and yellows and purples spiral together in a kaleidoscope of color as the sun eases over the horizon, hazing through a few scattered clouds that look like white cotton candy.

"I hate to be a party pooper," Scotty says, "but we're going to need some hydration.

He's not wrong. Even in this tropical humidity, I'm feeling dry. The last thing I drank was the beer several hours ago, and that was hardly thirst quenching.

I sigh. "I don't want to leave."

"We can come back tonight."

"Can we?"

"Of course! You think I'm letting you go after that? Tell me it was as mind-numbing for you as it was for me."

"More," I say.

He chuckles and cups my cheek. "We'll call it a tie, then."

"A tie." I close my eyes and breath in the fresh morning air. "I'm not sure I can move."

"Then I'll carry you. But I won't let you die of dehydration. Or starvation." He makes it to his feet and holds out his hand.

"Scotty?"

"Yeah?"

"If you didn't have to work today, would you stay here with me forever?"

He chuckles again. "Baby, I'd stay here as long as you want. But eventually we'd both need water."

I grab his hand and he pulls me into a stand and then into his bare chest. Scotty's shirt and shorts are a couple yards away, but...

"Scotty? Where's my dress?"

He glances around. "Should be right here somewhere. Oh, crap."

"What?"

"It may have gotten washed out to sea when the tide came in and covered us."

My jaw drops. "How am I going to get back?'

He hastily pulls his shorts over his amazing ass and hands his shirt to me. "This should cover everything that needs covering."

I laugh.

I can't help it. I give a fucking loud laugh.

And I wish this moment could last forever.

I drape Scotty's shirt over my naked body and button it up. Sure enough, it covers my ass...but just barely. Still, it's good enough to get back to the colony and to my hut. And the best part? It smells just like Scotty—an intoxicating combination of the bonfire, the beach, and his spicy, masculine scent.

We walk, hand in hand, a little more quickly than I'd prefer because Scotty has to get to his morning shift at the bar. We arrive just in time for him to begin his shift.

"Don't you need your shirt?" I ask.

"Won't be the first time I've tended bar topless." He winks at me. "I'll be late, though."

"Why?"

"Because I want to walk you to your hut."

"You don't need to."

"I know I don't need to, Em. I *want* to."

"I know you do." I press my lips to his stubbled cheek. "But I don't want you to be late. People are going to want their Scotty specials."

"I do make a mean pineapple and passion fruit smoothie," he says. "You should come by for one later."

"I will," I promise. "And I'll bring your shirt back."

"Keep it." He touches my cheek, making sparks shoot through me. "I kind of like the thought of you having it." He brushes his lips over mine and then hops over the bar. A second later, he tosses me a bottle of water. "Drink it all. Then have another when you get back to your hut, okay?"

I nod and smile, pulling the cap off the water and taking a long, soothing drink.

I walk back to my hut on a cloud.

I slide my keycard through the door, and—

I gasp.

Lucifer Raven.

Sitting on my bed, staring at one of the canvases I've been working on.

He doesn't look up.

He doesn't need to.

"Not your best work, Emily."

I don't reply.

"Then again, I was always your muse."

Still, I say nothing.

"You didn't truly think you could escape from me, did you?"

He rises, then, and turns toward me, his blue eyes on fire.

"Pack your things. We're going home. Now."

"No," I say.

He shakes his head. "Whose shirt is that?"

"No one's."

"You're not that good a liar, Emily."

"How did you get in here?"

He scoffs. "Really? You think I'm a vampire or something? That I need an invitation? We both knew I'd find you."

"But security—"

"I know my way around the best security in the world. How do you think I've remained in business so long? Now pack up."

"No." This time I plant my hands on my hips, determined. I just spent the most exciting night of my life, and I'm not ready for my time here to end.

I summon every ounce of strength I possess, every ounce of courage, every ounce of sheer guts.

Lucifer's power over me ends today.

"This isn't up for negotiation, Emily."

"I'm not going."

His fist comes toward me in slow motion. Nothing I haven't seen before, but this time—this time—I'm ready.

I know this man's moves. He doesn't strike me often, only when he feels I've disobeyed him.

Fleeing from him is the ultimate disobedience in Lucifer's eyes.

The best block?

The best block is to not be there. Another lesson from Buck.

I duck, and then I run out the door.

16

SCOTTY

"Scotty!" Nemo sidles up to the bar. "Someone didn't make it home last night."

"Someone thinks that's none of your business."

"Someone also forgot to put on a shirt this morning."

I don't respond. Normally I'd laugh off his comment, but I don't. I'm not irked. Not in the slightest. I just feel...

I should have walked Em back to her hut. To hell with my shift. She's more important.

"Last anyone saw, you grabbed two beers and disappeared."

"Still not your business."

"Well, if you're not interested in telling me about your evening, I'll tell you about mine."

"Lauren?" I ask.

"You betcha. And get this—she hates monogamy!"

"I know. She says anthropology doesn't support it."

"Yeah, whatever. I dig her outlook, man."

I laugh. Nemo always becomes a seventies reject after he gets laid. Never fails. "Glad you had fun."

"The whole thing became kind of an orgy after you left," Nemo says. "It rocked."

I nod. "Glad you had fun."

"You a broken record or something?"

"Huh?"

"You said that twice. 'Glad you had fun.'"

"Did I?"

"I figured once I said the word orgy your interest would be piqued."

Funny. Normally it would be. But not today. All I can think about is watching Emily walk away from me with only my island print shirt covering her. I can't wait to peel it off her later.

Damn.

I should have walked her back.

"What can I get you this morning, Nemo?"

"Still no comment on the orgy?"

"Not today. You want a smoothie? Juice? Water? Coconut water?"

"Give me a strawberry banana smoothie with a shot of wheatgrass."

I stare toward the path that leads to the colonists' huts. Something feels off to me. I can't put it into words, but the back of my neck feels like shards of ice are prickling it.

"Dude," Nemo says. "My smoothie."

I hop over the counter. "Do me a favor. Cover for me."

"I'm no bartender."

"Fake it."

"Scotty, what the fuck?"

"Sorry. There's something I need to do. Now."

"But—"

"For God's sake, Nemo, you know how to work a blender. All the recipes are under the counter. I'll be right back."

I'm still barefoot, wishing I had my Air Jordans, but I run. I don't know why, but I know I need to run.

I need to run fast.

I race through the common area and toward the colonists' huts—toward Emily's hut.

That's when I see her.

Still wearing my island print shirt.

My heart nearly jumps out of my chest as I swallow a gulp of air.

A blond man is holding her, a knife to her neck.

Security guards and island police officers have guns trained on him.

God, please don't shoot. Please don't shoot. If they shoot him, they might get her.

I can't bear the thought.

"Emily!" I shout.

She meets my gaze, pure fear in her brown eyes. She shakes her head slightly at me.

"Put the knife down," one of the officers says. "Put it down and we'll talk. You don't come out of this alive if you don't."

"Fuck off!" the blond man says.

My gut is twisting into knots. Acid claws up my throat.

"Emily!" I yell again, my voice hoarse.

The man whispers something to her. She shakes her head vehemently.

"Let her go!" I yell. "Take me instead!"

A security guard grabs me. "You've got to get out of here, Scotty. This isn't a game."

"Do I look like I think it's a game?" I wrench myself free from the guard, who I recognize as Jimmy Cox. We play poker sometimes.

"This guy's off his rocker," Jimmy says. "Get out of here before you get yourself in trouble."

"I don't care," I say. "I can't let him hurt her."

"We won't let him hurt her," Jimmy says. "You've got to trust us. He's way outnumbered."

"I'm not worried about his life. Kill the SOB for all I care. I'm worried about *hers*."

"Scotty, for God's sake, let us do our job. If I'm here worrying about you, I'm not focused on her."

That's all I need to hear.

I step back, my heart in my throat being eaten alive by the bile that's coating it.

God, Em.

I knew she was hiding something. I just had no idea it was a psycho boyfriend.

He looks vaguely familiar to me. He's tall, muscular, with light blond hair. Where have I seen him before?

My mind blanks.

Only Em. Her safety. That silver blade is right against the creaminess of her neck. The neck I spent last night kissing...

My God...

I can't lose her.

I can't lose Emily.

I rake my fingers through my hair, pace around behind the action. I could run forward, demand to help.

But Jimmy's right. I'm just another target the guards have to worry about.

I pace and pace and pace, until finally I turn back toward Emily and get as close as I can.

She meets my gaze.

And she mouths three words.

I love you.

God. I love you.

"I love you too," I mouth back.

I don't even have to think twice. The words tumble out on their own, as if they've always been inside me and always will be.

Is it forever love?

Does it even matter?

It's love, and if, God forbid, Em doesn't get out of this alive, I want her to know I love her.

In fact, I want to shout from the rooftops, but I don't want to startle the psycho.

My stomach churns. I haven't eaten anything. Just drank a quart of water when I got to the bar to begin my shift.

And now...

Now my stomach threatens to turn inside out on itself.

But Emily needs me.

She needs me to be strong for her.

Fuck! I feel so useless! So ridiculous standing here in nothing but board shorts, not allowed to cross the arbitrary line the guards have set up.

"Let her go," an officer with a bullhorn shouts. "You hurt her, you go down."

"If I die, we both die!" Psycho shouts back.

I curl my hands into fists. Not on my watch. I can't just stand here and do nothing.

I run.

I run full force through the makeshift boundary.

I run toward the woman I love.

I'm almost there when—

A shot. A fucking bullet.

17

EMILY

Lucifer drops the knife and falls to the ground. In a flash I'm running.

Running toward Scotty. "Scotty!"

I land in his arms and my mouth finds his.

We kiss hard. Deep. A kiss of life.

Time suspends itself.

We're in a warp. Everything around us ceases to exist.

We kiss.

We kiss.

We kiss.

"Scotty."

"Scotty."

"Scotty!"

He pulls away from me. Who's calling him?

"Scotty." From one of the guards. "We need to talk to the lady."

Scotty's lips are swollen and pink from our kiss. Our feral kiss that I wish were still going on.

"Come with me." I tug on his hand.

He simply nods.

A minute later, we're sitting with Roy Wolfe himself and—

"Buck!" I launch myself at my brother.

"God, sis. Thank God." He kisses the top of my head.

"When did you get here?"

"When Lucifer did. I've been watching him since you left. Somehow I lost him for a span of fifteen minutes, and the next thing I knew, he was on a plane. Once he was on his way, so was I."

"Were you the sniper?" Scotty asks.

"Who the hell are you? And why were you kissing my sister?"

"Sorry," I say. "Buck, this is Scotty. Scotty, my brother."

Buck holds out his hand.

Scotty takes it. "Thanks, man. You saved the day."

"All in a day's work."

"Buck's an ex-Navy SEAL," I say.

"Emily, Scotty," Roy Wolfe says, "I'm so sorry for all of this. We'll be taking a good long look at our security systems."

"It's not your system," Buck says. "It's top-notch. I should know, since I advised you on it. Lucifer Raven has gotten through top-notch security before. I'm just sorry I couldn't stop him from getting here. I'm sorry, Emily. I thought you'd be safe here."

I shake my head. "I know you did. This isn't your fault. I'm not safe anywhere as long as Lucifer is free."

"He's won't be free now," Buck says. "These are charges that will finally stick. We've got a ton of witnesses."

Roy's phone buzzes. "Excuse me." He puts it to his ear. "Yes?"

Pause.

"Thank you. I'll let everyone know."

"Mr. Ashton's injury is not life-threatening. He'll be transferred on a medical yacht to Hawaii where he'll be hospitalized and under constant guard. I assume you'll be filing charges, Ms. Moreno."

I nod, shivering. "Yes. Of course."

"We'll be doing a full investigation on how he got onto the island," Roy says.

"I can tell you right now how he got here," Buck says. "Money. He paid off a few of your people."

"Find them," Roy says, "and take care of them."

"Consider it done."

"People need to feel safe here," Roy says. "This can't ever happen again."

"Mr. Wolfe?" I say.

"Roy, please."

"Roy." I clear my throat. "He was determined to get to me. I should never have come here. I'm sorry."

"Don't be. Buck talked to me beforehand about your situation. I'm sorry we failed to protect you."

"You did protect me," I say. "All he had was a knife. His weapon of choice is a handgun, which clearly he couldn't bring here."

"I'm still very sorry, Ms. Moreno."

I smile. "Emily, please."

"Emily. What can Charlie and I do to make this up to you?"

"Nothing. You don't owe me anything."

"I've taken a look at your work. You're a very talented artist, especially with color mixing. Would you be interested in teaching here at the colony?"

My jaw drops. "You mean, live here?"

"Yes. You'll live over in the staff huts."

"With Scotty?"

Roy chuckles. "Well, not with Scotty. But in the same area."

I want to pounce on this offer, but—

"I'm not sure."

"Em," Buck says, "this is a great offer. You'll be able to paint to your heart's content. Work on your craft while you help others with theirs."

"It is a dream come true," I say.

I'll be free. Finally free from Lucifer's invisible bonds.

But Scotty...

I'm pretty sure he mouthed the words "I love you too" when I mouthed "I love you," but we were in a life-or-death situation.

I don't want him to feel trapped.

And he was here first.

"May I think about it?"

"Of course." Roy rises. "I'll leave Jimmy here to get your official statement. Come talk to me when you decide."

ONE OFFICIAL STATEMENT LATER, Scotty and I are walking hand in hand back to my hut. I'm shivering.

"I can't stay here any longer. All I see in here is him, sitting on my bed, as if he owns the place."

"Baby, why didn't you tell me?"

"Because you would have run away screaming."

"No. I wouldn't have. I already knew you had some kind of baggage. That you were running away. If you'd come to my place last night instead of here—"

"He'd have found me anyway, and he wouldn't have thought twice of hurting you to get to me. Nothing stops him."

"Except your brother's bullet."

"Lucifer—"

"I knew I recognized him from somewhere," Scotty says. "He's Lucifer Ashton. From the Ashtons of LA. Is it true? The rumors?"

"That he's an underground drug kingpin? Yeah, they're all true."

"Emily"—he caresses my cheek—"my God. How did you…"

"He lavished me with gifts. With a life a starving artist could only dream about. I was seduced by the lifestyle, and gradually, I…" I shake my head. How can I admit what happened? What I *allowed* to happen?

"Damn, Em. Thank God you're okay."

"He trapped me. Wouldn't let me go anywhere without him, until the day I escaped. Buck sent me here. Then…"

"It's my fault." Scotty rubs his forehead, messes with his hair. "I should have walked you back this morning. None of this would have happened."

"Oh, Scotty." I entwine my fingers through his. "This isn't your fault at all. It's my fault. I stopped watching my back. I shouldn't have, but I did. *Carpe diem*, as you say."

"I wouldn't have said it if I thought it could get you killed."

"No. Don't go there," I say. "Last night with you was the most amazing night of my life. I'll never regret it."

He smiles. "Then stay here, Em. On the island. With me. And I promise we'll have many more nights even better than last night."

"You mean it? You want me to stay here? I may need some… counseling. To get over what I've been through and all."

"There just happens to be a top-notch retreat center on the other side of the cliff with the best therapists in the world."

"You want me?" I ask. "Baggage and all?"

Scotty smiles, kisses my lips. "Baby, I want it all. And you've made me think about a lot of things."

"Like what?"

"Like maybe going back to school. I could take online courses and still work here. Maybe become a counselor myself."

"You did major in psychology. That's a wonderful idea." I

brush his hair off his forehead and return his smile. "I thought of a name for your cocktail."

"You mean *our* cocktail"—he trails a finger over my lower lip—"my love?"

"Yeah. We'll call it the Island Escape."

THANK YOU FOR READING ESCAPE! Read about the history of Wolfe Island here. https://www.helenhardt.com/book/?series=wolfes-of-manhattan

ISLAND ESCAPE

1 shot gold rum
    1 shot crème de banana
    1 shot crème de noyaux
    3 shots orange juice
    3 shots pineapple juice
    Shake with ice and strain into martini glasses rimmed with sugar.

ABOUT THE AUTHOR

#1 *New York Times*, #1 *USA Today*, and #1 *Wall Street Journal* bestselling author Helen Hardt's passion for the written word began with the books her mother read to her at bedtime. She wrote her first story at age six and hasn't stopped since. In addition to being an award-winning author of romantic fiction, she's a mother, an attorney, a black belt in Taekwondo, a grammar geek, an appreciator of fine red wine, and a lover of Ben and Jerry's ice cream. She writes from her home in Colorado, where she lives with her family. Helen loves to hear from readers.

http://www.helenhardt.com

EXES AND OHS!

Leah Marie Brown

Dedicated to my favorite Irishman, Alfonso. Thanks a million for the lethal craic. More than anything, thank you for your friendship. You make me grateful for it every day...and three times on a Thursday. And to Ciarán Johnston: I'll never forget the first time I heard you sing at McGann's in Doolin. It was like a golden ray of light on a dark winter night, which describes your personality, too.

1

JADED LADY

You are never single if you are in a long-term relationship with yourself.

"Get the fuck outta here."

I toss the glossy brochure onto the conference table and lean back in my chair, eyeing Kristin as if she has asked me to write a piece on genital mutilation—which, for the record, might be more appealing than a 3000-word article about some touchy-feely retreat designed to help sad singles "create healthy, fulfilling, long-term committed relationships."

I'm Marlow Donnelly, by the way. I write a column for *Conceit*, the consummate luxury lifestyle, travel and leisure magazine, and Kristin is my editor and bestie.

"*Exes and Ohs* is an innovative self-help program offered by Ian Chapman."

"Nuh-uh. No way. *So* not happening."

"It's Ian Chapman, Marlow. *Ian Chapman!*"

She says this as if I should recognize the name, and for one long embarrassing moment I wonder if the guy she tried to set me up with a few years ago was named Ian. *Ian. Ian. Fuck me!*

Was his name Ian? Think around it, Marlow. Tall, brown hair, Gregory Peck glasses. FBI hostage negotiator. Talked about the importance of understanding nonverbal communication and being able to read body language, while slowly reaching under the table and trying to slide his hand up my skirt. Yeah, I got nothing here. He could have been Ian or Tom or Freddie.

I finally shrug and lift my hands.

She exhales and her silky black bangs flutter off her forehead. "Ian Chapman. The Love Guru?"

"The Love Guru?" I snort. "*The Love Guru*? Please tell me you *are* joking, because if you're not, I will change into go-go boots and pepper my speech with phrases like, '*Oh, behave*' and '*Yeah, baby, yeah.*'"

Kristin narrows her gaze and crosses her slender arms over her chest. I know I should swallow back the bubble of laughter rising in my throat, but I imagine myself sitting crossed-legged on a grass mat interviewing a bejeweled and berobed man, a cloud of patchouli incense swirling around us, while he uses hokey phrases like *vibrational escrow*, and I am dying, hooting and wiping tears from my face.

The interns snicker.

Kristin doesn't even crack a smile. She was exposed to the Wide World of Marlow Chapman in full technicolor many years ago and is now blasé to my dramatic flashes.

"Are you finished?" she asks. "Ian Chapman is a psychiatrist and relationship expert with three million YouTube subscribers."

Oh, well, three million *YouTube* subscribers...

"His TED Talk on soulmates is one of the top ten most watched videos."

"Soulmates? You did *not* just say that word."

Kristin looks away because she already knows what I am going to say. She's heard it a bazillion times.

"I do not believe in soulmates. The idea that every person has a single mate they are meant to be with through eternity is a myth, like Marie Antoinette saying, 'Let them eat cake,' or creams that can get rid of cellulite, or George Clooney's charm."

"I love George Clooney," an intern in a bowtie and hornrims whispers.

I ignore the Clooney-loving minion.

"Do you know who made up the soulmates myth? A tragically lonely person—probably a spinster living in a ramshackle house filled with stacks of old yellow newspapers, and a clowder of cats."

"What's a clowder?" Bowtie whispers to the girl standing next to him.

"She made the idea up because she didn't want to admit she was a socially awkward recluse who would rather hole up with her fur babies than get out there and meet a man." I'm warming to the subject now. "'*I haven't met the one yet because there are seven billion people on the planet. He will find me, though. I am sure of it.*'"

"Are you quite through?" Kristin asks.

"I am." I grin before turning my attention to Bowtie. "A clowder is the word used to describe a group of cats."

"In the last ten years, wellness retreats have grown in popularity, particularly among the wealthy who have exchanged exclusive cruises for resort-based self-help-focused vacations." Kristin pushes a key on her MacBook and a PowerPoint pie chart appears on the conference smart board. "Wellness vacations have become a six hundred and thirty-nine-billion-dollar industry. Singles summits and relationship retreats are the biggest slice in that pie."

Props to my bestie. She gives an impressive presentation, but it hasn't juiced my mojo enough to make me want to set a date with the Love Guru. In fact, there is little she could say to convince me to spend a week having my head shrunk and my heart healed by some New Age charlatan spouting clever mantras. *Every choice you make helps align you for your mate.* Seriously? What if I choose chicken salad on a croissant instead of a tuna wrap for lunch? Does that throwaway decision bring my soulmate one step closer to me?

"Social media," Kristin says. "I believe our dependency on social media has inspired this travel trend. People feel more disconnected than ever before. A recent study found that people who use multiple social media platforms report more symptoms of depression, anxiety, insomnia..."

I sit up. My crafty bestie is speaking my language now. She knows my disdain for social media, especially dating apps. It's no accident she slipped that last part into her presentation.

"Marlow, this story needs your unique perspective to keep it from becoming a fluff piece. I'm looking for a docudrama here, not a rom-com."

"My unique perspective?" I laugh. "Would that be my jaded outlook on the happily ever after?"

"Precisely."

She is lethally serious.

I look at the brochure again.

Seven days of workshops, exercises, and mixers carefully crafted to help you...

I push the brochure away. Kareena, my archnemesis, reaches for it. Yes, I am aware the word *archnemesis* is only used by comic book characters and preteen girls, but I can't think of another word to describe a hyper-competitive, energy-sucking entity with talons for fingernails, and I'm a professional wordsmith.

"It's in Ibiza," Kristin interjects.

I snatch the brochure before Kareena can get her claws on it.

Determine what is blocking the deposits into your love bank.

"Yeah, I'm out." I toss the brochure back on the table. "There aren't enough pills in Ibiza to get me to spend seven days talking about my love bank."

2

HOW TO KILL A FRIEND

"I'd like a Tight Snatch."

"I am going to have a Ginger Bush." Kristin wrinkles her nose and purses her lips. "On second thought, make that a Creamy Pussy. Could you add a splash more Tequila Rose, though?" She hands her corporate credit card to the bartender. "You can start a tab. Thanks."

We're grabbing post-workday drinks at our favorite cocktail bar. Vesper has a chill vibe even though it's super swank. It was a theater during the Golden Age of Hollywood. The owner, the only daughter of an Academy Award-winning director, is an influencer with *serious* clout. She dropped a wad restoring the place. The banquettes are plush, the low amber lighting gives you flawless selfie-filter face, and the salaciously named drinks are super strong. The beautiful people come here to spill tea while getting drunk on top-drawer booze. Kristin and I come here to watch trends and abuse the company AmEx.

"You haven't told me what happened with Michael."

Michael is a music producer I met at the gym. After weeks of fitness flexing and flirting, he finally asked me out. We went to a

Post Malone concert, hung out at his studio, worked out together.

"Yeah, hard pass on the hard body."

"Why? You were having fun with him."

"I was until he took me to dinner at Circé."

Kristin stares at me blankly.

"He ordered *salmon*."

"I didn't know you had such an aversion to salmon. Is it freshwater sockeye, Chinook, or all species of salmon that offend you?"

"Ha-ha! He pronounced it *sall-men*. Once he said it, I couldn't unhear it."

"Are you kidding?"

"Nope."

"You broke up with a tall, dark, spicy snack because he mispronounced one word?" Kristin raises her glass in a toast. "Congratulations, Marlow. That might be the stupidest reason you've ever given for breaking up with a guy."

"We didn't break up because we were never *together*."

Kristin finishes her cocktail in one swallow, sets the empty glass on the table, and rolls up her sleeves. It's about to get real.

"You broke up with the real estate agent because he drank milk with pizza."

"That's just weird."

"The guy from New Jersey?"

"The accent."

"Fair enough. I'll give you that one."

"Thank you!"

The bartender brings Kristin another cocktail.

"What about the pilot?"

"He serenaded me."

"Awww." She tilts her head and gets the same dewy, dopey look she gets when she watches *Titanic*. "That's so romantic."

"He sang a Lady Antebellum song."

"Not..."

"Yep," I say. "'Need You Now.'"

Kristin groans.

"While playing the banjo."

"Shut up!"

"Serious."

"What about the boat broker?"

"Clammy feet."

"I don't want to know, do I?"

"Nope."

"The homicide detective?"

"Girl, that's dead, that's done."

She groans and rolls her eyes. "I'm worried about you, Marlow."

"Worried? Why?"

"You haven't had a serious boyfriend since Terrell."

Terrell Rose was my first love. We met my freshman year in the dorms. He was an upper-class football player with a muscular brown body, chocolate eyes, and a smile so sweet it made my teeth ache to look at it. He graduated, was drafted to play for the New York Giants, and blew out his knee in the fourth game of his first season. I went to see him in the hospital, but he was in a dark place. He told me he was over me, that I should go back to school like a good girl and find a guy that was going somewhere other than physical therapy.

"If a serial dater is someone who enjoys getting to know new people and isn't motivated to seal the deal with a wedding band and a four-bedroom in Santa Monica, then yes, I am a serial dater."

"Do you think you will ever be in a long-term monogamous relationship with someone who isn't your hairdresser?"

"You have like six skazillion television channels, right?"

Kristin shakes her head. "What does that have to—"

"Ride with me, here," I say. "Remember when you were recovering from your rotator cuff surgery and I took care of you? We were chilling on the couch, trying to find something on the telly. We flipped through all the local stations, movie channels, educational channels. Fuck me! We even tried Hallmark, and that cringe film about the American exec who went to Ireland to open a factory and fell in love with a pixie whisperer."

"*Chasing Leprechauns*," she says. "And she was a pixie charmer."

"How can you possibly remember the name of that movie?" My bestie has a brain like Wikipedia, crammed full of facts and useless minutia. "We only watched, like, ten minutes."

"Yeah," she says, sniffing. "I might have watched it the next time it was on."

"Who are you?" I shake my head. "If you tell me you've developed an affinity for cheesy, low-budget, made-for-cable romance movies, I'm going to block every channel except Skinemax. Don't make me do it. I'll force you to watch *Hollywood Sexcapades* and *Taxicab Confessions*."

"You say that like it's a punishment," she deadpans.

This is why I busted my prepubescent ass to make Kristin Bitter my best friend. Besides having a wicked cool name, she's been a spectator to my dramatic outbursts since we were seated next to each other in sixth-grade English class, and she's never batted a long black eyelash. Not once. She's funny even when she's stone-cold sober and one of the few people who keeps me on my conversational toes whether we're debating climate change, discussing Hemingway's influence on American literature, or trash-talking about celebs.

"Look at my girl fronting." I laugh, putting my hands to my

face and peeking at her through my splayed fingers. "You watched *Fifty Shades of Grey* with your hands over your eyes. Skinemax After Dark would drive you to a nunnery."

"Marlow!" Her porcelain cheeks suffuse with the prettiest rose blush. "What does my cable television line-up have to do with your inability to commit to a man for more than cocktails and...?"

"Cock?"

"Ew." She wrinkles her nose. "Gross."

I laugh. Shocking my bestie with my dirty girl humor is probably my favorite pastime—after sex. "My love life is like your cable television line-up. I can't find anyone who holds my interest."

"You've certainly flipped through enough channels. Like loads and loads—"

"Thanks."

"—and loads."

"Loads. Got it."

"No judgment. I'm not slut shaming."

"Gee, thanks."

She gives me a side hug, squeezing me tight. "I don't care if you sleep with every man in a fifty-mile radius, as long as you're safe and happy, but I'm not sure you are happy."

"You're right." I fake sniffle. "Dating a gorgeous guy and dumping him before the honeymoon stage wears off, before he's standing in my bathroom, scratching his ass while taking a piss with the door open, is making me *so* miserable."

She tilts her head and looks at me through the thick fringe of her black bangs. "Would you be real for three minutes?"

"Three, huh? That's an arbitrary number."

"Marlow!"

"Fine," I say. "What do you want me to be real about?"

"Admit dating a different guy every month isn't satisfying anymore."

I bust out laughing. "Okay, Boomer. Straight up, Kris? You're sounding like my mom right now."

"Whatever." She rolls her eyes. "Give me three reasons cycling through guys faster than Lance Armstrong on the Tour de France makes you happy."

"Again with the number three?"

She arches a brow and holds up one finger.

"Okay, fine." I sigh. "One. I can flirt with the hot barista at Starbucks or bang a high-key gorgeous suit in the Air France lounge bathroom whenever I want."

Her eyes widen. "Did you?"

I let my grin be the answer. "Two. I can leave his message on read if I'm not feeling it."

She holds up three fingers.

"Three. I can look at thirst traps on Insta and I don't need to do it on the downlow. Nothing ruins a good wank bank like a jealous boyfriend stalking your Insta follows."

"Lowkey? I can't argue with your reasons."

"Sweet! Because I could have said research has shown single people are more physically fit, mentally healthier, more productive at work, and better with their finances." I shrug out of my jacket and toss it onto the banquette beside me. "I never have to sleep in the wet spot. I don't have to fight anyone for the remote. I don't have to share the last bowl of Häagen-Dazs. I can wear flannel pajamas all weekend—"

"Marlow Ann Donnelly! You don't own flannel pajamas."

"I know"—I flick an imaginary piece of lint off my trousers—"but if I wanted to, I wouldn't have to hide them under my thongs and bombshell bras. Besides"—I pull my iPhone out of my pocket, open Instagram, and hand the phone to my bestie —"this guy just slid into my DMs—"

She turns her face away. "I will not look at another one of your Instagram thirst traps until you promise me you will go to Ibiza and interview Ian Chapman."

Honestly? I changed my mind about the Love Guru gig when one of the interns said she went to Ibiza for Spring Break and met loads of cute Spanish boys. If I'm completely honest, I would have agreed to take the assignment even without the temptation of meeting a Latin lover because it seems important to Kristin.

"Fine," I say in an exhalation. "I will meet your Love Guru."

She looks back at me, smiles, and claps. "Yay! You leave in a week."

"Can't wait."

"In the meantime, maybe you'll meet a guy at Taylor's wedding."

Taylor makes up the third in our trifecta of besties. She's getting married to a much older rando she met at a salsa class.

"Negative, goose. You're a stellar wing woman, but if I wanted to date a geriatric, I would take a cruise for seniors or join a gardening club."

"Marlow! He's not *that* old."

"He's ancient."

"He's forty-two."

I shudder. "He wears jeans from Banana Republic."

"So?"

"He smells like Old Spice and he has ear hair."

"You're being ridiculous. Harry is nice."

"Harry! Even his name sounds old."

"Prince Harry?"

"Balding before thirty-five," I sing. "Just saying."

Kristin rolls her eyes.

"Look, I'm sure Taylor and Harry will be happy clipping

groupons together for the early bird special at the Olive Garden, but I am not Taylor and I do not look for my rides on Silver Singles."

3

DIRTY MOTHER

I'm striding through LAX, pulling my Gucci Globe-Trotter carryon—swag I scored when I did a story about iconic travel bags—when my cellphone rings. I pull my phone out of my pocket, look at the screen, and smile when I see my mother's name on the caller ID. My mom is *extra* extra, but she's the only person I would answer the phone for while nursing a serious Tight Snatch hangover.

"Hi, Mom!"

"Marlow, darling," she says in a breathy, Marilyn Monroe-esque voice and I know she must have a man with her. "Where are you?"

"LAX."

"Oo, fun! Where are you headed?"

"A beach resort in Spain."

"New Latin lover?"

"I wish," I laugh. "I'm interviewing...ready for it?"

"I hope so."

"I am interviewing Ian Chapman, a relationship expert known as the Love Guru."

"Yikes," she says.

"Big yikes."

"Tell me you aren't headed to Mallorca?"

"Ibiza."

"Thank God," she says in typical Marla Donnelly dramatic fashion. "You do not want to go to Mallorca, darling. Anybody can holiday in Mallorca. The wealthy go to Ibiza."

"Seriously, Mother?"

"Seriously! You know what the Germans call Mallorca?"

"No."

"*Putzfrau Insel*, which means the low-rent island."

I snort.

"It's true! My friend, Gretchen Galloway, the German woman I met at *La Clinique*, she told me they call it *Putzfrau Insel*. Why would she lie?"

My mother loves to drop place names and *La Clinique* is one of her faves because the super luxe, super pricey Swiss spa has a history of attracting notable people like oligarchs, royals, and rock stars.

"*La Clinique*?" I say, feigning ignorance. "Is that the medical spa you went to for cosmetic surgery or menopause treatments?"

"Marlow!" she cries.

I laugh. I know damn well she went to *La Clinique* to have platelets injected into her clit and vahjay to tighten and heighten, but I get childish joy at hearing her shock. There are three things Marla Donnelly never discusses—money, my father, and menopause.

My parents divorced when I was eleven and it devastated my mother. She spent two years prostrate with grief and, frankly, a little out of her head. She talked about my father obsessively. *Cormac liked this song. Cormac took care of the mundane things like auto insurance and taxes. Cormac is dating a horse-faced woman, a medical assistant who works at the heart institute.*

Watching my glamorous and vivacious mother stumble out

of her room with two-day-old mascara ringing her eyes was traumatic. My mother has always been my hero. A Vassar grad who became the It Girl of the early eighties, with her big blond hair and dozens of signature pearl strands wrapped around her slender neck. She was a brand ambassador for several designers, and rumored in some circles to be the inspiration for Madonna's Material Girl look. That she used her fame and influence to become a bespoke luxury jewelry designer who counts the world's wealthiest as her clients is everything. Every. Thing.

I inherited my mom's blond hair, blue eyes, and facial features. Unfortunately, I also inherited my dad's height—five-eight without heels—and ridiculously large lips—one hundred percent natural, no filler or Kylie Jenner lip kit.

"I am almost to TSA, Mom. Did you want something?"

"Marshall asked if you'd like to join us in Croatia for Christmas.'"

"Marshall?"

"My boyfriend, darling."

"I thought you were dating someone named Grayton."

"Last season."

My mother is a statuesque blue-eyed blonde with a cool sophistication like old-school actress Lana Turner. At fifty-three she gets more male attention than I do...and I can pull. She rotates men like her wardrobe. She is goals.

"I'll have to get back to you on that, but please thank *Marshall* for the invitation."

"Ciao, darling. Have a safe flight."

"I love—"

The line goes dead before I say the last word.

I clear security and walk to my gate, lost in a maze of memories.

The next stage of my mother's grief was scathing anger. *Cormac met Seabiscuit on a dating site. Gold-digging tramps who want to land a sugar daddy use dating sites. Elaine said she saw Cormac's girlfriend coming out of the women's clinic. She probably has herpes.* The anger stage lasted the longest.

I don't know when my mom entered the final stage of grief: acceptance. One day she was talking about sending a bucket of oats to my father's horse-faced girlfriend, and the next day she was designing a collection to wear to Royal Ascot and dating her divorce attorney. With a snap of her perfectly manicured fingers, my mother banished my father's ghost and created an iconic jewelry line that is still worn by royals. After the divorce attorney, she dated an heir to the DuPont fortune, a sugar scion, and a Texas oilman. My mom showed me love, marriage, and a Silver Cross Balmoral baby carriage aren't the only ways to find your happy ending.

I'M STRETCHED out in business class, a champagne cocktail in my hand, my MacBook open on the lap tray. I've been scrolling through a dossier the research department emailed me on Ian Chapman. I am trying to figure out how a thirty-four-year-old Princeton grad from Strathpeffer, Scotland became a *New York Times* bestselling author, YouTube star, Sirius Radio talk show host, dating seminar sensation, and the most sought-after relationship expert on the planet. I lean my head back, close my eyes, and try to imagine a wee Scottish lad telling his gruff Highland father that he wants to grow up to be a Love Guru. Like, how the fuck does that happen? The United Kingdom is where you go for bland food that sticks to your ribs, thick rubber rain boots, getting properly pissed in a pub older than George Washington's dentures, and trying to charm a smile from men with stiff upper lips.

If you told me Ian Chapman came from a place where the

consumption of food and drink is viewed as a libidinous-enhancing pursuit, an endeavor meant to be embarked upon with the same unhurried focused effort as foreplay, I wouldn't bat an eyelash. France, Italy, Spain, and Portugal know food should be enjoyed slowly.

My mom took me to Paris for the first time when I was fourteen years old. Do you know what I remember most from that trip? Seeing the Mona Lisa in the Louvre? Riding the elevator to the top of the Eiffel Tower? Sipping foamy hot chocolate at Angelina Tea Room? Nope. I remember strolling through the Marais, a historic district in the fourth arrondissement, and gawking at the goods for sale in the shop windows—the laciest of lingerie, shiny chocolates shaped like nipples infused with aphrodisiacs, slender volumes of poetry, exotic perfumes in crystal bottles, bouquets of peonies tied with ribbons and raffia, and bottles of bubbly. Passion pulsed with every stray note from a wine bar or tap-tap-tap of stiletto heel striking cobblestone. It made a huge impression on my tender pubescent heart and is probably why I jones for Gallic guys in Giorgio Armani suits—hence, my one-off hook-up in the Air France lounge.

What could a pale-faced, porridge-eating Scot from Strathpeffer, a village famous for its gloomy Victorian architecture and even gloomier past as a retreat for incurables seeking restorative waters, know about the inner workings of the human heart?

I open my eyes, take a swig of champagne, sit up, and scroll through the file until I come to a photograph of Ian Chapman. I nearly choke on my bubbly when I see his handsome face. *Dammmmn, son. Porridge does a body good.* The pale-faced Scot is a babe in a button-down with a square jaw, cleft chin, and roughhewn, chiseled features that seem incongruent with a pinky-lifting, tea-sipping, Ivy League-educated snob. His relaxed posture and direct gaze suggest a confident, kind man, not a charlatan hocking hokey love mantras to the hopeless to fund his house in the Hamptons.

I open a new file and begin typing questions in a stream-of-consciousness format. The answers to some of my questions will be found within the dossier, but many will be edited and refined until there are a few dozen open-ended questions that will reveal the man behind the mantras.

I scroll to a *London Times* article published two years ago, titled "Chapman Kills Serial Daters Softly with His Song." In the first paragraph, Chapman defines a serial dater as someone who doesn't play by the widely accepted dating rules.

Seriously? Who in the hell follows dating rules? There are too many and they often conflict. Old-school dating rules say you shouldn't date more than one person at a time, but modern dating experts encourage a popcorn approach to finding *the one*. You always throw more kernels in the pot when you're trying to make a bowl of popcorn because you know there will be a lot of duds. So which is it?

Remember that episode on *Sex and the City* when Miranda asks Carrie's boyfriend, Jack, a writer with a jaded outlook on relationships, to analyze the behavior of her love interest? She wants to know why the dude didn't accept her invitation to come up to her place after their date, and whether his excuse—that he had an early meeting—was legit. Without missing a beat, Jack says, "Yeah, he's just not that into you. When a guy's really into you, he's coming upstairs, meeting or no meeting." That episode inspired a book, movie, and a fresh set of dating rules. A few years later, another author published *He IS Just That Into You*, which suggested women kill potential relationships by overanalyzing their date's intentions. The author included fifteen rules that contradicted the core philosophy of *He's Just Not That Into You*.

How's that for some serious mind-fuckery?

Is it any wonder courtship has been reduced to swiping left or right, followed by mad texting, a phone call, a dick pic, some sexting, a drive-by date at a coffee shop with multiple exits, and then, maybe, if you're lucky, dinner and a hookup?

I keep reading the article.

"'Serial daters aren't clear about their intentions, which are usually shallow and self-serving,' Chapman explains. 'They lead people on and disappear when things get too intense for them. They are experts at breadcrumbing and ghosting, sliding in and out of DMs like a phantom moving through walls.'"

Is it me or is the Love Guru coming off as a little judgy? Maybe serial daters aren't self-serving but self-*pre*serving. Maybe they disappear because they're not vibing with their date and they prefer to avoid the inevitable "Is it me? Is it something I did?" convo. Trust me, there is no right answer to that question. Don't believe me? Let's roleplay this shit.

"It's not you. You didn't do anything wrong. You're awesome."

"Then why don't you want to go out with me?"

This is where you shift around uncomfortably, avoid eye contact, and try to think of an answer that won't make them feel like they just took a bullet to the heart. So, you come up with lame-ass reasons they swat away like mosquitos.

"I'm still in love with my boyfriend."

"Then why did you go out with me?"

Fail. Try again.

"I think we just need to slow things down."

"But we've only had two dates."

Fail. Try again.

You can't tell them the truth, either. Not ever. Don't believe me? Here are some of the truth bombs I've dropped on guys I didn't want to see again:

You didn't talk enough.

You talked too much.

You're boring.
You showed up with spinach stuck between your teeth.
You mentioned your ex fifteen times—just over drinks.
You drank too much.
You didn't drink enough.
You're wearing dad jeans.
You have a dad bod.
You talked about wanting to be a dad.

I want to know what Mister Love thinks the best way is to tell a dude you don't want to see him again. Not for a bootie call. Not for dinner. Not even for a FaceTime.

I go back to the article. "'The serial dater is motivated by the thrill of the chase, the excitement of the first date, the exhilaration of sexual capitulation. Like any skilled predator, they move with devastating speed. They fall in and out of lust/infatuation/love before their prey even knows what hit them.'"

I let out a long, low whistle. The Love Guru packs a mean punch once he peels off his touchy-feely gloves, doesn't he?

4

STINGER

I'm staring at two bronzed nipples and realizing I have the best job in the world. Adonis—his real name—greeted me the moment I walked into the lobby of the adults-only resort, a beaming Colgate grin on his swarthy face, a fruit-filled glass of sangria in his hand.

"Welcome to Mar de Cobalto, Senorita Donnelly," he said, taking my carryon from my hand and replacing it with the sangria in one smooth gesture. "I will be serving as your personal attendant throughout your stay at the resort. Tickets, trifles, reservations, requests, whatever you desire. I am here to please."

The living, breathing, three-dimensional Calvin Klein underwear advert has the tightest, tannest nips I have ever seen. I wonder if allowing me to draw a tank top on him with my tongue falls within his purview? He did say he is here to please and that would definitely please me.

In the eight years I've worked for *Conceit*, I have landed some choice gigs—cooking with Gordon Ramsey, driving a McLaren supercar 130 miles an hour on a racetrack in Dubai, soaking in a jacuzzi in an ice spa in Norway—but having a hottie with Insta abs offering to serve as my personal attendant is the best perk ever, even better than my Gucci Globe-Trotter.

Adonis retrieves my room key from behind a screen made of blanched and bleached tree branches, giving me some time to take in the lobby with its breathtaking view of the sea and a massive rock formation the limo driver called Es Vedrà. Yachts float at anchor on the shimmering horizon. A few dozen downward doggers are doing yoga on the beach. The cloudless sky blends into the sea like an abstract cobalt ombré painting. I take a sip of my sangria to be polite. I want to pour out the wine and eat the fruit resting in the bottom of my glass. Besides a handful of vanilla and pomegranate cashews I devoured in the limo on the way from the airport, I haven't had anything solid in my stomach since yesterday.

Adonis gestures for me to follow him. We walk across the lobby to a glass elevator. The doors slide open as we arrive as if we are ballerz in a rap video. In my head, scenes from Post Malone's *Saint Tropez* vid flicker. The Mar de Cobalto looks like the sort of place Postie would use as a backdrop for one of his videos. I can see him pulling up to the lobby in a shiny white Bugatti, diamond-encrusted Rolex Daytona on his tatted-up wrist. We step into the elevator and Adonis jabs the down button.

"The resort has a hundred and fifty two-story suites situated in self-contained whitewashed homes, each with a private swimming pool. Mar de Cobalto has a lap pool, lounge pool featuring twenty-foot waterfall, state-of-the-art fitness center, holistic spa, four restaurants, three bars, a private *bitch*, and a seventy-foot yacht available for charter."

Adonis speaks in a calm, measured voice that reminds me of an ASMR recording I listen to when I have insomnia. Antonio Banderas reading *Don Quixote*—except Antonio doesn't pronounce *beach* as *bitch*.

"I understand you are here on business, but if you find you have time, and would like to book a spa treatment, dinner reservation, or space in a fitness class, please press the A on your telephone. It is your direct link to me."

"I will. Thank you."

The elevator doors slide open, affording us a view of a blue-tiled swimming pool framed by palm trees. We step out of the elevator onto a covered walkway. A warm breeze blows off the sea, carrying the scent of coconut suntan lotion, saltwater, and tropical flowers. A lock of hair has come undone from my high ponytail. The pale strands float in the air before getting stuck on my recently glossed lips.

Adonis waves the card key over the magnetic plate above the door handle. The lock emits a muted beep-beep-beep and then a click. He pushes the door open and steps aside, allowing me to pass.

The suite is super luxe and reminds me of a spa I visited in Bali. The sitting room has a low-slung, modern sectional upholstered in white fabric, whitewashed walls, and teak floors. Behind the sectional is a screen made of the same blanched and bleached branches I saw in the lobby. The far wall is made of sliding glass panels that are open to a private terrace and swimming pool. The suite even smells like a spa—eucalyptus, ylang-ylang, and cedar.

ADONIS PLACES my room key on the table beside the sectional. He grabs the television remote and gives me a down-and-dirty tutorial on how to navigate the features that allow me to order room service, watch a pay-per-view movie, check the resort calendar for daily events, or send a message to the front desk.

"This is from Señor Chapman." He gestures to a gift basket

on the coffee table. It's wrapped in cellophane marked with red Xs and Os. "He asked me to confirm your meeting with him at five this evening in the conference room in the business center."

Adonis leaves with a bow.

I tear the cellophane off the basket and look at the goodies inside—a box of chocolates, a heart-shaped stress ball, a T-shirt embroidered with a small *x* and *o*, a folder containing information about the week's workshops and mixers, and autographed copies of Ian Chapman's books *Land the Man* and *Fill Your Love Bank*. I kick off my shoes, tuck *Fill Your Love Bank* under my arm, grab the box of chocolates, and head to the pool.

By the time Adonis returns with my luggage, I've tossed my jacket over the chaise longue, rolled my pants to my knees, and am dangling my legs in the pool. I've murdered the box of chocolates and left the blood-red wrappers strewn about like a confectionary crime scene.

Adonis carries my luggage up the stairs to the bedroom and returns with a travel-sized bottle of sunscreen with the hotel logo on it. He hands me the sunscreen, and I hand him a generous tip. He bows and leaves. I change into my bathing suit and stretch out on the chaise with *Love Bank*. I'm on chapter seven and have filled the margins with notes and questions when I get the feeling someone is watching me. I look around, half-expecting to find Adonis waiting with another glass of sangria, when I notice a muscular hottie in a black button-down standing on an upper balcony looking at me. There's a fluttery feeling in my stomach like I'm a silly teenager who has just spotted her crush at the mall. I'm flustered and flushed. Should I wave? Should I pretend I haven't noticed him? Am I giving side boob lying on this chaise?

Jesus, Marlow! Pull it together. You're not a fifteen-year-old girl at her first school dance. You're a sophisticated twenty-eight-year-old woman who's looking snatched in a Versace bikini. Thank you very much.

I roll onto my side, facing away from the hottie, arch my back, and let my bootie pop a little. I can feel his gaze on me. I like it.

That's right, baby. Look at my cake, because I'm serving it thick like Entenmann's.

~

"You've a chocolate wrapper stuck to your shoe."

These are the first words Ian Chapman says to me.

A week of research, a notebook full of clever questions, and a chic new sheath dress were supposed to set the tone for my rendezvous with the Love Guru. Confident. Hard-hitting. Instead, I shuffled into the conference room like a vaudeville clown, dragging a red foil wrapper behind me.

He's smiling at me. A wide, white toothy grin that defies the stereotype of the orthodontically-challenged Brit. His eyes sparkle like an up-and-coming model smizing her little heart out for the camera. He is *money* in his impeccably tailored Windsor check sports coat, monogrammed button-down, and dark jeans. I pull the chocolate wrapper off my shoe and return his smile. I don't know what I expected—a hippie-dippie Scot with a thick brogue, maybe. Instead, I'm picking up *Kingsman* in bespoke oxfords.

We exchange pleasantries and then get down to it.

"In a recent interview with the *New York Times*, you said singles are lonelier, but less likely to connect than any other time in history despite the technological advances that have made the world a smaller place. Why is that?"

"We have become addicts." He leans forward and rests his arms on the conference table. "We are addicted to the quick fix.

The twenty-four-hour news cycle, UberEats, video on demand, instant messaging. Technology has conditioned us to expect immediate gratification, but you can't order a soulmate the way you order a pizza. It doesn't matter how many dating sites you join. You're not going to have a meaningful relationship if you're only willing to invest the time it takes to swipe your finger across the screen."

Kristin would be happy to know I suppressed my automatic gag reflex when the Love Guru said the world *soulmate*.

"Some might say swiping allows singles to separate the wheat from the chaff."

"Finding a love connection isn't like winnowing grain," he says, rolling the *R* in *grain* ever so slightly. "Separating the wheat from the chaff. That idiom suggests swiping on a dating app is sorting the valuable from the worthless. No human is worthless."

"You wouldn't say that if you met some of the guys I've dated." I chuckle.

He doesn't laugh. He just stares at me through slightly narrowed eyes, as if I'm a brainteaser and he is trying to find hidden objects.

"Are you able to determine someone's value merely by looking at him?"

"I'm able to determine whether they are worth my time."

"How?"

I shift. In my mind, I see the Road Runner standing beneath a cliff with a boulder teetering on its edge. I feel like the Road Runner. I shift again. "I read it takes one-tenth of a second for someone to judge another person and develop a first impression. In one-tenth of a second we can determine someone's approximate age, race, gender, mood, and physical characteristics. Their posture, hygiene, body movements, and eye contact are clues that help us determine their self-esteem."

"What if one of your clues is a red herring?"

"Like..."

"Like a chocolate wrapper stuck to the bottom of a shoe."

Fuck. I knew the ghost of chocolates past would come back to haunt me. That thud? Yeah, that was the boulder falling off the cliff and crushing my argument. Props to the Love Guru. He's definitely wily.

"I dig what you're saying. The wrapper stuck to the bottom of my shoe could indicate I am scattered, distracted, hurried."

"Or that you just like chocolate." He grins.

I laugh. "Guilty."

"If we dismiss someone solely on their profile picture or dating bio we kill the magic before it happens."

"The magic?"

"You're right. We do form first impressions. The magic happens when we discover our first impressions were wrong. The person who looked so serious is actually a laugh. The vapid pretty boy has deep thoughts. The player wants a committed relationship. Swiping kills the magic before it has even happened." He leans back in his chair. "The flip side of that is social media. Social media creates false magic. We read someone's pithy comments in two hundred and eighty characters or less, and we think they're always pithy. How many people are actually living the life they portray on their Instagram feed? We filter our thoughts, actions, feelings, and selfies."

Social media hate. I'm here for it.

"People use filters whether they are looking for a date on the internet or in some old-school way, like in a grocery store or at hot yoga class. Though, I would argue it's hard to filter when you're twisted into an unnatural position in a room with fifteen sweaty people."

He laughs again.

"Do you think everyone wants a long-term, committed relationship?"

"Yes. Have you ever heard of Abraham Maslow?"

"No."

"Brilliant psychologist and philosopher. He wrote *A Theory of Human Motivation*, which, in essence, states that all humans have basic needs they strive to satisfy. Socialization and mating are two of those basic needs."

I want to ask him if mating has to be forever and ever, amen? Is it natural for two people to mate and remain monogamous for the rest of their lives? We have many friends throughout our lifetimes. Why not lovers? I am afraid the interview will get lost in the fog of soulmates.

"In *Fill Your Love Bank*, you wrote all people can be put in one of four categories with how they approach intimate relationships. The Avoidant, who is uncomfortable with intimacy; the Anxious, who fears loss of connection; the Fearful, who has a combination of traits from the Avoidant and the Anxious; and the rare beast, the Secure. Is that right?"

"It is."

"You claimed you can determine which category a person belongs to and why in ten questions or less."

"Yes."

I tilt my head and look at him through narrowed eyes.

"Would you like a demonstration?"

"Me?"

"Who else?"

Bring it, Love Man. "Okay."

"Are your parents still married?"

"No." I lean back in my chair. "My father divorced my mother when I was eleven years old."

"How did you feel when they told you they were getting divorced?"

"Two years before my parents got divorced, we spent Christmas holiday in the Swiss Alps. I had been skiing before—Aspen, Vail—so I thought I had mastered the bunny slopes and was ready for a blue square *piste,* an intermediate slope. First run, I fell flat on my back, hard. One moment, I was confident, flying over the snow, and the next I was staring up at the sky, confused, embarrassed, and unable to get my breath." I remember the snowflakes stinging as they landed on my tear-filled eyes and the whoosh in my ears as more experienced skiers raced by. "When my mother told me my father had left us, that he had packed his bags, and wouldn't be coming back, I felt like I did that day in the Alps, like someone had knocked the confidence and wind out of me."

Fuck me, Freud. That's some heavy stuff to lay on a light-filled Love Guru.

Ian reaches into his suitcoat pocket, pulls out a hankie, and hands it to me.

"I don't need—" A fat tear plops on my notepad and I realize I'm crying. I take the hankie and gently dab under my eyes. "I'm sorry. I don't know where this is coming from. I'm not usually this emotional."

Ian reaches across the table and places his hand over mine —a brief, warm expression of sympathy that causes fresh tears to fill my eyes. What in the hell kind of Charlie Manson head-trickery is this Love Guru practicing? I'm not a crier. I don't get misty-eyed at sappy love songs or weepy while watching commercials that shamelessly attempt to tug at the heartstrings with images of warm family gatherings. Machine Gun Marlow —that's what Kristin calls me, because I can destroy a sentimental advert or love ballad with a spray of sarcastic comments, riddle the fantasy with bullets of reality. That commercial that follows a grandfather and his granddaughter from childhood to adulthood, where all of her milestones are marked by Gramps giving her a candy bar? That's a glimpse into the making of an obese diabetic with a mouthful of cavities.

"Tears are proof that there is a well of emotion inside you. Shedding tears is proof that you are brave enough to be vulnerable with another. Never apologize for being vulnerable."

Vulnerable? Me? Marlow Donnelly? *Not bloody likely, Scot.* I blink back the tears while I fold the hankie into a neat square and then hand it to him with a flat smile, gaze direct, chin lifted. "Next question?"

He takes the hankie and places it on the table between us. "Did your mum remarry?"

"No."

"Why not?"

"Excuse me?"

"Why hasn't your mum gotten married again?"

I could say my father broke a part of my mother and she's never been able to lower her defenses, to be vulnerable, to rely on another. She looks happy and healed, flitting to the French Riviera or French Polynesia, always with a new man, but her broken part wasn't set properly, and now she's crippled. I could say that, but I don't like the picture it paints.

"I don't know."

"Is she happy?"

I stare blankly. Is my mom happy? A memory plays in my brain, like the first flickering frames of a movie. I went to see her after one of her cosmetic tweaks. The painkillers had her higher than Snoop Dogg. She got all in her feels and told me she thought she would die alone. Of course, I told her she would never be alone as long as she had me, but I knew my mother's admission spoke of a loneliness and yearning that couldn't be fixed with a daughter's love. A surgeon's scalpel and a morphine drip had left my beautiful mother exposed. The mask of the confident jetsetter, the ageless It Girl, removed, revealing an ordinary woman with ordinary longings.

"Is my mom happy?" I repeat his question, employing a basic tactic to stall for time. "She's a successful businesswoman. She has many friends, travels the world, and never struggles to find a date. She's beautiful, always has been, even before the face lift and cosmetic tweaks. Why wouldn't she be happy?"

Nice try, Charlie, but you are not going to brainwash me with your hankies and hypnotic gazes. You got the waterworks once, but you won't get them again.

His lips curve in a slow knowing smile, and I wonder if this mystical matchmaker is a mind-reader.

"Have you ever been in love?" he asks.

A memory of Terrell scoring the winning touchdown against Notre Dame and then forming a heart with his hands and pointing at me flashes in my mind.

"Yes, I've been in love."

"How did it end?

"Painfully," I say, my flat voice matching my expression.

"How long ago was that?"

"Eight years." Eight years and two months, to be precise. "You have two more questions."

"I don't need them." He folds his hands and rests them on the table. "You are an Avoidant. I suspect your mother suffered from serious depression after her divorce and it took her a long time to accept that her marriage was over. Your father became the absent parent, focusing on his new life while forgetting his old one. You were close with him before the divorce and you took his abandonment personally. You felt abandoned again after your love affair ended eight years ago. Your mom didn't process her pain. She pushed it away. She keeps it at bay by never being alone, never being without attention, because her self-esteem remains inflated as long as she is chasing or being chased. You have done the same thing. You, Miss Donnelly, are a serial dater. Aren't you?"

Fuck me. I didn't see that coming. The Love Guru sucker-punched me.

"Okay." I sit forward. "You've got my attention."

5

SHAMROCKED

I am totally drained after the psyche-probing interview with the sucker-punching Love Guru. I feel like I was mind-raped. I want to numb the pain with alcohol. Lots of alcohol.

I know. I know. Alcohol should not be used for emotional medicinal purposes. Vodka is a temporary anesthetic for sadness, grief, loneliness, fear, and low self-worth, but popping a borrowed Xanax before you get on an international flight doesn't make you a junkie, just as drinking your daily intake of calories occasionally doesn't make you an alcoholic.

The resort's main bar faces the sea, with floor-to-ceiling sliding glass doors open to the balmy night breeze. The lights are low, the music a libido-stimulating R&B song. A few guests are seated at tables, but the stools lining the bar are empty. I head for the bar and sit at one end. The bartender is a tall, tanned, muscular hottie.

"Hiya," he says.

"Hello," I say.

"What's the craic?" he says in a thick Irish accent.

Crack? What the actual hell? I knew Ibiza was turnt up, but I didn't expect the bartenders to offer crack. Wonder if a Molly left on the pillow is part of the resort's turndown service?

He must notice the confusion in my eyes because he laughs and says, "I asked how ye were. I didn't offer ye drugs."

"Ah," I say, relieved.

"What can I get ye?"

"Something strong."

"Are ye wanting a drink or a man?"

"A drink."

"Either way, I would recommend something Irish." His blue eyes sparkle.

"Whiskey will be fine."

"Grand choice."

"Leave the bottle."

"Not a bother." He slides the bottle toward me.

Fuck me! He looks like one of the thirst traps I follow on Instagram, all chiseled jaw and dimpled cheeks. His dark blond hair is styled in an undercut, like he just took off his flat cap and stepped off the set of *Peaky Blinders*. His black button-up is straining to contain his chest and bulging biceps. He winks before walking to the other end of the bar to take an order. Broad shoulders and an ass so sweet it makes me want to sink my teeth into it. Not that I'm into asses...or biting them. Don't know where that came from.

I drain my whiskey in one swallow. I'm reaching for the bottle to pour a finger or two of the emotion- and tongue-numbing liquid into my glass when I notice a tall, slender woman hovering at the entrance. She's wearing a J. Crew little black dress with an *Exes and Ohs* nametag slapped to her chest—more in the region of her shoulder than her breast. She's clutching her purse to her stomach as if she expects to be accosted by a knife-wielding hooligan. Poor thing looks like one of those cartoon fraidy cats—eyes wide, shoulders dropped, back hunched, like she will startle at the slightest noise. She takes a deep breath and hurriedly walks to the bar, practically collapsing onto a stool near me.

She notices me watching her, slides her glasses up her nose, and offers me a tremulous smile before pulling her phone out of her purse. Classic self-conscious single woman move. I want to snatch the phone out of her hand and replace it with a bottle of vodka and a straw. Everyone knows drinking alcohol through a straw accelerates its effects, and this girl needs twenty-five ounces of liquid courage, stat.

I glance at her nametag, but she's written her name in script so small I can't read it. The big glasses, odd nametag placement, teensy-tiny handwriting, and cellphone held like a shield scream, "Get back, muthafucka."

I lean over the bar, grab another glass, and pour some whiskey into it.

"Hello." I slide the courage toward the cat. "You look like you could use a strong drink."

She peeks over the tops of her massive eyeglasses. The blue light from her phone reflected in her lenses is making it difficult for me to see the middle third of her face. She could use a little lip tint, but she's bringing some serious eyebrow game. This is a girl who knows how to wield a pair of tweezers. *Serve it, sister.*

"I...I could, actually," she says, dropping her phone on the bar and seizing the proffered glass with both hands. "Thank you—"

"Marlow," I say. "My name is Marlow Donnelly."

"Thank you, Marlow. I'm Brandy. Brandy Brewer."

"Get the fuck outta here," I say, laughing. "That is *not* your real name."

"Afraid so." Her smile wobbles.

"Man, are you lucky."

"I am?"

"*Shyeah*," I say. "A name like that is an instant ice breaker."

Her wobbly smile straightens. She brings the glass up to her face and takes a deep breath. Her nose wrinkles as if she's walked into a fish market. I expect her to put the glass down without taking a sip, but she presses the rim to her mouth, throws her head back, and downs two fingers in one swallow.

Respect. Okay, girl born with the perfect stripper name. I see you.

I'm pouring another finger into her glass when the Irish thirst trap returns.

"Come here," he says, eyes sparkling. "You're after doing me job."

"I'm sorry, Irish." I smile. "Brandy was having an intoxicant emergency."

He crosses his lethally sexy guns over his chest and laughs. The sound shifts my libido into fourth gear like Dale Earnhardt making his final lap.

"I'll let it slide this time," he says, his eyes sparkling. "But only if you promise to keep calling me Irish."

"Done."

"What should I call you?"

Fuck Buddy? Booty Call? Friend with Benefits?

"Marlow," I purr.

That's right. I purred. You would purr too if you could see this big hunk of Irish catnip. A little more flirting and I'm going to throw my cat at him so hard he won't see me coming.

"Hiya, Marlow." He holds out his hand. "Fionn O'Connell."

Of course he's a Fionn. Aren't all Irish bartenders named Fionn or Patrick? I put my hand in his and a spark of sexual energy passes between us.

"Nice to meet you, Irish Fionn." I pull my hand away, suddenly inexplicably shy. "This is my friend Brandy."

Fionn holds my gaze and several more jolts of electricity travel through my body. Jaysus! This must be what it feels like when you get hit with a bolt of lightning. My skin is all tingly and hot. My limbs are jumpy. Finally, after what seems like a very long time, he breaks eye contact.

"Hiya," he says to Brandy. "Is that really your name, like? Brandy?"

Brandy's cheeks flush with color. She's wilting, retreating into herself under Fionn's direct gaze. Something tells me it is going to take more than a wellness retreat to coax this flower off the wall.

"Brandy Brewer," I say, drawing Fionn's attention away from the painfully shy woman. "I was just telling her she has the best name, ever. Brandy Brewer."

"Brilliant."

"Right? A name like that is an instant ice breaker. 'Hello, my name is Brandy Brewer and I go down smooth.'"

Brandy giggles. Fionn laughs.

"'Hiya, I'm Brandy,'" he says, uncrossing his arms. "'Would you believe I improve with age?'"

Damn! Gorgeous and quick.

"Okay, Irish," I say, laughing. "Bring it. What else you got?"

"Oh, I have loads and loads." He grins. "'Hiya, I'm Brandy. You can mark me VS, Very Special, because I am definitely more than three stars.'"

"Nice," I say, giving the gorgeous bartender the props he deserves. "'Hello, I'm Brandy. I go good with dessert.'"

"Brilliant," Fionn laughs.

He leans against the bar and fixes me with his twinkly-eyed gaze. Dingle Whiskey must have something special in it because the world beyond my peripheral vision has faded away and all I can see is the Irishman's handsome face, the sparks of silver in his blue eyes, the tiny scar just below his hairline, the hole in his right earlobe the size of an earring post.

"Come here. If ye're on the lash, forget the whiskey."

The golden liquid has me feeling comfortably fuzzy all over. I've never found a whiskey I liked—because I don't dig swallowing razor blades—but I think I'm falling in love with Dingle Batch Five.

"What do you recommend?" I ask.

"My specialty," he says, his sexy smile teasing the dimples onto his cheeks. "Three and ye'll be well and truly pissed."

He drops the *h* in *th* words so three sounds like tree.

"Bring it, Irish," I say, the whiskey and the sensual Spanish air making me bolder by the second. "Whatcha got?"

He turns around and pulls a chilled martini glass from a cooler behind the bar, grabs a shaker, and fills it with some sort of seeded fruit and a splash of vanilla vodka. He moves so fast I can't identify the other ingredients. He is impressive behind the bar—not in a cheesy, theatrical way like Tom Cruise juggling beer glasses in *Cocktail*. This Irishman isn't a Hippy Hippy Shaker. He's skilled and quietly confident. His hands are broad, his fingers long, and I wonder if the hand-penis ratio holds true.

He looks up, watching me through his thick blond lashes, and a flush of heat spreads through my body. His lips pull up in a small, knowing smile that makes me wonder if he is the mind reader. A dirty, dirty girl mind reader.

He grabs a shot glass and pours a measure of champagne into it. He puts the martini glass and Brut shot in front of me. Lowkey, it's a work of art. An orange concoction with a passion fruit slice floating atop its foamy surface.

"It's lovely. What do you call it?"

"Porn Star Martini," he says, his thick Irish accent turning my insides as mushy as a slice of overripe passion fruit. "Alternate between the martini and the shot. One beautiful woman between two strong drinks—the *menage à trois of cocktails*. Think ye can handle it?"

Oh. No. He. Didn't. Did this fit-as-fuck Irishman just throw down with me?

"Humble brag." I lift the martini to my mouth and press the rim to my lips. "I'm an American, gorgeous. There isn't much I can't handle."

"Fair play to ye," he laughs.

Fionn winks before going to the other end of the bar to take orders from a group that has just arrived. Brandy is staring at me with fraidy cat eyes wide, mouth agape.

"You are amazing," she says.

"Yes, I am." I punch the air above me.

"I can't believe the way you just flirted with the bartender." Brandy shoves her glasses back up her nose. "You were so cool and clever. I could never do that."

"Sure you could."

"No way."

I lean forward, snatch the napkin she's been shredding out of her hands, and drop it on the counter. Then I grab her cellphone off the bar and slide it into her purse.

"The first rule to successful flirting is to be present. You can't flirt if you don't find someone to flirt with, and you won't find someone to flirt with if you're distracted by your phone, or napkins, or twizzle straws, or your glasses. Do you wear contacts?"

"Yes. Why?"

"Wear them. You have beautiful eyes. Why would you want to hide them behind an oversized pair of glasses?"

"You think my eyes are beautiful?"

"Absolutely." I take a sip of my drink. "Velvet brown eyes with thick eyelashes that don't even need mascara. Envy."

"Thanks, Marlow," she says, beaming.

She really is quite pretty when she isn't slumped over or hiding behind her purse.

"You're here for the singles retreat, right?"

"Yes, is it that obvious?"

"The *Exes and Ohs* nametag kinda gave it away."

She looks down at the sticker on her dress and rolls her eyes. "I forgot I was wearing a nametag."

I laugh.

"You're not here for the retreat, are you?"

I shake my head. "I'm a reporter with *Conceit*—the magazine. I am here to do an article on Father Chapman and his faithful flock of singletons."

"How exciting."

"Do you mind if I ask you a few questions?" We spend the next hour talking about Brandy's tragically stunted dating life. If you measured a person's love life in height, Brandy's would be a dwarf. She's a twenty-six-year-old cyber-security expert with a serious case of Sarmassophobia.

Sarmassophobia. Sounds like an issue made up by someone trying to score a free emotional support puppy, doesn't it? It's a totally legit phobia, though. It means fear of dating. Brandy is a Sarmassophobie-ite. Okay, I made that one up because I don't know what they call people who have Sarmassophobia. Sarmassophobians? Sarmassophobia is a social phobia that makes it difficult for people to engage with members of the opposite sex. Brandy tells me she has tried cognitive behavioral therapy, hypnosis, and anti-anxiety meds to treat her phobia. She tells me her fear of being medicated for the rest of her life motivated her to throw down the big bills for the retreat. Ian Chapman's love fest doesn't come cheap. Horny hopefuls pay fifteen thousand dollars to attend *Exes and Ohs*, and that doesn't include airfare and lodging. Brandy tells me she is attending a workshop in the morning—*Exorcise Your Relationship Demons,* an intensive session designed to heal old wounds and break the negative mental patterns preventing singles from becoming doubles.

"Do you want to go to the workshop together?"

"Seriously?" She looks like she just won the Power Ball. "That would be great."

"Why don't we meet for breakfast first?"

I am not a brekkie kinda girl, but Brandy is sweet, and she looks like she could use the moral support. I'm always down to make a new friend. Vacay friends are my favorite souvenirs.

We agree to meet at the poolside restaurant at eight the following morning. Brandy finishes her drink, slides off her barstool, bids me *adieu* with a tipsy wave, and leaves the bar without putting her glasses back on.

I look down the bar at Fionn pouring tequila into a shot glass. Watch the smooth way he moves his muscular body and imagine him moving it on top of me. I imagine what it would feel like to have those arms wrapped around my waist, to have him pushing inside me from behind. He notices me watching him and winks.

When a second bartender arrives, Fionn finishes pouring shots and comes back to me.

"What brings ye to Ibiza?"

"The singles retreat."

His blond eyebrows arch sharply. "Why would a dashing woman like ye need a singles retreat, for fuck's sake? Trust me, love, ye don't need help finding a ride. Have ye seen some of the people that go to those things?"

Tose tings is how he pronounces it, which pleases me more than it should.

"I'm a reporter with *Conceit* magazine. I'm here to write a piece on the retreat."

He whistles. "Impressive."

"Not really," I say, suddenly shy.

"Really."

"Thank you."

"Not a bother."

He reaches for my empty shot glass and his hand brushes against mine. An electric jolt passes through my body, like the shock you get when you drag your feet on the carpet and touch something made of metal. He freezes and looks at me. I think he felt it this time, too. I play with the slender stem of my martini glass, sliding my fingers up and down.

He splashes some champagne into my shot glass and sets it on the bar. His hand brushes against mine again, longer this time.

"What's a lad from Ireland doing working in a bar in Ibiza?"

"Ah, sure, look. That's a long story."

"I'm not going anywhere."

"How about I tell ye the abbreviated version right now and the longer version over dinner tomorrow?"

Oh fuck, fuck yeah.

"Sure." I take a sip of my martini. "Or I could buy you a drink when you're off tonight."

"I would like that, but I don't drink."

"An Irishman who doesn't drink? Isn't that an oxymoron?"

He laughs, but something flickers in his eyes—pain, embarrassment, irritation—and I instantly regret my words. *Nice, Marlow. Nothing like throwing down a politically incorrect insult to attract a gorgeous guy.*

"I'm sorry. That was rude."

"Go on with ye."

He shrugs it off, but I sense my thoughtless comment cut deeper than he is letting on.

"What do you do for fun in Ibiza?"

"I surf and go dancing.

"You've got moves?"

"I'm an Irishman, gorgeous. There aren't many moves I can't make."

Okay. I see you, Boo.

"Oh, really," I laugh. "That's a bold claim. Don't be surprised if I ask to see the proof."

"Not a bother."

We stare at each other until I am practically vibrating with sexual tension. I wonder if he can feel what he's doing to my body.

"I am a reporter. I like a good story. Let's hear yours."

"Oh, ye know. The usual story." His tone is chill, but the arms crossed defensively, the muscle working in his handsome jaw, tell me he doesn't feel chill. "When ye grow up in a village with only five hundred residents—and loads of them family members—it can feel like the world is closing in on ye. Like if ye don't break free ye'll be trapped there forever, seeing the same faces, listening to the same stories."

"I get it."

"Do ye?"

"No," I say, laughing. "I grew up in Los Angeles, population four million super shallow, super self-impressed people who are too busy chasing fame or the almighty *dollah dollah* bill to slow down and tell a story."

"Is that why ye became a professional storyteller, then?"

Wow! I love words and stringing them together in a way that entertains a reader, but I never considered my deeper motivation for being a reporter. Fionn's dead on the money. The best part of my job is the interview, when I sit face-to-face, coaxing a story from a stranger.

"You're more than just a hot bod and a pretty face, aren't you?" I say.

He laughs. "Was that a compliment or an insult?"

"A compliment. Definitely."

"So, ye think I have a pretty face?"

I want to tell him he has the face of an angel and a body built for sin. I want to say I could dive into his blue eyes, lose myself in their depths. Wait! What in the Hallmark movie is happening to me? Lose myself in his eyes?

"Don't let it go to your head."

"Never," he says, grinning. "I won't let your comment about my—what did you call it again? Oh, yeah. *Hot bod*. I won't let that comment go to my head either."

"Good. I wouldn't want you thinking I've fallen for you."

He gasps and he presses his hands to his heart. "Ye mean ye haven't? I've fallen for ye, Marlow Donnelly."

I roll my eyes and pull my credit card out of my pocket. "You're a shameless charmer."

"Guilty as charged, but something tells me ye bring the shameless charmer out in every man ye meet, love."

"Careful, Irish." I stand. "You don't want your compliments to go to my head, do you?"

"No. Your heart."

Fuck me! He's good.

"Shameless."

I hand him my credit card to settle my tab, but he pushes it away. I slip my AmEx back into my pocket.

"Thank you."

"Come here. Tell me your room number."

"Ten twenty-one."

"Ten twenty-one. I'll call for you tomorrow at six o'clock. Dress for dancing."

I walk out of the bar onto the empty terrace, shivering as a balmy breeze blows over my bare arms. Damn! That Irishman has me so hot and bothered I'm actually perspiring. Beads of sweat started forming between my breasts the moment he said, *"I've fallen for ye, Marlow Donnelly."* His accent made the sweet admission sound dirty, sexy dirty. I lift my thick hair off my shoulders and let the breeze cool my damp neck. *Get a serious grip, girl. So what if a fit-as-fuck Irish bartender flirted with you? He probably flirts with everyone.*

I'm on the path that leads to my room when I hear the thud of footsteps behind me. My stomach clenches and a dozen thoughts race through my mind. *What if it's Fionn? I hope it's Fionn. It's not Fionn. I need to get laid because I am acting thirsty.*

"Marlow."

I turn around and my stomach clenches again as soon as I see him standing on the path, the moonlight making his chiseled face even more handsome, if that's possible. He closes the distance between us in two long-legged strides. We're close enough for me to smell the soap on his skin. Remember that scene in *From Here to Eternity* when Burt Lancaster is making love to Deborah Kerr on the beach with waves washing over them? That's what Fionn smells like. Sex on the beach.

He leans down and presses his lips to mine. A tender kiss that makes my knees as mushy as overripe passion fruit. I want to press my hands to his chest, feel the solidness of him, but he stops kissing me before I can make my body follow my thoughts.

"I have wanted to do that all night," he whispers in my ear. "Goodnight, Marlow."

And then he's gone, and I'm standing alone in the moonlight, wondering if I just imagined the feel of his lips on mine.

6

GAME DAY SANGRIA

"*Marlow.*"

I turn around slowly. My breath catches in my throat. Fionn is standing behind me, shirtless and even sexier than I remember. He wraps his arm around my waist, pulls me close, and kisses me. I move into him, melt into him. I thrust my tongue into his mouth. Bolder this time. My breasts against his rippled chest. His hands cupping my bum. His cock throbbing against my stomach. My hand aching to feel the weight of him, suddenly sliding into his waistband, my fingers wrapping around his—

"Marlow. Hello?" Brandy waves her hand in front of my face. "Are you okay? Your body is here, but your mind is somewhere else."

"Jet lag. Sorry."

The truth? I've been in my head since Fionn kissed me. I replayed the moment in my mind like a video on loop all night, fantasizing different endings, playing with myself until I fell asleep exhausted, frustrated. I stay in my head through breakfast and on the walk to the ballroom where the workshop is being held.

I assumed the hotel would use a partition to create a smaller, more intimate space for the handful of attendees wanting to exorcise their relationship demons. There are more possessed singles than I realized. The ballroom is packed. There must be three hundred people waiting for Ian to splash some holy water on them and drive the desperate from their dating lives. Who knew there were that many English-speaking singles with enough scratch to spend a week at an exclusive resort, listening to wisdom being dispensed by a twenty-six-year-old relationship expert, who is—*no shade here*—still *single*?

A stage stretches across the front of the ballroom. It's designed to look like a multi-dimensional set, with a series of screens layered in the back. Focused pink, white, and red lighting gives it a slick, theatrical feel. The only seats available are located in the first two rows. Apparently, there aren't many eager-to-impress overachievers in this crowd.

"Ohmygod!" Brandy clutches my elbow. "There aren't any seats left."

"Sure, there are. Up front."

She squeaks. Literally squeaks. "We can't sit up there."

"Why not?"

"It's too close to the stage"—she lowers her voice to a reverential whisper—"to *Ian*."

"Good!" I fix her with an encouraging smile. "You forked over some serious cheese for this retreat. You might as well get everything out of it you can. What better way than to see Ian Chapman up close and personal?"

She squeaks again.

"Come on," I say.

Flipping my hair over my shoulders, I walk up the middle aisle before fraidy cat has a chance to run back to her room. I reach the middle of the first row, shrug out of the tight-fitting jacket that matches my strapless jumpsuit, and toss it over my chair. I'm already sitting and patting the empty chair beside me by the time Brandy arrives, her shoulders hunched to her ears, a fine line of perspiration beading her forehead.

"That was awful." She collapses onto the chair beside me.

"I know." I squeeze her hand. "You did great, though."

The lights slowly dim. The hum of conversation fades away. When we're sitting in a dark, silent ballroom, the screens over the stage flash black-and-white images of random singles interspersed with clips of Ian dispensing his wisdom.

You have to heal the past if you hope to thrive in the future.
Reprogram yourself so happiness is your default setting.
Building your core is the only way you can have a fit relationship.
Personal transformation is the first step to a perfect pairing.

By the time the stage lights flicker on and cast the ballroom in a happy, rosy glow, I'm nearly as amped up as the hundreds of hopeful romantics hooting and clapping around me. Ian is such a dynamic, empathetic speaker I find it easy to focus on him for the duration of the two-hour workshop. The last forty-five minutes are enthralling. Ian brings random singles on stage and does that whole Jedi mind-reading trick thing he did on me. Straight up? I'm blown away by his ability to ask the right questions and then accurately describe the baggage keeping each single from moving onto a healthy relationship. One hundred and twenty minutes of the Love Guru pumping his players up like Knute Rockne giving his Fighting Irish a pep talk before the big game. I expect him to turn to the audience and say, "They can't lick us!" and for them to respond with a resounding, *"Fight! Fight! Fight! Fight! Fight!"*

I only think about Fionn once or twice throughout the workshop, but as soon as Ian bounds from the stage, I'm back on that damned path, wrapping my legs around the Irishman's narrow waist. I'm lost in my dirty girl thoughts when someone taps me on the shoulder. My skin tingles and I wonder if Fionn is standing behind me.

"Marlow Donnelly!"

I turn around and just like that my thoughts shift from my *Oh* to my Ex. Terrell Rose is standing in a beam of pink light, like I'm a silly eighteen-year-old looking at her first love through her Dolce & Gabbana rose-colored sunglasses.

"Terrell Rose." I blame that mind-reading, ghosts-of-boyfriends-past-conjuring Ian Chapman and his exorcising workshop for this moment. I have been to New York dozens of times in the last eight years and never once have I crossed paths with my first love. "I can't believe you remember my name."

He pulls back like I delivered an uppercut to his whiskered chin. I'd be a liar if I told you it didn't feel good to verbally knock the cocky grin off his handsome face. I'm just so pissed. Our reunion wasn't supposed to go down like this—at some sad singles retreat, with him looking like he's *People Magazine*'s Sexiest Man Alive, his tight-fitting black tee clinging to every damned muscle, a two-carat solitaire sparkling in one ear, his espresso skin as unlined and yummy as ever.

Brandy clears her throat.

"Oh, I'm sorry." I smile at Brandy before returning my gaze to Terrell. "Where are my manners? Brandy, this is the man who tossed my love away like it was a deflated scrimmage ball."

Brandy squeaks.

"I deserved that." Terrell looks deep into my eyes before turning to Brandy. "Hello, Brandy. I'm Terrell Rose, the idiot who let this beautiful woman walk out of his life. Pleased to meet you."

"It's nice to meet you, Terrell," Brandy says.

"Good to see you again, Terrell." I turn away.

"Wait!" Terrell grabs my arm. "You can't just leave."

"That's not what you said eight years ago."

I hate that I sound like a bitter bitch. Bitter never looks good on a woman, not even when she's rocking an on-point jumpsuit and deep cut décolleté Louboutins. For eight years, Terrell was a ghost, trapped in the dusty attic of my memory. Sometimes, when I'd drink too much and get all in my feels, I'd mentally climb the stairs to that attic, unlock the door, and confront Terrell's ghost. I'd ask him why he stopped loving me. I'd tell him about the nights I fell asleep staring at my phone, willing him to call.

"Can we go for a walk?" he asks.

"Sorry." I shake his hand from my arm. "I'm not an attendee. I'm here to write an article about Ian Chapman. I'm a reporter. For a magazine."

"I know." He smiles.

"You do?"

"I was flying to Chicago a few years ago. *Conceit* was one of the magazines in the seatback. I was bored so I started flipping through the pages, and there it was, an article about the architect who designed Leonardo DiCaprio's Malibu beach house written by Marlow Donnelly." He's grinning now, the same way he used to grin at me when I would show up to a game wearing a barely-there minidress and thigh-high boots—his favorite. "I was so proud when I saw your byline. I ordered every back issue I could get and read all of your pieces."

No. No. No. No! He doesn't get to grab my arm, to look at me with his soulful eyes, to say he's proud of me. He lost those rights when he told me to get out of his hospital room, to forget about him, that I was just a college fling. I want to shrug off his praise like I shrugged off my jacket, but learning that my first and only love has read all of my articles warms me more than the sweltering Ibiza sun.

"Um." Brandy shifts from one foot to the other. "I have to... go...make a...phone call."

Brandy is gone before I have a chance to stop her.

"Let me buy you lunch," Terrell says.

"No, really"—I shake my head—"I have to get started on my article."

"Dinner, then?"

"I can't."

"You have to eat, Marlow."

"I plan to," I say.

"Then have dinner with me."

"Sorry, I can't."

"Okay, how about you let me buy you a sangria?"

I imagine how it would look to Fionn if I walked into the bar with Terrell.

"I have a date."

He grins again. "You do, huh?"

"Yes, I do!" I snap. "Believe it or not, I can pull."

"Oh"—he gazes slowly up my body, from my heels to my perfectly styled hair, and everything in between—"I have no doubt you can pull, Mad Girl."

Mad Girl is the name he called me when he discovered my name was Marlow Ann Donnelly. Later, he said it was because he was "mad about the girl." I look at his grin, remember the way he wore my initials on the back of his helmet, and a smile tugs the corners of my mouth.

"There she is!" He claps his hands. "There's my girl. I knew you were in there somewhere under that sexy suit and serious expression."

"I am *not* your girl, Terrell. Not anymore."

"You will be." He winks and walks away.

7

IRISH BUCK

"You're a smashing bit of stuff," Fionn whispers, kissing my cheek.

I'm wearing a black lace mini dress with a deep V-neck, short sleeves, a cinched waist, and short-ruffled skirt. A wisp of fabric more than a dress. My legs are bare except for the shimmering bronze body oil I applied after my bath. The only things keeping me from being naked under my dress are a spritz of Flowerbomb and a strappy thong. I'm bringing my A-game for the Irish player.

"Thanks." I press a hand to my stomach to still the wild fluttering that started the moment I caught a whiff of his cologne—exotic and spicy. "You're rather smashing yourself, Irish."

If smashing translates to stud I've spent the entire day thinking about riding, then yes, by all means, Fionn O'Connell is smashing, crazy smashing. He's wearing dark, skinny summer-weight trousers rolled at the ankle, a crisp white button-down unbuttoned just enough to see a tantalizing hint of his tanned chest, and a black Rolex Submariner on his wrist. His Italian buttery-soft leather loafers are money. I wrote an article about Federico Santoni, the leather shoemaker in Bologna known for making luxury loafers like the kind Fionn is wearing, and since then I've had a bit of a thing for men in bespoke shoes.

Fionn rests his hand on the small of my back and guides me out of the hotel.

"I've made reservations at a new restaurant," he says, hailing a cab. "I hope you like curry."

"I do," I say. "Curry. Bold move in Ibiza."

"Bold moves are the only kind of moves I make, love."

Oh, fuck, fuck yeah!

A taxi pulls to a stop. Fionn opens the door and steps aside. I slide into the back seat and he climbs in beside me, his thigh pressing against mine—a warm, muscular promise of the bold moves I hope he intends to make later.

The curry restaurant, it turns out, is less than a mile from the hotel, but the Irishman didn't want me to walk in my heels. I'm trying not to go all head over red-heeled Louboutins for Fionn, but he's making it difficult with his Irish Coffee composition, a perfect combination of frothy whipped sweetness and heady full-bodied sinfulness.

A hostess shows us to a table on a patio lit by colorful paper lanterns suspended from the branches of a gnarly algarrobo tree. Fionn pulls out the chair facing the sea and waits for me to sit before folding his massive body into the chair opposite me. A waitress appears to take our drink order. I order chardonnay. Fionn orders a sparkling water.

"Am I blocking your view?" he asks.

"Baby, you *are* the view," I say.

"Ahha!" He laughs, but spots of color appear on his cheeks. "Stop! No compliments."

Ireland has the reputation of being the most magical place on earth—the land of pookahs, selkies, fairies, and leprechauns —but the most mystical creature of all has to be the one sitting across from me—a panty-dropping gorgeous man in possession of humility. How often do you spot one of those?

"Fionn?"

"*Marlow?*"

"You mentioned you don't drink alcohol." I keep my shoulders relaxed, look him in the eye, and smile softly, the approachable posture I adopt when I ask tough questions during interviews. "I don't want to be a buzzkill, but my reporter sense is tingling. There's a story behind your sobriety, isn't there?"

He leans back in his chair and inhales until his shirt is stretched so tight across his chest, I expect the buttons to pop off and whizz through the air at me. The open gaze becomes shuttered like Ibizan windows against the afternoon sunshine. This. This is the classic defensive interviewee posture. I expect him to evade the question, but he doesn't.

"Timothy, my older brother, was murdered. Stabbed on a football pitch in Dublin two years ago."

He holds my gaze, but a current passes below the surface of his sea blue eyes, something dark and dangerous, and I know he's struggling against waves of pain. I hate that I caused those waves. I reach across the table and rest my hand on top of his.

"Were you close?"

"He was my best mate."

"I'm sorry, Fionn."

"Ah, sure, look. Death is a part of life."

The waitress returns with our drinks.

"I'm sorry"—I lift the chilled chardonnay glass off the table and hand it back to the waitress—"but I've changed my mind. Could I please have a sparkling water with a twist of lime? Thank you."

"Ye didn't need to do that," Fionn says, after the server hurries away to replace my white wine with lime water. "It doesn't bother me when people drink around me."

"I would hope not, because"—I glance around quickly and lower my voice to a whisper—"Fionn? You work in a bar. People drink around you every day."

He laughs and the sound fills me with the same warmth and contentment I felt yesterday, when I was stretched out on the chair beside the pool, the sun on my bare skin, a book in my hands.

The waitress returns with my lime water. She asks us if we need more time to peruse the menu. Fionn orders for us to share —spicy red seafood curry, chicken coconut curry, and jasmine rice. Once the waitress takes our menus and hurries off to place our order, Fionn tells me about the days following his brother's murder.

"I was gutted, like someone reached inside and ripped out my heart and lungs."

His voice catches on the last word and I feel gutted for him. The only other time I've felt this desperate need to ease someone's suffering was when I found my mom curled up on her bathroom floor, sobbing into a wad of mascara-stained Kleenex because she found out my father had popped the question to Amy, the cat-loving, Yoga-pants-wearing, Herpes-infected, horse-faced medical assistant.

"I went on the lash after Timothy died."

"On the lash?"

"Go out drinking," he says. "I spent the better part of the year wrecked. One night I stayed in the pub after closing, determined to drink myself stupid to numb the pain. I don't know how many pints I had that night. I don't remember leaving the pub. My uncle found my car wrapped around a light pole the next morning. I had gone through the windshield and spent the night lying unconscious and bleeding in a field."

"Oh my God!" I curl my fingers around his hand. "You could have died, Fionn."

"I nearly did," he says, lacing his fingers through mine. "Fractured skull, broken ribs, punctured lung."

"I am glad you didn't die."

"Me too." He rubs his thumb against the back of my hand.

"I am sorry about my comment yesterday."

He frowns.

"I said an Irishman who doesn't drink is an oxymoron."

"Jaysus, go on with ye."

There is something more, something deeper and sweeter, about this guy. He's more than his Hollywood hot looks and gym rat bod. He brings out my deeper, sweeter, softer side, and it scares me. I catch flights, not feelings.

"What about you?" he asks.

"What about me?"

"Tell me about Marlow Donnelly."

"What do you want to know?"

"Everything." He grins. "I want to hear the story of your life. Where were you born? Do ye have a big family? Are ye close?"

I tell him about growing up in Los Angeles, the daughter of a powerful, wealthy man and his beautiful style icon wife, about the pressure I felt to be as spectacular as my mother, the pressure I still feel. You can't grow up the daughter of the woman who may have inspired the Material Girl and not feel pressure to be fabulous, like wearing pearls to bed when you're eight years old, fasting the week before prom so you could fit into one of your mom's double zero Dior gowns, or landing an internship at the most famous luxury magazine in the world and then clawing your way up the corporate ladder to become their premiere lifestyle reporter. I tell him about my parents' divorce, my father's new family, and my mother's phoenix-like rising from the ashes of her heartbreak.

When the waitress arrives with our food, pungent-smelling fish and chicken in fluorescent sauces, I'm grateful for the interruption. Thank God something has happened to stem the verbal diarrhea that's been flowing freely from me for the last half hour. Fionn knows more about me than my last twenty dates combined.

Fionn serves me a helping of each dish before serving himself. I'm mesmerized by his hands, the graceful way he moves them despite his obvious masculinity, the numerous small scars on his knuckles that suggest the boy has brawled.

"Do ye have a fella, Marlow? Anyone you're kissing on?"

"Kissing on?"

"Anyone you're serious about?"

I laugh. "I don't do serious."

He frowns. "Ye've never had a serious boyfriend?"

"I did, once. In college."

"What happened?"

"He was two years older, a football player. He was drafted to play pro ball and was injured his first season. I went to see him in the hospital, and he broke up with me. Broke my heart."

"That's it? Ye never saw him again?"

"Actually..."

He looks at me, brow raised.

"He's here."

"Here?" He looks over my shoulder. "In this restaurant?"

"No," I laugh. "In Ibiza. At the singles retreat."

He frowns. "Is that why ye came here? To see him again?"

"What?" I try to keep the incredulity out of my voice because I know if the roles were reversed I'd find it difficult to believe Fionn and his ex-girlfriend ended up at the same singles retreat by coincidence. "I am not in Ibiza to stalk Terrell Rose. I didn't know he was here until today."

"Did seeing him bring up any feelings?"

"Anger." I pick up my fork and move the disturbingly yellow chicken around my plate. The truth is, seeing Terrell brought up all the feels, from anger to sadness to lust, but I'm not emotionally sophisticated enough to deal with more than one feeling at a time, so I'm sticking with anger. "He rolled up like he was still BMOC and I was his girl."

"BMOC?"

"Big man on campus."

"Ah." Fionn takes a bite of the seafood curry. "Any chance ye could be his girl again?"

"None."

He wrinkles his nose.

"What? You don't believe me?"

"I believe ye." He presses his fist to his lips and clears his throat. "It's the curry."

"Spicy?"

"Shite."

"No way!" I look from his face to the food coagulating on his plate, feigning surprise. "Are you telling me the fish glowing on your plate like radioactive waste is unpalatable?"

"Can ye believe it?" He forks a piece of chicken and offers it to me.

"Nah, baby," I laugh, turning my face away. "I'm good."

He laughs and returns his fork to his plate. I know this moment is going to become our inside joke. If we live until we're ninety-three years old, we'll remember the shite curry we shared in an empty restaurant in Ibiza, and we'll laugh.

"Fionn?"

"*Marlow*?" he says, drawing my name out.

"I'm sorry for going so deep on our first date."

"Go on with ye." He pushes his plate away. "I like to go deep."

He presses his knee against mine, sparking my desire and dozens of dirty, dirty thoughts. I imagine myself straddling his leg, my hot, wet sex against his knee, him bouncing me up and down until my breasts jiggle out of my dress, my nails digging into his thighs, his hand tangled in my hair, pulling my head back, until my throat is raw from moaning his name. Jesus! If a simple touch of his knee against mine brings me to orgasm, what would happen if he pushed my legs apart and buried himself in me to the hilt?

"Wait! First date?" He grins. "Does that mean there will be a second one?"

"Maybe."

"Maybe?"

"It depends." I lean forward, tilting my head. "You talked a big game yesterday, Irish. Telling me what a great dancer you were. If you want a second date you'd better bring your moves tonight."

He stares at me for several excruciatingly long, delicious seconds before pressing his knee harder against mine. "Not a bother."

The curry-scented air is crackling with sexual tension. He's giving me serious lady wood. What would happen if we dropped to the floor and fucked until the candles in the paper lanterns melted down? *Focus Marlow. Unless you want this to be another meaningless hookup with a rando, forget the way his knee feels against yours and focus on forming sentences that don't include double entendre.* I turn to the side and cross my legs.

"Tell me something I wouldn't expect about you," I ask, using my serious reporter voice.

Fionn smiles in a way that tells me he knows about my lady wood. "I love Motown."

"Motown? Like Smokey Robinson, James Brown, The Temptations?"

"Yeah."

"You got me. I wouldn't have expected a ripped, surfing, dancing Irish bartender living in Ibiza to listen to oldies. You intrigue me, Fionn O'Connell."

"Good. I want to intrigue you."

"Okay, next question. If you could go on a date with any celebrity, who would it be, and where would you take her?"

"Is that the best question ye've got?" He grins again. "Easy. Marlow Donnelly, world famous journalist. A shite curry place on Ibiza, of course."

Why are my cheeks suddenly so hot? For fuck's sake. Am I blushing?

"Thank you."

"My turn," he says. "Finish this sentence, 'Never have I ever...'"

"Never have I ever"—I lick my lips—"wanted to kiss someone more than I want to kiss you, right now, Fionn O'Connell."

He leans across the table and presses his lips to mine. I keep my hands curled around the arms of my chair to stop myself from sweeping the dishes to the floor and climbing over the table onto his lap. The kiss is over before I have the chance to close my eyes or flick my tongue over his lips.

"I've another question," he says, sitting back down. "If you could spend the day with anyone, who would it be, and what would you do?"

"Easy. Fionn O'Connell. Eating shite curry in Ibiza."

"Brilliant."

"What's your favorite food?"

"Good curry." He grins. "What's your favorite food?"

"Steak and truffle fries."

"You're joking."

"I joke about many things, but never truffle fries," I deadpan.

"I've never met a woman as fit as ye who ate anything beyond salads and kale smoothies."

"Thank you. I'll take that as a compliment."

"Do."

Some people smile with their mouths. Fionn smiles with his whole body.

"Tell me something ye do in the shower ye wouldn't want everyone to know."

"Pass."

"Ye can't pass. It's the rule."

"What rule? There are no rules."

"There are now. Answer the question."

"I sing freaky songs operatic style."

"Freaky? Like scary?"

"Freaky like dirty."

He sits forward, resting his forearms on the table. "Example?"

"Have you heard the song 'Broke Leg' by Tory Lanez and Quavo?"

He shakes his head. "Sing it for me."

"Not happening, Irish. Google the lyrics and you'll see why."

He pulls his phone out of his pocket, moves his thumbs over the screen. His eyes dart back and forth as he reads the lyrics. He stops reading and looks at me, whistling.

"Marlow Donnelly. Ye are a dirty, dirty girl."

"Guilty." I look at him through lowered lids and twist a lock of hair around my finger. "Lady in public and dirty, dirty girl in private."

He lifts his arm and looks at the heavy Rolex on his tanned wrist. "Is it too soon to go back to your room?"

Um, no. Fuck no. Saddle up, cowboy, because I am ready to ride.

The waitress arrives. She must not notice the uneaten food on our plates because she asks if we're ready to order dessert. Fionn looks at me. I shake my head.

"No, thank you," he says.

She hands him the bill and hurries away before he has a chance to say anything else, as if she's used to customers refusing to pay their bill. Fionn is not that guy. He throws down a wad of bills and we leave the restaurant, his hand on the small of my back again. When we're back on the street, Fionn grabs my hand, laces his fingers through mine.

"Ye must be starving. I know I could murder a pizza."

"I am a little hungry."

"I know a place..."

We walk to a place that could only be described as a hole in the wall. The mouthwatering scent of garlic and melted cheese tickles my nose before I see the thick-crust pizza they're selling by the slice. Fionn orders us each a slice and two bottles of Coke. We sit on two stools, "murdering" our pizza.

"I am sorry about the shite curry, Marlow," Fionn says.

"Not a bother," I say, doing my best to copy his accent.

"It is a bother." He unfolds a napkin and lays it over my skirt. "You're dashing, Marlow. You deserve better than a stool and a slice."

"I've been to some of the finest restaurants in the world and not enjoyed myself half as much as I am right now, sharing a slice with a sweet guy."

"Ye mean it?"

He tucks a lock of hair behind my ear, his fingers brushing against my throat, and my bones suddenly feel like they've turned to jelly, like I might slide off the stool, and pool up around his feet.

"I mean it."

"Brilliant," he says, staring into my eyes.

Fuck me! I do. I really do mean it.

I don't get it. If any other guy had taken me to a crappy curry place on our first date, I would have mentally checked out before the bill arrived, but I'm still here, present, focused on this perfectly imperfect date.

"Fionn?" I shake off my sappy, soppy thoughts. "If you could have a superpower, what would it be?"

"I would manipulate time. How great would it be to go back and relive your happiest moments?"

"I love that answer," I say, honestly. "Which moments would you revisit?"

He closes his eyes for just a second. "I would relive a day from three years ago. It was October, after the high season. Timothy and I went for a hike on the cliffs, from Doolin to Liscannor. We climbed down into a cave and sat in there talking for hours. I don't remember what we talked about, but I remember it was great craic. One of those perfectly imperfect moments ye forget until ye realize there's no chance of ever having one like it again. Do ye know what I mean?"

I nod, not wanting to break the spell of his words, stunned he used the phrase I thought to describe our date—*perfectly imperfect*.

"I would relive that moment with my brother"—he balls up his napkin and tosses it into a nearby garbage can—"and the one where ye walked into the bar for the first time."

"Seriously?" I tilt my head and look at him through narrowed lids. "Of all of the moments you've had in your life, you want to relive the one where I thought you were offering me drugs?"

"Serious. I looked at ye and my heart stopped. I wanted to text Timothy."

"What would you have texted?"

"I've just met the love of my life."

Love? Whoa. What the actual fuck? I imagine the robot from *Lost in Space* waving his arms and intoning Danger! Danger!

"What do you think Timothy would have texted you back?"

"Stop acting the maggot and get back to work," he says, laughing. "Then he would have called me a thick cunt or dope."

"Thick cunt," I chuckle. "I love it! What a fabulous insult. Timothy would have been my people."

He grabs my hand and kisses the back of it. "You're gas, Marlow Donnelly. Lethal craic!"

We finish our sodas, toss the empties in the garbage can, and walk outside.

"Some lads I know from back home are performing in a pub not far from here," he says, holding my hand. "Do ye want to go listen to them?"

"Of course." I nudge him with my shoulder. "You don't think I'm going to let you off the hook, do you? You owe me a dance."

"Marlow?"

"Fionn?" I draw his name out the way he does when he says mine.

"I don't want to be off the hook. Ever."

8

SEX ON THE BEACH

The line of casually dressed twenty-somethings waiting to get into the club snakes around the side of the building. I'm wondering if the curse of the shite curry has carried over to the club, when Fionn wraps his arm around my waist and leads me to the front of the line. The bouncer greets Fionn by name and waves us inside. The club is packed with beautiful young things nursing overpriced beers. We make our way to the bar.

"Whadya have?" he asks.

"Surprise me," I say.

The bartender returns with a seltzer with lemon and an icy bottle of Irish cider. Fionn hands me the bottle, grabs my free hand, and leads me through the crowd. We find a free stool close to the stage. Fionn offers it to me, but I shake my head. He sits, and I position myself between his legs, leaning my back against his solid chest.

Four guys take the stage, each carrying a different instrument. The singer has a sweet face and a shock of long, frizzy hair secured into a manbun, like Post Malone without the face tatts. He has a guitar strapped around his chest.

The singer sits on a low stool, adjusts his guitar, and starts strumming the strings, playing the first chords of "Take Me to Church" by Hozier. His voice is soulful, haunted, like he's lived a thousand lives. I'm mesmerized by it, by the way he pours feeling into every word, the way each note hangs in the air. The other musicians join in at the chorus and the song picks up tempo, transforming into something other than just another derivative cover. They reel through a dozen songs before jumping down from the stage to deafening applause. I've finished three ciders and am feeling a happy, warm buzz.

The sweet-faced Post Malone doppelganger with the guitar comes over to us and Fionn stands up. They do one of those side bro hug things, slap each other on the back, and speak in a flurry of indecipherable Irish.

"Marlow," Fionn says, wrapping his arm around my shoulder. "This is one of my best mates, Cillian. Cillian, this is Marlow Donnelly."

"Hello, Cillian." I hold out my hand. "I am in love with your voice. Love or lust, I haven't decided which yet."

He swings his guitar to one side and grabs me in a big, sweaty bear hug. I laugh. I've heard the Irish believe there are no strangers, only future friends. Cillian is proving that stereotype true. We talk about music, the embarrassing political situation in America, and the best beaches on Ibiza. Cillian tells me about Fionn's triumphs on a football pitch.

"Your one is a legend in Clare. A legend, for fuck's sake," Cillian says, looking at me. "He holds loads of records."

I'm about to ask him which records when a gaggle of girls who were hanging back finally pluck up the courage to approach Cillian. One of them is wearing a T-shirt that reads, *"I'm with the band."* It takes all of my self-control not to laugh out loud when she sticks out her chest like she's a fembot about to fire bullets from her breasts. Cillian looks back over his shoulder at Fionn and waggles his eyebrows.

A DJ takes over and the club is filled with an upbeat, sexy jam.

"Come on." Fionn grabs my hand and leads me to the dance floor. "They're playing our song, love."

Fionn puts his hands on my hips and pulls me to him, holding me so close I have no choice but to wrap my arms around him. He leans down and presses his lips against my ear, singing a song about a man who wants to break some rules and have a rendezvous. His hands are firm on my hips, moving me back and forth like a boat swaying on the water.

By the time the song ends, my body is vibrating. I imagine tearing his clothes from his body and riding him until I'm too weak to stay upright. When he puts his hand on the small of my back to lead me from the dance floor, I orgasm—a warm, wet rush that soaks my G-string and thighs. I like to think I am sexually responsive, but I've *never* orgasmed from a simple touch.

He must be able to read my body language, because he leads me out of the club and hails a taxi. The ride back to the hotel passes in a blur.

He walks me back to my room. We're standing at my door, a sexually electric charge passing between us, when I rise onto my tiptoes and kiss him until we're both breathless.

"Do you want to come in for a drink?" I say, gasping. "I have sparkling water."

When he looks into my eyes, I know this evening isn't ending with a polite drink. It's ending with dirty, dirty sex. The kind of sex you think about when you're alone in bed, one hand in your panties, the other squeezing your breast. The kind of sex that becomes a movie in your mind, one you replay in slow motion.

I slide the key over the magnetic sensor and push the door open.

He's going to lift my dress, hit it from the back, and drive me wild.

I go to the minibar, pull out a can of sparkling water, and hand it to Fionn.

I'm suddenly nervous.

"You should see the view." I walk to the balcony. "It's amazing."

You should see the view? For fuck's sake. I sound like one of those basic bitches on Instagram—Like, OMG, you're fire—not someone who can pull from Doonbeg to Dallas. Not someone who works for a luxury lifestyle magazine writing articles about the super-swank.

I walk out onto the balcony and stare at the ocean shimmering like mercury in the moonlight. The sea air blows against my heated cheeks, warm and salty. He comes up behind me. I feel him even before he touches me. He moves my hair to one side and presses his lips against my bare neck. I moan, low and throaty. I lean my back against his muscular chest, wiggle my bottom against his bulging cock. He moans and bites my neck. I turn around, slide my hands under his shirt, over his hot muscular chest. Pinch his nipples.

And then we're all over each other, hands on bodies, frantic. He lifts my skirt up, just as I imagined he would, looks from my bare legs and barely-there lace thong and says, "Oh, fuck yeah."

He turns me around.

He reaches around and cups my bare bottom, squeezing my flesh with his broad hands, until I think I'll orgasm again before he even pushes inside me.

He lifts me up as if I'm an empty shot glass and carries me to the bed. Then we're all over each other, tearing at clothes until we're skin on skin. Tongue on tongue. His body is spectacular—even by the dim light of the moon I can make out the tatts covering his chest and biceps. I want to trace every line of the intricate Celtic knots and crosses with my tongue.

He cups my mound and uses a finger to slowly, expertly stroke my clitoris. I slide my hand between us—down, down—until I feel the weight of his heavy balls and thick shaft in my hand. He moans and plunges his finger into my slick folds.

When he hits my G-spot I turn into a mad woman, bucking and grinding against his hand. I want him to keep going, but I want his cock inside me and his mouth on me. It's like having a fever, aching all over. I've never felt this aroused and agitated at the same time.

He pushes inside me, and we move to a silent, ancient rhythm, as if our bodies have known each other through many lifetimes. I know the heft of him against the palm of my hand, the length of him pushing deep inside me. It's familiar. *He's* familiar. I look deep into his eyes, lose myself in their sea-blue depths, drown as wave after wave of desire drags me into a dark, disorienting abyss. I hold my breath until my lungs ache. When he grows thicker, harder, I will him to come with me.

He draws a shuddering breath. He breaks eye contact, his long blond lashes drawing a veil over his gaze.

He is going to come. God, let him come. Please let him come.

His eyes snap open. He pulls out, lifts me off the bed, and carries me to the balcony. He sits on the sun lounger, still holding me in his arms, against his perspiration slick chest. I'm about to lick his tattoo when he turns me around to face him.

"Wrap your legs around me, love."

I obey, lowering myself onto his hard cock, and we make love—a slow, sexy grind. Forehead to forehead. Oblivious.

"You are so fucking fit."

His Irish accent does it for me and just like that I orgasm again, tight spasms, squeezing him, deeper. Moaning, clawing at his back like a wild animal.

"Fionn…Fionn…"

"Yes, love. Say my name."

"Fionn..."

He says something in Irish, brushes his lips against my ear, and the world goes dark.

I AM IN MY HEAD.

I'm naked except for Fionn's cologne and a thin sheet of perspiration clinging to my skin. The fit AF Irishman spent several hours making slow, smoldering love to me better than any man has before. He's asleep next to me, his beautifully tattooed body on full display, and I am stuck in my fucking head. I'm brilliant at being in my head, at complicating simple moments by overthinking. What am I doing here? Why am I with this guy? What happens if he wants to cuddle or stay for breakfast? What happens if he doesn't want to cuddle or stay for breakfast? What will he do when he finds out I am not like other women? I am not normal. I don't do the whole boyfriend-girlfriend thing. I don't daydream about a guy standing under my bedroom window holding a boombox over his head while it blasts our song. There has never been a Marlow and "fill in the blank" song.

I hear Fionn's voice in my ear.

"I'd like to get to know you better..."

I don't know what it means to be a girlfriend. My picture of what it means to take a relationship from booty call to boyfriend is gleaned from romcoms. Am I supposed to wear his T-shirt? *Gag!* Make a relationship playlist? *Seriously?* Leave love notes? *Kill me now.* Hide my quirks and flaws? *Impossible.* Wake up early and so I can put my makeup on before he wakes up? *So not happening.*

What happens if I do all of those things and end up getting kicked to the curb again, like I was after Terrell? What happens if we marry and then he leaves me, like my father left my mother? I don't think I could handle that pain.

I've protected my heart like Scrooge hoarding his gold coins, never allowing anyone close enough to covet my treasure. Terrell broke me, and I've spent the last eight years breaking others before they could break me more.

I stride around in towering Louboutins, my chin lifted at an angle somewhere between confident and come-at-me-bro.

The designer heels? Purchased secondhand on the RealReal.

The lifted chin? I'm running a Statue of Liberty play. I dated a quarterback once and he told me about this trick play he ran to get a touchdown. He pretended to snap the ball, but really he tucked it behind his back for another player to grab and carry down the field to the end zone. A fake. I'm good at faking it. I act confident, and people believe I am confident. I wonder if Kristin is right. Maybe my serial dater thing is an act. Maybe, deep down, I want someone to love me forever and ever, amen.

Maybe fate has brought me to Ibiza. Maybe I was meant to meet Fionn O'Connell. Maybe I am meant to unfuck myself.

Wait! What the fuck am I thinking?

My biggest fear is I will have a one-night stand that goes horribly wrong. Like, I wake up the next morning in some strange guy's bed wearing his boxer briefs and a sparkly wedding ring. I know what you're thinking. That's a weird fucking phobia. Most people are afraid of heights or spiders or slasher movies. Not me. I'm afraid of having a *bad* one-night stand.

I love having sweaty sex with some fit-as-fuck rando, and I'm not afraid to wake up in his briefs either. It's the ring. Just talking about waking up to find a wedding ring strangling my happily liberated ring finger has me breaking out in a cold sweat.

I sneak a look at the Irishman sleeping beside me. I study his profile, the thick blond lashes resting against his tanned cheeks, the model perfect nose, the juicy lips that kissed me from lips to hips, and my heart does a ridiculous little flip-flop in my chest, like I'm on my first date and my boyfriend has put his arm around me in the dark theater. What the hell is happening to me? There must be something in this sultry Spanish air, or the Porn Star Martinis, that is turning me into a silly teenager daydreaming about her crush. I'm not mentally writing our names in loopy script and surrounding them with a big heart —*thank Jesus*—but I am acting like a gone girl, all in my feels, because some fit-as-fuck Irishman stroked my G-spot.

My throat closes. I can't breathe.

I want out. Out of this bed. Out of this room. Out of this situation.

I scooch sideways, inch by inch, until I feel the edge of the bed against my back. I'm on all fours in the dark, trying to gather enough clothes to make my escape, when I hear a sound that makes my heart skip a beat.

"Marlow," Fionn says, in a sleep-roughened voice. "Where are ye?"

I stand, shivering against the arctic A/C.

"Come here," he says, lifting the blankets. "Roll into me, love."

This would be the time for me to make an excuse about having to be up early and send him on his walk of shame...but I don't give him an excuse and I don't send him on his way. I climb back into bed and roll into him, and I fall asleep replaying the sound of him calling me "love" in my head.

I wake just before dawn with Fionn's arms around my waist, his hard cock pressed against my bottom, and his fingers sliding between my slick folds. I move my hips so I'm slow-fucking his fingers, arching and rolling my spine, biting my lip to keep from crying out. I roll onto my stomach and push myself onto all fours. Fionn positions himself between my legs, grabs my hips in an erotically bruising grip, and guides me onto his cock. I catch our reflection in the mirror—me on all fours, vulnerable, hair tangled around my shoulders, Fionn kneeling above me, his tattooed chest slick with perspiration, his gaze on my arched back. He looks up and notices I am watching him in the mirror.

"You are so fucking fit," he moans.

The sound of his sexy Irish accent does it for me. My body tightens. I orgasm even before he reaches around and plays with my clitoris. He grows harder, pushes deeper, and spills himself inside of me.

9

KISS FROM A ROSE

By the time Fionn leaves to run to his place for a change of clothes before starting his shift in the bar, we have banged in the pool and the shower. I missed the day's workshops but not the cocktail hour speed-dating event. I get dressed in a simple black maxi dress with slits to the thigh and strappy silver gladiator sandals and head to the resort's pool. Brandy texted me earlier and asked if I would meet her at the poolside bar for a cocktail before the cocktail slash speed date. She's waiting behind a potted palm. I only spot her because I recognize her dress. Actually, I loaned her the dress after a flurry of texts she sent asking me to help her pick something to wear. I asked Adonis to deliver the backless dress—which I spritzed with Flowerbomb—and a sexy backdrop gold necklace.

We are two pre-cocktail cocktails into our speed-dating pep sesh, and Brandy is feeling it. Her glasses are in her room, replaced by contacts, and she's bringing big lip game with a sexy red pout courtesy the tube of Yves Saint Laurent lip stain I bought her from the gift store. She's Cinderella at the ball and I am as pleased as a plump wand-waving fairy godmother. So when a hottie in a blue button-down and khakis approaches our table, I'm ready to sing "Bibbidy-Bobbidy-Boo." Okay, he's not fit AF Irishman hot, but he would defo rep one of the months if someone decided to do a Sexiest Accountants Alive calendar. Prince Calculator barely acknowledges my presence. He focuses on Brandy, who looks more relaxed than I've yet seen her, even though her shoulders are still a little hunched.

I make an excuse about needing to powder my nose and offer my seat to Prince Calculator. I catch Brandy's eye, shrug my shoulders to get her to relax, and give her a *"you've got this, girl"* thumbs up before heading to the beach for a solo stroll.

I untie my sandals, leave them on the steps leading to the beach, and then wiggle my toes in the warm sand. The sun is slipping into the Mediterranean, casting the beach in seductive golden light—the sort of light that makes for Instagram-worthy selfies, or romantic rendezvous against a palm tree.

"Marlow?"

My heart does a silly little traitorous skip.

I turn around slowly. Terrell is standing behind me, his pants rolled up to above his ankles, his diamond stud winking at me in the setting sun. Same juicy lips, same devastating smile.

"What do you want, Terrell?"

What do you want? Where have you been? Why are you at a singles retreat?

"Come on, girl. I just want to talk to you."

"What is there to talk about?"

"Don't be like that, Boo." He reaches for my arm.

"Be like what? You've had eight years to reach out to me, to explain why you broke my heart, but you didn't. And don't call me Boo. I am not your Boo or your Bae or your...your..."

He laughs. "I can't believe I have lived to see the day when Marlow Ann Donnelly is at a loss for words."

"Fuck off." I shake my arm free of his touch.

"Mad Girl in the house." He raises his hands like he's up in the club, raising the roof. "Whoop! Whoop! There she is!"

I look at his stupid grin, his hands still in the air, and I laugh. I can't help it. Terrell could always make me laugh, especially when I was angry.

I see some movement out of the corner of my eye, on the pool terrace overlooking the beach, but Terrell grabs my hand, distracting me.

"Come on, Mad Girl." He pulls me down the beach. "Take a walk with me. A little stroll on the beach. Give me a chance to explain."

"Fine." I yank my hand away. "But you're not holding my hand."

We walk side by side, and it feels as if the setting sun is working magic, transporting us back to the time when Terrell was the Big Man on Campus and I was his hopelessly devoted, miniskirt-wearing Mad Girl. Terrell takes me back to the day he broke up with me, tells me what was going through his stupid head, that he didn't think he would be able to offer me the life I deserved.

"What could a washed-up pro ball player with a bad leg and bullshit degree in criminal justice offer Marlow Donnelly, daughter of the fabulous Marla Donnelly?"

I stop walking and look at him. "That's not fair! I didn't want my mother's life. I wanted you."

A breeze lifts a lock of my hair, whipping it across my face. Terrell reaches down and tucks the strand behind my ear... something he used to do all the time. It's familiar yet jarring. We stare into each other's eyes, and the time and distance that has stretched between us seems to shrink. I'm twenty again, being kissed by the star of the football team beneath the branches of a maple tree, the autumn breezes causing leaves to fall around us like red-and-orange raindrops.

He bends down, presses his luscious lips to mine. He tastes like oranges and that Carmex lip balm he used to slather on his lips before a game. For a second, I think about sucking one of his lips into my mouth, running my tongue over the citrus-sweetened skin. A fleeting second. Then I remember Fionn—the way his lips felt against mine—and the feelings that have been haunting me for eight years just disappear. *Poof!* Just. Like. That.

I pull away. Wipe my lips with the back of my hand.

"Marlow?"

Oh, fuck me! This is not happening.

I turn around. Slowly.

Fuck me! This is happening.

"Fionn!"

10

DRUNK IN LOVE

He's wearing his black button-down and holding a big, beautiful bouquet of flowers. The look on his face could eviscerate a girl. Like gut her from stem to stern.

I look back at Terrell and I know exactly what I want.

"Goodbye." I stand on my tiptoes and press a platonic kiss on Terrell's cheek. "Thank you for explaining what happened eight years ago. No hard feelings."

"Goodbye, Marlow."

I watch him walk away and then turn to look at Fionn. My heart lurches when I see the look on his face.

"So that was Terrell?"

"Yes."

"Are ye getting back together?"

"What? No! Terrell is my ex."

He shifts the flowers from one hand to the other. "And what am I, Marlow?"

"You're my..."

"What? What am I?" He tilts my chin up, forcing me to look

him in the eyes. "Some *rando* you flirted with in a bar in Ibiza? A vacation hookup?"

"No, it's not like that."

"How *is* it, love?" His voice is deceptively placid, but his eyes are turbulent with emotion. "If I am not the fella you rode to make your ex jealous, who am I? From my perspective, you left my bed to go kiss on your ex."

"It's not like that."

"How is it?"

I want to tell him I've spent the last eight years going out with different guys because I had a need, a consuming desire, I couldn't express. I wanted to stay in, to curl myself around *the* guy, my guy, to let go of the world of dating apps, sexting, ghosting, breadcrumbing, random hookups, waking up in a stranger's bed, and dipping out before he wakes up and wants to cuddle.

I inhale and hold my breath, because I'm in over my head now.

"Terrell is my Ex, Fionn, but you're my Oh. You're my '*Oh my God, he is it! He is the one I've been looking for my whole life. The one who makes me want to stay in when everyone else I know is going out.*'"

My stomach is queasy, but I'm not sure if it's because I'm revolted by the cheesy dialogue coming out of my mouth or because I'm afraid Fionn won't believe the cheese is legit, one hundred percent true. My *Exes and Ohs* monologue is almost as bad as the one Julia Roberts delivered to that floppy-haired British actor when she told him she was just a girl, standing across from a boy, telling him she loved him. Almost.

"Are ye saying ye want me to be your fella?"

"Y...Yes. I want you to be my fella, ye 'tick cunt. I want to eat shite curry with you. I want you to take me in your arms, to kiss on me, to call me *love*. I want you to give me loads and loads of ohs."

"Go on, with ye."

A slow smile spreads across his handsome face and I realize he is having a go at me.

"You're my Oh, Marlow Donnelly. My, *'Oh fuck, fuck yeah! I'm going to be this smashing bit of fluff's fella.'*"

"Oh fuck, fuck yeah, you are, Irish," I say, kissing him.

AUTHOR'S NOTE

Last year, I fulfilled my dream to move to Ireland. On New Year's Day I moved into a cottage in Doolin, a crayon box village located a short walk to the majestic Cliffs of Moher. If you've read my books, you've probably developed an impression of me: verbose, outgoing, politically incorrect. These traits have often made me stand-out, and not always in a good way. That was not the case in Ireland, a land of grand stories and deadly craic. I am blessed to have made friends with several locals. One of my friends, Sean T. O'Connor, works in his family's pub in Doolin. O'Connor's is the best place to have a pint and listen to trad. Sean is a fit AF Irishman with a Hollywood-worthy smile. He has the sweetest soul, a great singing voice, and he knows how to give a sexy cocktail. When I asked him for the recipe for a popular cocktail served in Ireland, he sent a video of him making this, the Porn Star Martini. *Sláinte!*

PORN STAR MARTINI

1.5 Fresh Passion Fruit
    2 fluid ounces Absolut Vanilla Vodka
    ½ fluid ounce Passoã liqueur
    ½ fluid ounce Vanilla Sugar Syrup
    2 fluid ounces Brut Champagne

Wash and cut 2 passionfruit, scooping out the seeds and flesh of three halves into your shaker (keep the last half for garnish). Add all of the ingredients except the champagne, shake with ice, fine strain into a chilled glass. Separately pour champagne into chilled shot glass to serve on the side. Sip alternately from each glass.

ABOUT THE AUTHOR

Leah Marie Brown is a *USA Today* Bestselling Author and professional photographer. Before writing novels, she worked as a print journalist, radio announcer, and television broadcaster. An avid world traveler, her (mis)adventures often inspire her contemporary romantic novels. When not writing or traveling, she's mentally eating fish and chips with Colin Farrell in a pub in Doolin, Ireland. Connect with her on social media or her website. She loves to hear from readers!

NEXT ROCK ON THE RIGHT
AN ISLAND GIRLS NOVELLA

EmKay Connor

1
BRITT

Unlike most people, I love Mondays. There's nothing more thrilling than coming into the office early on the first day of a new week, energy replenished, creativity pulsing, the week a pristine canvas just waiting to be filled with new ideas, new campaigns, new collaborations, and new achievements.

It was barely ten a.m. on *this* Monday, and I wanted nothing more than to crawl under my desk. Or better yet, crawl back under my covers and turn the clock back a year.

"You have to come, Britt. We want you to be the baby's godmother, and the godmother has to be there for the gender reveal."

I pulled the phone away from my ear but still heard the conciliatory undertone that colored every single conversation with my sister like a filter on a camera.

Twelve months later, she still felt bad.

A vicious jolt of satisfaction shifted to a guilty pinch. I rubbed my forearm, as if to ease the unpleasant sensation. Mona and Nick—my ex-boyfriend, who was now my brother-in-law—

hadn't meant to fall in love. It "just happened." Yeah, that statement includes air quotes.

What "just happened" was the three of us were supposed to meet up for a ski weekend in Steamboat Springs so I could introduce Mona to my new guy. I got stuck at work and left later than planned, and then a record-breaking March blizzard dumped four feet of snow, making the roads impassable. Mona and Nick were snowed in together for three days—long enough to figure out they were "soulmates."

It was fate. Destiny. Cupid. Kismet. Call it whatever you want. They never meant for it to happen and were so genuinely remorseful that I couldn't remain angry, even though a tiny black corner of my heart was still vindictive. Nick and I had only been dating for a few months, so I was more disappointed than devastated. Still, it seemed we—I?—couldn't shake an underlying sense of betrayal.

Or was it jealousy?

"I'll do my best." I pressed the phone against my ear. "I'm in the middle of a huge campaign right now, and I'm not sure I can get away."

"It's a week from Saturday. Surely, you can give us an hour." Now her tone was a combination of remorse and reproach, heavy on the latter.

Her expectation that I should be as excited about her pregnancy as she and Nick were was like a gust of wind across a bed of coals. Red-hot resentment flared in my chest. I clenched my jaw to avoid saying something I'd later regret.

Mona had my life—my beautiful, going-according-to-plan life—and I was supposed to be happy about it.

Late at night, I scrolled through my Instagram feed, torturing myself with reminders of how perfect things had been. Photos of my girlfriends and me on vacation in Maui. The nameplate on my new office when I was promoted to junior account executive at Drummond Advertising. Sunday brunch with Mona and my parents at one of Denver's many downtown bistros. Killing a CrossFit workout at the gym. Saturday nights on the town with Nick, my sleek red hair, green eyes, and slender frame a perfect match for his dark Italian good looks. Then there were the images of the life I dreamed of, planned for, was making happen.

Nick took a knee after two months, offering Mona a two-carat, oval-cut diamond platinum engagement ring—exactly like the one I had posted on Insta. Five months later, they got married at The Little Nell in Aspen, exchanging vows at 11,212 feet, a gorgeous autumn view of the Maroon Bells and the Rocky Mountains behind them—just like the photos on my Insta—while I stood off to one side, hoping my smile didn't look like a grimace.

After a two-week honeymoon in Italy—okay, I didn't have any of those photos on Insta because I wanted a honeymoon cruise—they moved into a gorgeous condo in Highlands Ranch, an upscale neighborhood outside of Denver. The gleaming tigerwood floors and metallic granite counters? Yep, straight from my Instagram pics.

Right on schedule—*my* schedule—Mona and Nick announced they were expecting. Aw, it was a honeymoon baby. Of course. Because Mona had my perfect life, while I had—

A fabulous career.

Yeah, that was about it. Dad was retiring after thirty-five years as a high-school math teacher, and Mom was swiping left and right on Zillow, looking for something smaller than the tri-level where they'd raised Mona and me. Even my girlfriends were a fail. Like Mona, two were recently engaged or married, and the fourth of our BFF Quad as we called ourselves in college was putting herself through med school.

I realized Mona was still on the phone, waiting for a response. "I'll be there—"

She sucked in a relieved breath, which I felt not an ounce of apology for turning into a disappointed sigh.

"—unless something work-related comes up."

"You know Nick and I—"

Oh, no. No, no, no, no, no. We weren't going down that road again.

"Don't you have prenatal yoga on Mondays?" I didn't give her a chance to answer. "Gotta go. Talk to you later." I dropped my phone and threw myself back in my chair.

Let it go, Grasshopper.

For some reason, my inner voice—the one that dispensed wisdom at odd moments—sounded like an old Chinese man and called me Grasshopper. Who knew watching reruns of the seventies western *Kung Fu* with my dad would make such an impression?

I gave my mental Master Po a flick and huffed in determination, sitting upright in the chair and scanning my desk.

Mona and Nick had taken enough of my time and emotional energy. They weren't snatching away my Monday morning joy.

Two hours later, I'd mostly forgotten about the gender reveal party, immersing myself in creatives and ad copy for the grand opening of Bite Me, a new vegan restaurant in town. Satisfied with the presentation I'd put together for the client meeting later in the week, I stood and stretched. I grabbed my Yeti Rambler and headed for the office water dispenser for a refill.

"Hey, Britt. I need a few minutes of your time." Seymour Drummond, the ad agency founder and big boss, called out to me as I passed his office.

Seymour was somewhere between sixty and a hundred and believed in reincarnation. If I shared his belief, which I did not, I'd say he's done stints as a hippie, a mule, and Julius Caesar.

Most of the time he was chill, managing the agency with the most expansive open-door policy I'd ever experienced. When he dug in his heels on something, though, it would be easier to move a mountain than shift his stance. Like Caesar, he was strategic, political, and there were probably a few people planning his assassination. Somehow, the combination of laidback and determined worked because Drummond was one of the top ad agencies in the country.

I counted myself lucky to be learning the business under his tutelage.

"What's up?" I leaned against the doorframe, the water bottle dangling from one hand.

"Sit down." He poked a finger toward a chair across his desk.

It wasn't unusual to be called into Seymour's office, but something in his voice made the skin on my nape prickle.

In a good way.

I dropped into the seat and set the water bottle on the floor, meeting his gaze and waiting for him to continue.

"We've been approached by a new client."

He smoothed a hand mottled with age spots over the luxurious white mane he wore in a short ponytail. He reminded me of Karl Lagerfeld...without the fashion sense. Seymour favored jeans, old rock band T-shirts under flannel shirts, and Doc Martens.

"Is it something you want to bring me in on?" I asked, a flutter of anticipation tickling the inner side of my navel. One of the reasons young advertising professionals scratched and clawed for a chance to work at Drummond was Seymour's rep for promoting talent sooner rather than later.

He cocked his head and regarded me with brilliant blue eyes.

Be still, Grasshopper.

I heeded Master Po's advice and endured Seymour's contemplation without giving in to the urge to fidget.

"Are you familiar with Care For All?"

"Never heard of it." I hated to admit I was unfamiliar with it, but Seymour had zero patience for suck-ups.

"Care for All is a private nonprofit." Seymour leaned on one elbow in the massive executive chair that dwarfed his short, stringy build, reaching to tap his keyboard. "It's an international humanitarian organization that funds healthcare initiatives in impoverished communities. Their goal is to 'establish permanent community resources.'" His brows rose as he quoted the corporate-ese.

"Sounds like a noble mission," I murmured.

"Hell, yeah, it's noble." His casual tone belied the ferocity of his words. "The problem is that funding has dropped off, and their budget is shrinking. They've relied on grants and federal subsidies for the past two decades, but that isn't working anymore."

The buzz of anticipation kicked up a notch, sending goosebumps over every inch of my skin.

"They want to reach out to the public for contributions. Last night, I chatted with Alistair Deacons, who's on the board of directors."

I sat up, my brain already riffling through ideas. I'd been at Drummond long enough to have learned the secret to its success.

"What's the *story*?" I couldn't hide my excitement. Drummond didn't create ad campaigns; it created story campaigns. Storytelling marketing relied on a narrative that created a visceral response, prompting consumers to take action. Seymour was a master—probably *the* master—of the art form.

"You tell me." A smug look of satisfaction creased Seymour's face.

"Me?" The word squeaked out as surprise, and delight hit me with a one-two punch.

"If you're up for it." He leaned forward, all business now. "I need someone who can give me a hundred percent for at least a month. Maybe longer."

"Not a problem." The only commitment on my horizon was the dreaded gender reveal party.

"No. I mean one hundred percent, twenty-four-seven." His fuzzy caterpillar brows kissed over the bridge of his nose. "If you take this assignment, you'll be spending two weeks on a tropical island in the middle of nowhere."

2

LUKA

I gradually came awake from the light doze I'd settled into and took inventory of my surroundings to determine if I needed to get up or if I could allow myself to return to sleep. The clinic was quiet except for the tick of the ceiling fan and hum of the refrigerator where I stored medication. Outside, the deep navy-blue of night was just starting to lighten with the approach of dawn.

Nothing but silence from the treatment room across from my office where I'd stretched out for a nap in the worn recliner inherited from Doc Rodriguez, the previous physician-in-residence on *Isla Tortuga Verde*. The leather stuck to my skin when I tried to shift position, holding me fast like a bug caught on fly paper. The ripping noise as I peeled my thigh off the seat seemed extra loud against the stillness, and I cocked my head, listening to see if the sound had disturbed Florencia or Juan. After a moment of continued silence, I was reassured that mother and child were still sleeping.

I exhaled, knowing I'd never get back to sleep. My medical residency cured me of needing a decent night's sleep; I was used to operating on two or three hours and then crashing for twelve.

Shifts as an island practitioner were significantly less grueling, although yesterday's emergency with four-year-old Juan took me back to my early days as an intern when my God Complex was still developing.

Fear. Panic. Indecision.

Florencia and Juan lived on one of the nearby islands served by the *Isla Tortuga Verde Clinica Medica*. The young mother arrived after a forty-minute boat ride, Juan limp and pale in her arms. My Spanish was limited, so I had trouble understanding her rapid-fire explanation, but when the little boy began convulsing, I recognized the febrile seizure.

High fever, vomiting, loss of consciousness, repeated episodes of seizing. Florencia confirmed all of the symptoms.

I quickly diagnosed a severe middle ear infection as the cause of Juan's high fever. Treating something like this on the mainland where modern equipment and medication were readily available wasn't a big deal, but on a remote Caribbean island, medical situations could quickly go south with little warning.

After administering antibiotics and starting an IV to keep the boy hydrated, Florencia and I sat watch as the hot, sunny day faded into a balmy twilight, eventually passing into nighttime. Juan's temperature dropped without another seizure, easing our concerns.

I stood and stretched, unknotting my cramped muscles. As soon as Martina, my part-time aide, arrived, I promised myself a leisurely swim out to Shark Rock. Maybe catch a few winks on the warm sands that ringed the tiny chunk of land a quarter mile offshore.

Until then, strong, hot black coffee would keep me going. I levered the footrest back into place and then pulled the back of the chair into an upright position. Worn and cracked and God knew how old, the recliner was surprisingly comfortable. I'd discovered that about many things on the island. Old, dented, a missing piece or two, the shine long ago worn off but still useful. Hell, that described me.

Yep, time for coffee. When my thoughts started leaning toward the philosophic, melancholy wasn't far behind.

I paused to pull the treatment room door closed and then padded down the hall to the kitchen, the tile floor cool and a little gritty. Salt and sand were part and parcel of life on a tropical island. The salt air rusted anything metallic while the wind-blown sand scoured away the rust, along with paint, fabric, the top layer of epidermis...you get the idea. What it couldn't remove was the islanders' resilience and *joie de vivre*.

I filled a kettle with water and set it on the stove to boil. One of the perks enjoyed as the island physician was round-the-clock electricity. A small electric plant generated power for the island, but consumption was restricted to the hours between seven a.m. and nine p.m. Some households had small generators powered by diesel fuel, but most, especially the older folks, made do.

The soft shuffle of footsteps alerted me that Florencia was awake. I added an extra scoop of coffee to the French press and grabbed another mug.

"Juan, he is sleeping." She tugged nervously at the neckline of her shirt. "No more *sacudida*?"

"I'm not sure what that means." I held my thumb and index finger apart about half an inch. "*Yo solo hablo un poco de español.*"

"*Solo hablo un poco de ingles.*" She laughed, teeth white against her golden-brown skin.

"Little bit of English?" When she nodded, I pointed at my chest. "Little bit *de español*. What is *sacudida*?"

She thought for a second and then jerked her arms and rolled her eyes. "Juan? All done?"

"*Si.*"

Martina was more than my aide. She was invaluable as a

translator, fluent in Spanish, a bit of French, and the local patois. I'd have to ask her to explain about the infection and the seizure so Florencia would be prepared if it happened again.

Florencia eyed the coffee, raised her brows, and reached for a nearby cabinet.

I nodded approval for her to make herself at home in the kitchen and moved out of her way as she assembled eggs, leftover rice, and a couple of mangos. Ah, breakfast. My stomach rumbled, reminding me Juan's emergency pre-empted dinner.

I handled coffee while Florencia prepared the rest of the meal. The horizon was pink when she handed me a plate loaded with sticky rice, sliced mango, and scrambled eggs. I filled both of the mugs and wandered out to the veranda while she returned to Juan's room.

I ate. I drank. I inhaled and exhaled. I listened to the rustle of palm fronds. I watched the surf run up to the edge of the sand and chase itself back to the ocean. I just *was*, and it was enough.

Sitting in silence, without thoughts circling through my head like a runaway carousel, was as much a learned skill as drawing blood or setting a broken bone. When I first arrived on Green Turtle Island, I rushed through each day like I had at Boston Medical Center.

Doc Rodriguez taught me to slow down. How to sit still and relinquish the need to control my thoughts and feelings, and how surrendering was actually empowering. The man saved my life, and I would do anything for him.

Anything.

So far, he hadn't cashed in that chip, but I'd be ready when he did.

I made a circuit back through the clinic to rinse my plate, refill my coffee, and check on the boy. Florencia had drifted off again, so I collected her dishes, dumped them in the sink, and ran water over them.

I dropped into the metal chair on the veranda, a comfortable seat that accommodated my long torso and legs. It didn't rock but had enough spring in the design to achieve a pleasant bounce.

I sat. I drank coffee. I bounced.

I'd saved Juan.

Life was good.

∼

MARTINA MARCHED INTO MY OFFICE, her flip-flops smacking against the tile. "Dey boat is here to take Florencia and Juan home. Okay for dem to go?"

I looked up from the backpack I was stocking with supplies and read the text in my line of vision.

I'm a Virgin (But This is an Old Shirt)

Martina, a fifty-something widow with skin the color of cinnamon, collected slogan T-shirts, which she wore over long skirts banded with multicolored horizontal stripes. I hadn't seen this one before.

"Nice shirt. Curious fact to advertise." I tipped my head toward the bold lettering.

"No time for dah small talk. Edgar ready to go now."

"Fine. Did you check Juan's temperature one last time and prepare the medication I ordered?"

"Of course, Doctor Man," she huffed.

"I have to ask, Martina. It's just a way of making sure we don't overlook something that could jeopardize our patients' health and wellness."

"I know dat, Doctor Man." She grinned, wide enough to reveal the spaces where she was missing all four first molars, and then shuffled back down the hall. "I just give ya hard time."

"I love you, Martina," I shouted after her.

"I know dat, too, Doctor Man." She cackled, the sound triggering my own laughter.

The recliner wasn't the only thing I'd inherited from Doc Rodriguez. Martina was a second or third cousin on Doc's mother's side of the family tree, and she'd worked at the medical center since she was fifteen. With no children of her own, she poured her heart and soul into those served by the clinic, dispensing unsolicited wisdom and advice along with medicine and bandages. Most days, I operated under the delusion that I ran the clinic. When I got a bit too full of myself, she wasn't afraid to remind me who the real boss was.

I added another bottle of ibuprofen to the pack and zippered it shut. Slipping on a grungy pair of Nikes and shoving my Oakleys atop my head, I slung the bag over my shoulder.

"I'm leaving, Martina," I hollered into the clinic and headed out the back.

"Don't run over dey turtles."

I rolled my eyes, but warmth spread through my chest. I heard that corny line every time I headed out for my weekly round of house calls. Martina was a cross between a doting grandmother and sarcastic teenager. She and Doc were the closest thing I had to family and part of the reason I was happy to remain on the island.

I unlocked the small shed behind the clinic and wheeled out the all-terrain mountain bike I'd splurged on so I had reliable transportation. Most of the folks came into the clinic, but a few lived up on Corcova Mountain. Older islanders who weren't always receptive to medical advice but who welcomed a visit from Doctor Man.

First stop was Alonso Rodriguez, Doc's younger brother, who owned a small farm at the base of the mountain. I coasted down the dirt trail leading to his small tin-roofed house, squinting against the sun's glare to locate Al. His favorite place to avoid the noonday sun was the shade of a huge tamarind tree in front of his house. I realized he already had company and then recognized Doc.

"Luka!" Al bellowed a greeting as Doc waved.

I leaned the bike against a scrubby palm and strode across the short patchy lawn. Doc stood and held out his arms for a brusque embrace, a little unsteady on his feet. Al settled for a handshake.

"Looking a bit shaky there." I supported his elbow as he sat back down, eyeing him with concern. "How are you feeling?"

"These legs've been walking the earth for eighty years. They get tired now and then." Waving a hand dismissively, he grunted. "I'm fine. A few aches and pains, but I woke up this morning. Makes it a good day. Seeing you makes it a great day."

I poured a glass of guava agua fresca, topped off the men's drinks, and then snapped open one of the battered lawn chairs Al kept stacked against the tree trunk and got comfortable.

"Why didn't you come by the clinic?" I asked.

"Al picked me up at the dock. He had a load of produce going over to Belle Isle on the ferry."

"How long are you staying?" I chugged half the refreshing drink and wiped the sweat off my forehead.

"Until Friday. Island hopping is taxing when you're my age."

Two references to his age in under a minute. My stomach coiled in on itself like a rolling hitch knot.

"I'm glad you came by," Doc said. "I need your help."

The solemnity of Doc's gaze warned this wasn't a simple favor. Didn't matter. All he had to do was ask. "Name it."

"The clinic is at risk of losing its funding through Care for All." Half-turning toward his brother, Doc explained the significance. "CFA is a nonprofit that funnels financial support for medical resources in communities where none exists. They provided the seed money for our clinic twenty-five years ago.

Without their help, there's no money for salaries or supplies and zero chance of upgrading the equipment."

Doc's news was a shock but not a surprise. Everything in the clinic was secondhand. Medication was in short supply so reserved for critical situations. Even something as basic as an IV, like the one I set up for little Juan, was a carefully calculated decision. Did the patient *really* need it?

"I can afford a salary cut." I curled tense fingers around the canning jar that held my agua fresca. "The clinic provides housing for me, and you know how many of the patients barter food or labor to pay for their care."

"Thank you, Luka." Doc's voice thickened. "That's very generous, but a temporary solution, at best. We may not have to resort to drastic measures if CFA can develop another channel for funding."

"It sounds like they already have a Plan B." I wiped the condensation from the glass and flicked it away.

"I went to medical school with Stanford Deacons," Doc said. "His son, Alistair, is on the nonprofit's board of directors. They've hired an advertising agency in Denver to create a public awareness campaign to drive donations to CFA so they can continue their work. So we can continue *our* work."

"How long before we know if their plan pays off? *Isla Tortuga Verde Clinica Medica* probably receives a tiny percentage of the aid they hand out. The money is life-or-death for us but nothing more than a few digits on one of their spreadsheets." I didn't bother hiding my cynicism. I'd seen how big hospitals prioritized budgetary line items. A small clinic like ours was way, way down on the list.

"That doesn't matter, my friend." Doc patted his hand on my arm. "We're in this together. If CFA fails, we'll have to secure funding elsewhere. Do you want to spend your time caring for patients or meeting with men in suits and ties?"

Damn. The old man knew exactly what button to push to get the response he wanted from me. Wasting time on hospital politics was one of the reasons I quit Boston Medical Center.

"Great." I slapped a hand to my knee, the crack of skin on skin loud in the humid air. "I'm not sure how we can help Care For All raise millions of dollars, but if I have to stand on the corner with a bucket and a cardboard sign, I'll do it."

The lines radiating from the corners of Doc's eyes deepened as he smiled. "That won't be necessary. They need something different, and I volunteered *Isla Tortuga Verde Clinica Medica* to help."

I lifted the glass to finish off the agua fresca.

"Someone from the advertising agency will be here on Friday. She's spending the next two weeks with us to learn more about the clinic. She'll be collecting photographs and video footage for the campaign." Doc cashed in his chip, and I almost choked. "Luka, you're the new spokesman for CFA."

3

BRITT

"Is this your first visit to the islands?" A guy giving off beach-bum vibes joined me at the prow of the passenger ferry, leaning his forearms along the metal railing.

"It is obvious?" I gave him an appraising look from my peripheral vision.

Deep tan a shade or two darker than fried chicken. Long hair he kept shoving out of his face. Baggy khaki shorts, a faded tank, and beat-up canvas slip-ons.

Nope. Not what I had in mind for a no-strings vacation fling.

"Only the virgins ride up front. Taking pics to show their coworkers back home. Hootin' and hollerin' every time they see a dolphin."

"Not a fan of tourists, are you?"

"Nah, they're all right. Just predictable." He inched closer. "Now you... I can't get a read on you. You're dressed for a week at one of those all-inclusive resorts. I call 'em Disneyland for grownups. I heard you tell the captain you're going to *Isla Tortuga Verde*, and there isn't a fancy resort on that rock. They don't even have WiFi."

I stared, not willing to believe something so outrageous from a stranger. Okay, maybe the resort was wishful thinking, but I thought WiFi was a given except in the most remote corners of the world. Wasn't that why Elon Musk kept launching new satellites?

No internet? He had to be wrong.

"You called *Isla Tortuga Verde* a rock. Is that like a cay or atoll?"

The guy snickered, and I made him a double nope.

"Rock. Island. Same thing."

A sinking sensation warred with motion sickness. I'd come to the front of the boat in hopes it would ease the nausea. Now my travel guide was shattering my tropical island fantasy.

"Maybe you're scouting out a place to retire. Lots of expats relocate to the islands. Nice weather. Laidback lifestyle. White sand beaches. Friendly locals." He pretended to stretch his arms and moved toward me. "You're kinda young to retire. Unless you're independently wealthy."

"I'm here for work. Two weeks and it's back to the nine-to-five grind. No time to get friendly with the locals." I felt like a mean girl when his cocky attitude deflated. "Thanks for the conversation, though."

He looked at me with puppy-dog eyes and an icky grin, and I regretted the impulse to be nice. Some guys interpreted any signal you gave them as a one-way sign pointing to the sack.

"How long before we arrive at *Isla Tortuga Verde?*" I couldn't stand much more time with this Caribbean Casanova.

"Next rock on the right." He pointed to a green mound rising out of the azure water.

In the distance, beyond *Isla Tortuga Verde*, I saw dark humps —more islands. When I'd boarded the ferry, the captain told me the region was dotted with small islands. As I looked at each separate bump of land, they appeared lonely and isolated. I could relate. Ever since Mona and Nick "just happened," I felt like an outsider, like I'd lost my place in the grand scheme of life. *My* life. The perfect life I'd been living and creating, hammered into smithereens by their happiness. I hated feeling like that, but what bothered me more was how bitter and petty and wretched I was becoming.

I grabbed my backpack and walked to the other side of the ferry. The boat was about forty or fifty feet long, had a covered seating area under the pilothouse, and an engine that wheezed like a smoker with emphysema. Its green-and-white paint was faded, the metal fixtures rusted, but the vessel plowed smoothly through the water, churning up a white wake.

The Caribbean Sea was breathtaking, but I was too exhausted to appreciate the view. I dropped onto a wooden bench, put my feet up on the railing, and watched the island take shape as we got closer. Seymour had given me three days to prep for an intense two-week assignment—the campaign that could make or break my career. He'd lent me his executive assistant to make sure everything got done, but it was still a scramble. I hadn't read any of the research Louella assembled and was walking in cold. I'd snatched a few hours of sleep each night and then was up at four this morning for the trip. Two planes and a ferry to get from Denver to a rock in the Caribbean.

It was the perfect excuse to skip Mona and Nick's gender reveal.

Time to take off the cranky pants, Grasshopper.

I bet Master Po never told Caine to take off his cranky pants.

Still, the old Chinese guy was right. Letting my attitude show was unwise. For this campaign to be a success, I needed the cooperation of Dr. Luka Stanic and his patients. I had two weeks to collect enough material for an integrated marketing communication. Photographs, video, and personal interviews that I'd take back to Denver, piece together with corporate facts and figures, weigh against market and demographic research, and unveil as a series of compelling stories designed to inspire people to open their wallets and give, give, give.

No pressure, Master Po.

Isla Tortuga Verde loomed straight ahead, a green, rounded mountain rising from the turquoise depths. In the later afternoon sun, it was dappled with shadow and light. The ferry followed the curve of the island to a wide cove split by a long wooden dock. On one side, a white sand beach was framed by palm trees and a few wooden structures. On the other side was... a town? Crooked streets lined with buildings—some neatly painted, some slanted as if a giant had tried blowing them over, none taller than two stories. Shops? Homes? I couldn't tell. I didn't see anything that looked like a medical clinic.

Dread settled over my shoulders like a fifty-pound mantle. I slumped down on the bench, wondering what I'd gotten myself into.

"This is your stop." The friendly local who'd tried picking me up jerked his thumb toward the back of the boat where a few other people were waiting to step off the ferry.

I forced myself up, tugging the straps of the backpack over my shoulders. Add another thirty pounds. The pack held my laptop, a video camera and digital camera—both waterproof—and a digital voice recorder. Pens, notepads, my money and wallet, and a string of just-in-case condoms.

I could dump those overboard right now. The probability of a holiday hook-up wasn't looking good.

"Enjoy your visit, miss." The captain, a craggy-faced man with a faded Scottish accent that matched his gone-gray ginger curls, waved from the pilothouse.

One of the crew, a slender young man with inky skin and a lilting island accent, carried my suitcase to the end of the wooden pier. "Dr. Stanic, he be meeting ya. Cap'n McDougal radioed ahead for ya."

"Thanks." I tipped the crewmember, adjusted the backpack, and looked around for Luka Stanic. There hadn't even been time to read his bio. God, I hoped he wasn't a lush or some kind of quack or a witch doctor who believed in black magic. Wasn't voodoo a thing in the islands?

I glanced over my shoulder as the ferry pulled away and pictured myself running down the pier, yelling, "Stop. Come back. Take me with you."

I pictured Seymour, in a Rush T-shirt and flannel button-up, firing me and then I'd have to get a job taking orders from people who wanted it their way.

I turned and took a step.

I pictured Mona and Nick popping a huge balloon that spewed pink and blue glitter because...twins!

I turned around and gripped the straps of the backpack until my knuckles were white, inhaling and exhaling to regain control. I popped the handle on my roller bag and went in search of Dr. Stanic. The sooner I started this assignment, the sooner I'd be off this godforsaken rock.

4

LUKA

"Doctor Man. Psst! Hey, Doctor Man."

I pulled out my earbuds as Martina peeked around the doorjamb and rested my hand on the grant application I'd been filling out, the tinny sound of 2CELLOS' cover of "Smooth Criminal" echoing out of the headphones.

"Der's a pretty lady here. Says she needs a doctor."

"Shit!" I launched out of my chair and hurried to the front door. I was supposed to meet the advertising executive at the dock and then got distracted by the paperwork. Doc Rodriguez's warning that the clinic's future was in jeopardy goaded me to look for other funding options. I'd become a bit obsessed. "Where is she, Martina?"

"Right behind you."

The honeyed feminine voice was like a feather being trailed over my spine. I shivered at the unexpectedly sensual effect of her words. Good manners dictated I turn around. Two and a half years of celibacy insisted I wait to see if she'd say something else.

"Dr. Stanic?" All business.

I wheeled around and forgot what came next.

She was gorgeous. Long sangria-red hair framed a heart-shaped face. Wide light-green eyes, tilted up at the corners. Delicately arched brows a shade lighter than her hair. An expressive mouth, the lower lip lush and pouty. She had the fair complexion of a natural redhead, and a dainty gold ring pierced her left nostril. She wore navy walking shorts, a white sleeveless blouse, and white leather sandals. About five-six, she was slim. Plump, firm breasts—a C-cup or better—saved her figure from being boyish.

"Britt—" I couldn't remember the rest of her name.

"Connolly." Her eyes crinkled as the corner of her mouth tilted up. "Did I catch you at a bad time?"

"No. I...er...I..." Was that really me stammering? "I was in the middle of something and lost track of time. I'm sorry I wasn't there to meet you at the dock."

"The island isn't that big. It wasn't hard to find the clinic." A note of derision in her voice cooled my libido.

"How was your trip?"

"Long. I'd like to get to the hotel...or wherever I'm staying." She jutted a hip, planted a hand on it, and cocked her head. "Is it true you don't have WiFi? That's going to make it very difficult to do my job if there's no internet here."

I bristled at her patronizing attitude. "Grab your stuff, and I'll show you to your thatched hut. We put up a new hammock just for you, and the women checked every inch of your mosquito netting to make sure there are no tears. We wouldn't want you inconvenienced by something like a bug bite or no internet."

She glared at me, and I glared back. I didn't want to be the Care For All spokesman, and I didn't want to deal with a spoiled city girl throwing a temper tantrum because she couldn't check her social media. The commitment I'd made out of respect for

Doc felt like rough rope binding my hands and feet and neck. It chaffed and burned and made it hard to breathe.

"Doctor Man not so good at da hospitality." Martina popped out of the kitchen. She bustled down the hall and wedged herself between us.

Britt Connolly's gaze dropped to read Martina's T-shirt and then jumped to me, a pink blush tinting her cheeks.

Hah. I'd teased Martina about the slogan this morning.

Doctors Do It with Skill and Love

"You stay with Oz and Nina. They da owners of Sandcastle Bungalows. Nice place. Good food." Martina shrugged. "Maybe technology."

"Maybe?" Britt looked past Martina to me. She dipped her head.

"Our infrastructure is limited." I regretted my own outburst. "A power plant built in the eighties provides enough electricity for fourteen hours of service each day. There's no power before seven a.m. and or after nine p.m., although Oz has a generator he uses for paying guests. BrightStar Telecommunications provides satellite internet access to most of the islands in the Caribbean, but the signal isn't reliable."

"Thank you for explaining." She lifted her backpack. "If you'll give me directions to this bungalow place, I'll check in."

"Doctor Man, he show you da way." Martina glowered at me, giving me no choice. She could make my life miserable if she wanted to.

It was easier to comply.

It would also give me a chance to clear the air with Miss Connolly. I resented being thrust into the role of spokesman. I disliked Big Pharma and distrusted Corporate America. Even nonprofits like Care For All made me leery. Too many rules and too many hoops meant people went without timely, affordable medical care.

Bureaucrats cared about money. I cared about people.

I'd agreed to work with CFA because Doc asked me to and because the islanders would suffer if I let pride get in the way. I could suck it up for two weeks. That fact that Britt Connolly was hot as hell might even make it fun.

I swooped down to grab the suitcase before she could add it to her load. The backpack looked like it carried bricks, the straps digging into her shoulders, pulling her blouse tight against her breasts. Tight enough reveal the lacy pattern of her bra.

Blood raced to my groin, my cock engorged in seconds. I flashed back to life in the States and the casual availability of sex. Young women at nightclubs in slinky dresses or on beaches with everything hanging out. Singers and performers whose careers exploded, not because of talent, but how well they bounced their tits and ass. The infamous *Sports Illustrated* swimsuit issue.

Don't misunderstand. Totally not judging. I love eye candy just as much as the next guy.

There aren't many eligible women my age on this or any of the nearby islands, so my visual sweet tooth has long gone unsatisfied. Catching sight of Britt's bra was a tease, a tiny bit of deliciousness, like the corner broken off a chocolate bar and laid on your tongue to slowly melt.

"Are you hungry, Miss Connolly?" I led her out the front door, down the short walkway, and out to the street. "Because I am suddenly ravenous."

5

BRITT

Dr. Stanic took a right outside the clinic, and I followed. Left would have taken us away from town, the narrow coastal road that eventually curved behind a rise of land. In the direction we were going, the two-laner wound through the hodge-podge assemblage of structures and then continued along the cove and disappeared around a bend.

Luka was not what I expected. I'd pictured Jimmy Buffet with a stethoscope. Instead, I got dark and brooding. Luka was at least six feet tall, with thick longish black hair that fell over his forehead, and dark, intense eyes under dense brows. A heavy scruff emphasized the angular hollows of his jawline, and dark hair covered his arms and legs. His name and features hinted at an Eastern European heritage, maybe Croatian. Definitely vacation fling material, except he was grumpy as hell and I was here to work.

From an advertising perspective, he'd make a great spokesman—intense, charismatic, capable. The more I side-eyed hot Doctor Man, the more he reminded me of a swoony TV drama doc.

"Does this road go around the whole island?" I pulled on the straps of the backpack to lessen the drag on my shoulders. The weight of my exhaustion, combined with the pack, pressed down so heavy each step felt like slogging through mud—the kind that sucks at your foot like it doesn't want to let go.

"Yes. *Isla Tortuga Verde* is only three square miles. There's the perimeter road and then another that leads up the mountain. Lots of dead-end dirt roads off that for the inland homes and farms."

"How many people live here?"

"Three hundred, give or take."

"That seems like a manageable population for your clinic to serve."

"It would be, except we're the closest medical resource for about five times that many." He raised his arm and pointed from one end of the horizon to the other. "There's a dozen or so small islands like ours scattered over a two-hundred-mile area. If someone gets sick or hurt, it can take an hour to get here by boat. If it's an emergency, we have to call for an air ambulance."

"How often does that happen?"

"Once, in the two and a half years I've been here. One of the day visitors had a heart attack."

My dad had a heart scare a couple years ago. I remember the ambulance careening away, siren blaring, rushing him to Denver Health Medical Center, less than ten minutes from our house. How scary would it be to have that happen when you were hours away from emergency care?

"Did he make it?" I asked.

"No." Luka's jaw clenched. "If we'd had a defibrillator, he might have survived."

He stopped in front of single-story white stucco building and knocked on a wooden screen door. "Hello. Oz? Nina?" When there was no response, he said, "Come on."

We went around the back of the house, up a short winding path through a patch of dense vegetation and palm trees to a rise of land where three tiny bungalows sat in a row. Each was painted a different color—sky blue, coral pink, and sunflower yellow.

"Pick one. Oz and Nina don't have any other guests right now."

"How do you—"

"It's a small town." Head cocked, eyes sharp and bright and fixed on my face, he gave me an assessing look that made my belly somersault. "Let's go with yellow." He crouched to retrieve a key from under a flowerpot outside the door of the tiny house, giving me an impressive view of his muscled back and shoulders under the black T-shirt he wore.

Propositioning the Care For All spokesman for a few nights of sweaty sex probably wasn't a good idea.

He unlocked the door and set my roller bag inside.

"Give me a minute." I shut the door, leaving him on the doorstep.

The bungalow consisted of one room with a double bed, table and chair, and private bath. The walls matched the yellow exterior, and a tall window looked out onto the town and cove. I set the backpack on the chair, dug my toiletries out of the suitcase, and freshened up. It didn't do much for my fatigue, but at least I felt human again.

Luka was leaning against the wall, arms crossed over his chest when I came out.

"Ready?"

We walked from one end of the cove to the other. Luka gave me a choice between Fred's Place or Ginger's Palace after explaining the bars, which stood nearly side by side, were owned by a divorced couple who had an entertaining love/hate relationship.

"To avoid favoritism, I patronize both." He stood on the sand, feet shoulder width apart, hands on his hips with the fingers angled toward his crotch, as if he had all the time in the world.

"Whose turn is it?" I didn't need to be starting trouble on my first day.

"Ginger."

Decision made, he led the way to a bunch of wooden tables and benches grouped under a huge, weathered tarp suspended from four posts. Each was painted a bright color—red, yellow, orange, and blue. We sat across from each other, and I kicked off my sandals so I could dig my toes into the sand beneath.

"Hey, Luka."

A tiny woman, not more than five feet tall, with a long gray plait down her back and deep creases at the corners of her friendly brown eyes bopped out from the dim interior of the bar, which was open its entire length. A long counter with stools for seating ran parallel to the front of the place. A TV with a staticky display was tuned to Spanish *telenovela*, the volume loud enough to catch an occasional phrase from the actors on the screen.

So far, we were the only people in the place.

"Hi, Ginger. How's Fred?"

"Validating my decision to divorce his skinny behind." Ginger dropped a peck on Luka's cheek, brushed a bit of sand off the table, and bent her leg to kick the bench behind her back into place. She looked me up and down. "Is this the advertising chickie? I thought they'd send someone older. With balls. They always think the ones with balls can get the job done better." She shook her head and winked at me. "Women do it just as well as men, except backwards and in high heels."

She reminded me of a hummingbird—suspended in mid-air as if unmoving until your eyes found the blur of their wings. She darted around the table, pulled my fingers into a quick handshake, and then zipped back into the restaurant.

"People around here really do know everyone else's business." I looked around for a laminated page or chalkboard listing options. "Is there a menu?"

"There's a drink menu for tourists in search of cocktails like a Painkiller, Hurricane, or Pina Colada. If you like beer, they have Corona. If you want something different, something light and refreshing, I've got you covered. As far as eats, there's jerk chicken, burgers, conch fritters, pulled pork, or fish tacos."

"Order for me. Nothing too exotic and no mayonnaise. I hate mayo." Just saying the word was enough to make me shudder.

"I like to dip my fries in it." His eyes gleamed, as if he'd made the comment to deliberately taunt me.

Ginger came back with chilled bottles of water and a basket containing napkins, plastic eating utensils, and condiments.

"We'll have the fish tacos and bellinis." Luka opened his water and took a swig, his tanned throat rippling with each swallow.

Ginger whizzed away.

Watching his Adam's apple bob emphasized his masculinity. Maybe it was the setting or maybe it was the man, but Luka's virility was raw and real, stripped down to the core of his manhood. His hands were big and strong, callused and capable. The muscles in his arms and legs were well developed and wiry, clearly earned through hard work, manual labor, and sweat equity. Walking over to the bar, I'd noticed how his khaki shorts hung off lean hips and the sculpted plane of his abdomen revealed by the close fit of his T-shirt.

I went for guys who were meticulously groomed and maintained a nice physique by working out three times a week in an air-conditioned gym. Sophisticated urbanites who paid as much for their skincare products as I did. Ambitious white-collar professionals who wanted the same things I did—a luxury condo in one of Denver's up-and-coming neighborhoods, a summer vacation to somewhere exotic and a winter vacation to one of Colorado's ski towns, kids after thirty, a strategic investment plan that allowed for the purchase of a second home and retirement at fifty.

"Do you ski?" The question popped out before I knew I was wondering.

"No. Never had an interest."

Ginger returned and plunked down two tumblers filled with an orange liquid topped with a fizzy froth.

"I thought bellinis came in champagne flutes." I lifted the glass and examined it.

"You're not in Kansas anymore, Dorothy." He raised his drink in a mocking salute.

"Bellinis are a girly drink. The kind of thing served at brunch or a baby shower." *Or a gender reveal.* "You seem more like the type to order a Red Stripe or shots of tequila with a side of lemon and salt."

"Can't a guy show his softer side?" He took another sip and smacked his lips. "I like the bubbles and the sweetness of the mango. Ginger plucks them from a tree out back and juices them by hand."

"I'd love to see you order a bellini during happy hour at the sports bar back home." I swirled the Prosecco and mango puree.

"Would never happen. The mangos you get in a grocery store are a poor comparison to ones still warm from soaking up the sun. Try it."

I brought the glass to my lips, tilted it back, tasted the drink, and moaned. "Oh, my God. That is sooo good."

Luka's heavy lids dropped, hooding his eyes, but not enough to disguise his reaction to my X-rated sound effects.

"Told you."

The husky dip to his already gruff baritone twisted my

nipples into tight points. Something melted low in my belly, puddling into instant want.

Not good, warned Master Po.

Damn, I hated when the old Chinese dude with spooky white eyes was right.

Backpedal! Backpedal!

"So...I understand a Doctor Rodriquez has been the go-between for you, Care For All, and the Seymour Agency. Did he fill you in on the campaign details? Let you know what I'll need while I'm here?"

What I *needed* had nothing to do with advertising or philanthropy...

"Yeah, Doc gave me the basics." His mouth twisted and his icy disdain washed away any sexual undertone. "I'll make sure you get what you need."

I wasn't sure I wanted anything from Luka if it was delivered with loathing reluctance. His furrowed brows and scowl left no doubt he'd been strongarmed into his role as spokesperson.

People were beginning to wander into Ginger's Palace, filling seats at the bar and a few of the outdoor tables. They waved or nodded to Luka but didn't interrupt. Aware of the small-town scrutiny, I dropped the conversation and enjoyed the mango bellini until Ginger scurried out with two large baskets in hand.

Luka ordered another round of drinks, and we munched through the meal in a not unpleasant silence.

Okay, so maybe *Isla Tortuga Verde* had a few redeeming qualities. The fish tacos with papaya salsa were the best I'd ever had. The jeweled sunset gilded the ocean gold and bronze, with nary a skyscraper to block the view. And while moody Dr. Stanic was off limits, that didn't mean I couldn't enjoy my time with him.

Even Master Po couldn't argue with that logic.

6

LUKA

Fuck. This fucking Care For All campaign thing was not fucking working.

At least, not for me.

I stood, back against my closed office door, and grabbed my cock through the soft fabric of my shorts. As a physician, I knew the dangers of a prolonged erection, and I'd had a boner worthy of a Viagra overdose since Britt arrived five days ago.

How could I not?

She was shadowing me, day and night. A not unobtrusive presence in the corner of the treatment room as I dispensed medical treatment to the islanders. Her laugh ringing out through the clinic as she chatted with Martina or interviewed patients. The scent of her spicy body lotion and floral shampoo, twin olfactory memories that stayed with me after she returned to her bungalow for the night. The silky brush of her skin against my hair-roughened arm when we sat side by side to go through the daily accumulation of photographs and footage after the clinic closed.

"Who is this?" she would ask, taking notes while I fantasized about slipping my fingers under her skirt and working my way up her thigh to the sweet juncture between.

"Petra Jones. Diabetes. She lost a leg because she wasn't getting the treatment and medication she needed," I would answer distractedly.

"And these three men?" She would frown, bending closer to peer at the trio of Creole fishermen from Belle Isle.

"Peter, Paul, and Matthew Darbonne. Brothers. They have a rare genetic disorder that can cause heart damage if not managed properly." I would take advantage of her posture to sneak a look down her shirt as her lush breasts jiggled in their pink lace cups.

I'd never wanted to be anything other than a doctor, but I'd trade duties with Britt's bra and panties any day.

Any. Day.

"Doctor Man. What you be doing in der?" Martina pounded on my door. "It be lunchtime. I make da fish stew with da red snapper Royal Phillips dropped off to thank you for da house call to his granny yesterday."

"I'll be right out, Mar-tin-a." I spit out each syllable of her name. Somehow, the damned witch knew I had it bad for Britt.

"You wait too long, der be none for you." Her footsteps faded back to the kitchen.

I got the impression she wasn't talking about fish stew.

Pumping my fist around my cock to ease the discomfort, I vowed to keep my distance. Britt was nothing more than a temporary temptation. She'd be gone, back to civilization with its coffee chains and nail salons and health clubs and manscaped bachelors, while I remained on *Isla Tortuga Verde*.

Fuck. I hated the conflict Britt was stirring up inside me.

I whipped the door open and stomped down the hall.

Martina and Britt looked up as I dropped into the third chair, both wearing the same amused expression.

"Is he always this cranky?" Britt faked a stage whisper.

"Oh, Doctor Man never be dis cantankerous." Martina ladled spicy fish stew into my empty bowl. "Everybody loves him. So nice and kind. Most da time."

"Don't talk about me like I'm not here." I hunched over my stew and spooned up a bite.

"This is delicious, Martina. You said it was a gift from a patient?" Britt tore a chunk of bread from the loaf in the middle of the table and dipped it in her bowl.

"No, not da gift. It da payment. Many island people money-poor. Happy-rich. Love-rich. Family-rich. No cash." Martina ripped the loaf in half and shoved it at me. "Maybe Doctor Man hangry. Eat more."

"I'm not hangry."

Britt's smile fell away and her eyes went flat, like the green oxidized patina on brass, as she dropped all pretense of tolerating my bad mood. "Spit it out, Luka. You're turning into a pain in the ass. I can't use any of the images where you're grimacing like you're trying to pass a three-pound kidney stone. I have a job to do, and it's getting to the point where I can't stand being around you."

I looked at Martina, expecting a smartass comment, but she just lifted her brows and shook her head as if to say, "You on your own, Doctor Man."

"Sorry." I forced the apology through gritted teeth. This wasn't Britt's fault, and I shouldn't be taking out my frustration on her.

Well, she was the cause of some of my frustration, but not the portion feeding the dark part of my soul.

"I didn't want to be a part of all this." I waved a hand over my head. "I walked away from a six-figure career at one of the country's leading hospitals because I couldn't tolerate the bureaucracy. People were *dying* because of red tape. Waiting for approval from their insurance company. Turned away because the hospital didn't accept their insurance. Misdiagnosed because doctors didn't spend enough time to thoroughly evaluate them—they had quotas and documentation requirements that took precedence over patient care." I shoved my chair back, my chest heaving.

"Is that what you think this is? 'Bureaucracy?'" Following my tirade, Britt's voice sounded especially soft, reasonable.

"Isn't it?" I shoved an angry hand through my hair, then crossed my arms is if holding back more vitriol. "Care For All needs to refill their coffers so their organization remains prosperous. And yes, I know our clinic can't operate unless CFA remains viable, but at what cost?"

Martina, gaze bouncing from me to Britt, remained uncharacteristically silent.

"You sold *out*." Britt's eyes darkened from moss green to viridian. "That's what you're telling yourself."

Bingo! Give that girl a Kewpie doll.

My heart felt the size and texture of a shriveled bean. Dried out, ugly runnels marring the surface. No room for anything but rot.

"I can't deal with this right now." I stood, leaving the fish stew unfinished. "Martina, please reschedule Ana Mendoza's pregnancy check. Call now before she leaves to catch the ferry. I'll be at Shark Rock if you need me."

"Okay, Doctor Man." Martina left the table to use the phone in my office.

"What is Shark Rock?" Britt had also risen.

I stared at her, indecision twisting my innards. Her dark red hair was twisted up into a messy knot, and she wore a casual black halter-top sundress. The only thing indecent about the dress were my dirty thoughts about pulling it off so I could suck and fondle her beautiful breasts.

Her hand went to her neck, fingers slowly drawing my attention to the valley between her plump mounds as she held my gaze.

"You'll need a bathing suit and water shoes or sneakers. And sunscreen. Otherwise, you'll burn. Meet me at the dock when you're ready."

"I know, Doctor Man." Her coy whisper, the flush rising up her neck to her cheeks, and the pebbled nipples poking through the fabric of her dress made *me* burn.

I was going to fuck Britt Connolly. Right then, I didn't care if it was the worst or best decision of my life.

My hands shook as I changed into orange board shorts, the drawcord tangling as I fumbled to tie it. I dragged on a T-shirt I'd picked up at some Caribbean surf shop, stared at my reflection in the small mirror above my dresser, and wondered what the hell Britt saw that made her want me.

I was a cynical, thirty-five-year-old doctor who'd given up the big money payoff after investing fifteen years to earn his credentials. I lived on a tiny island, hours from a decent-sized city, with the most rudimentary basics for a civilized existence. I didn't own a home, didn't have a 401K, and the only wheels I owned were on a $1,500 mountain bike.

It had to be my movie-star good looks, washboard abs, and witty banter.

"Just go with it," I told my reflection, sliding my Oakleys into place.

I could easily have made the half-mile swim to Shark Rock, but Britt didn't have the stamina I'd built up over two years of regularly swimming long distances in open water. Instead, I borrowed a wooden fishing boat from Fred and loaded it up with towels, bottled water, a first aid kit, snacks, and a handful of condoms from the stash I hadn't touched since moving to *Isla Tortuga Verde.*

"Ready!" Britt trotted down the wooden dock, her backpack over one shoulder, a navy baseball cap shading her face.

"I'm off the clock," I reminded her.

"I know. I brought my gear in case there was an opportunity to capture some of this gorgeous scenery." She gave me an impish grin. "I promise not to capture so much as a snapshot of your big toe."

"I'll hold you to that promise, Britt." Seeing her backpack triggered some of my negative feelings about agreeing to serve as CFA's spokesman. It also reminded me Britt was here for a short assignment. In less than ten days, she'd be headed back to Denver.

I knew what Martina would say about that. *"Get in da boat and quit wasting da time."*

"Let's go." I scrambled into the boat, waiting for the rocking to settle, and held out a hand to Britt.

She slid her fingers across my palm and stepped off the dock. I didn't want to let go, but I needed two hands to row the small boat.

The physical exertion helped to improve my mood. The sun, hot and oddly reassuring as it beat down, played hide-and-seek between mile-high banks of fluffy white clouds. A salty breeze dried the sweat beading on my face and dripping down my back. Seagulls cawed as they swooped and dived overhead. The water was a gentle slap against the side of the boat as I found my rhythm over the oars.

This was what had been missing—fresh air and the endless expanse of sea and sky. I spent a good part of every day outdoors, but Britt's project had me on lockdown. Calling a time-out was proving to be a smart move.

"That tiny inlet there"—I pointed to a small sandy cove at the base of a steep incline—"is Nursery Harbor. Green turtles, the island's namesake, lay their eggs there between July and September. It's a popular species to harvest for turtle soup."

"Gross." Britt scrunched her lips and she stuck out her tongue.

"How is it any more gross than eating hamburger or bacon?"

"I don't know, but it is." She stared at the inlet as we went past. "I had a turtle when I was young. One of those little green and yellow ones you keep in an aquarium. I can't imagine turning Timmy into soup."

Yeah, Britt was a city girl, through and through.

"Is that Shark Rock?" She pointed to a rocky outcropping that jutted out of the aquamarine water.

"Yes. There's a nice beach on the other side of those palm trees."

"Why is it called Shark Rock?" She gripped the sides of the boat.

"Truth?" I chuckled, knowing she'd be amused by the story. "It's actually Sharp Rock. When tourists began visiting *Isla Tortuga Verde*, they thought the islanders were saying 'Shark Rock.' That scared them away. The locals liked having a place of their own to escape to, so the name stuck."

"What are the chances we'll run into other people?" she asked casually.

"On a Wednesday afternoon? Even islanders have workdays, Britt. I can almost guarantee we won't be interrupted."

Our eyes met.

"Good." She rubbed her collarbone.

When the water was shallow enough to see bottom, I levered myself over the edge of the boat and pulled it up onto the shore. I wound the nylon rope around a limestone ledge, securing the craft.

"Hand me your backpack. I'll come back for the rest." I waded through the water, up the hardpacked sand, and carefully settled her pack in the shade.

She waited inside the boat to hand me the other supplies. "Need me to carry anything?" She propped herself on the edge of the boat, ready to jump.

"Nah, I got it."

The water was only knee deep, but she splashed enough to soak her oversized cotton tee. It clung to her breasts and the flat contours of her belly, causing my heart to race. She beat me to the beach and shucked off her shirt, dancing in a circle to face me, where I still stood in the water.

"You're sure no one else will come along?" She held both hands to the front closure of her bikini top.

"Reasonably."

"Good enough." She unfastened the clasp and whirled the hot-pink top over her head while I feasted on the glorious sight of her breasts—round, heavy, tipped in rosy nipples.

I didn't know if I was going to fuck Britt Connolly...or if she was going to fuck me.

7

BRITT

I didn't know what possessed me to go topless in front of Luka. I talked a good game when it came to casual sex, but Master Po was like, "Hey, Britt, why are you packing condoms when the odds of you letting a guy you met over Mai-Tais all up in your vajayjay are less than zero?"

Wishful thinking, I guess. Nick and I had been dating for four months and still hadn't done the dirty. In hindsight, that was a good thing. Can you imagine knowing what your brother-in-law's come-face looked like? You know, that face men make when they shoot their wad—eyes squeezed shut, the space between their brows all puckered, mouth twisted in a grimace like someone just shoved a monster dong up their butt.

My ego took a hit when Nick "just happened" to fall in love with my sister. I packed the condoms to feel sexy. To pretend that someone, somewhere—maybe on a tiny island in the middle of the Caribbean Sea—would find me sexy.

I never, ever expected it to happen.

But Luka was looking at me like he wanted a season pass to my lady parts.

He shoved his sunglasses atop his head, and we locked eyes.

I swear I could feel the weight of his stare, solemn and earnest, as if there was some unspoken agreement yet to be made. His mouth was a flat line, his nostrils flared, his jaw tight.

I dropped my chin to peek at him through my lashes and arched my back, thrusting my boobs up and out. He didn't even blink. Just held my gaze and walked toward me.

"Are you going to lose the bottoms, too?" He slid the tip of his middle finger under the elastic at my hip and teased it slowly back and forth.

"Not yet."

I'd forgotten how good the wanting felt. So breathless with desire you got a little dizzy. Tiny injections of lust into your bloodstream that traveled through your body until every nerve ending was sensitized, especially that royal cluster that sat on the throne in your clitoris. I wanted Luka, but I *wanted* to want him more. I wanted to be so turned on that my clit *throbbed,* so close to a climax that all he had to do was blow on it.

Luka pulled the elastic away from my skin and smiled a bit savagely when it snapped back with a brief sting.

"Ow." I backed away, grinning to reassure him I was okay with a little hanky-spanky.

He adjusted his package and sucked in a deep breath.

"Drop that stuff by my backpack so we can go for a swim." I'd never been skinny-dipping. My skin went ultra-sensitive, anticipating the sensation of sinking into the warm, buoyant water. Or was it the fact that every second ticking by brought me closer to getting my hands and mouth on the luscious doctor?

Luka plucked the bikini top from my hand and added it to his bundle. As I waited, I looked out across the ocean, the horizon a dividing line between the sapphire sea and cerulean sky. Closer to shore, the water was a crystalline turquoise—so smooth and flat, it was like looking through colored glass.

"Are you a decent swimmer?" Luka stood next to me in his orange board shorts.

"I don't need floaties, if that's what you're asking."

I waited for a crass joke about my built-in flotation devices, but none came. I'd seen Luka smile with patients and tease Martina, but there was an underlying intensity that seemed as much a part of him as his black hair and dark eyes.

There would be no casual sex with Luka. He didn't do casual.

The realization was simultaneously thrilling and terrifying.

My desire deepened, shifted, slipped through my skin and sank into my bones. It became more than a physical craving. I needed to connect with Luka on an emotional level or the sex would just be...sex.

Fun, maybe even incredible, but it wouldn't satisfy this soul-deep hunger.

"Sunscreen, Britt." Luka pressed his fingers into my shoulder, angling me toward him.

He'd retrieved the tube from the side pocket of my backpack. He squeezed a generous dollop into his hand, screwed the lid on, and tossed it back into the pile of our belongings under a palm tree. Spreading the cream between both palms, he started at my shoulders, slathering it over my chest, back, abdomen, and —finally!—bare breasts. His touch was light but firm, moving in lazy circles to rub the sunscreen into my skin. I'd picked up some color since arriving on the island, but my boobs had never seen the bright light of day like this. I looked down to watch his hands, tanned and nimble, stroke white smears of lotion over the globes of my breasts, paying special care to the tips.

"Mmmm."

My long, low moan and the stiffening of my nipples pleased him; his half-smile was possessive, arrogant, masterful.

"Sunburned nipples are no fun." He ran a finger along my

lower lip, tugging it partly open. "Same for lips. Next time get sunscreen lip balm with an SPF of at least fifty. As a redhead, you're more sensitive."

I giggled. Couldn't help it. Standing half-naked on the beach with a gorgeous doctor sporting an obvious erection, and he was worried about my Sun Protection Factor.

Luka took my hand and led me into the undulating waves.

"We have to go farther out. The water is shallow here."

He was right. We waded out about a hundred yards—the length of a football field—before it got deep enough to submerge completely.

"It feels like bathwater." A leisurely breaststroke kept my head above water as Luka floated on his back nearby.

"It's about eighty degrees this time of year. That's the coolest it gets. In August and September, it warms up to eighty-four, eighty-five."

"Last March, Denver got two feet of snow. Steamboat Springs got four." I waited for the pang that accompanied reminders of Mona and Nick's unintentional betrayal...but none came. "Do you miss snow or the change of seasons?"

Luka paused for a moment. I liked that he considered my question before answering, knowing his answer would be thoughtful.

"I spent so many years working on my medical degree that I didn't pay attention to anything else. Both of my parents are dead. I didn't have time for friends or dating. Because I don't have family, I volunteered to cover holiday shifts. Snow and cold were something to deal with driving to and from work. There are times when I miss autumn. That was my mother's favorite time of year."

"My mom likes springtime. She's big into gardening. She'd go to the nursery and come home with the entire back end of the minivan full of seedlings and starter plants. My sister and I hated it. We wanted to hang out with our friends, and instead, we had to help Mom put in all those plants." I rolled in the water, looking up into the sky.

Mona knew how much I hated working in the dirt, so she always volunteered to do my share. After the plants were in, Mom took us for mani/pedis. Mona liked fun colors like blue and green while I was ruby red every time. My eyes stung as I remembered those happy times. For the past year, I'd done nothing but envy Mona. She was my sister, and I loved her. Instead of being glad she'd found her special someone, I clung to my self-righteous resentment. Shame added to the burn of tears.

"You're close to your family?" Luka splashed at a seagull diving too close to the surface of the water.

"Oh, yes. We all live in the same area and get together once or twice a week. Brunch every Sunday and Taco Tuesdays or Friday Game Night. My sister...just got married."

"Do you like your brother-in-law?"

That was a question I frequently asked myself.

"I dated him before he hooked up with Mona." I wiggled my fingers in the water, and my heart gave me my answer. "Nick is a nice guy. He and Mona didn't cheat or anything like that. It just happened."

I closed my eyes, imagining the air quotes around that phrase drifting up and away, into the white marshmallow clouds.

"It just happened," I repeated. "They're really, truly, deeply in love. I'm glad I found out Nick wasn't the guy for me before our relationship went any further. Even if he hadn't met Mona, we wouldn't have lasted."

Master Po had been urging me to let go for months. I should have heeded his advice. Without the jealousy and bitterness, my heart felt lighter.

"They're pregnant," I told Luka. "I'm going to be Aunt Britt in a few months."

The waves had pushed us back toward the beach. Luka planted his feet on the sandy bottom, wrapped his fingers around my wrist, and pulled me to him in the waist-deep water.

"You're going to be a very cool aunt."

"You think?" I found my footing and steadied myself with my hands on his shoulders, my breasts pressed against his chest. When his hand slid to cup my butt, pressing me against his erection, I curved my leg around his hip, aligning his cock with my cleft. I slowly ground against him, the subtle push and pull of the tide adding to the rhythm.

"You're gutsy and independent. Smart. Fun. Creative." He coiled a strand of wet hair around his finger and tugged. "You'll be the aunt who lets them eat ice cream for dinner, stay up past bedtime when they sleep over, and as they get older, the one they come to for advice when they can't talk to their parents. Everyone should have an aunt like that."

I pictured myself painting glitter nail polish on tiny toes or cheering from the top of the bunny slope. I suddenly couldn't wait to find out if Mona and Nick were having a girl or a boy.

"You're bold and sexy and adventurous." Luka caressed the swell of my breast. "Every man wants a lover like that."

"I'm all yours, Doctor Man." I circled my arms around his neck and locked both legs around his waist, aligning our bodies from hip to chest. He throbbed against me in counterpoint to the slow beat of the waves.

Luka splayed his hands across my back and bent to kiss me. He brushed his mouth across mine and then traced the seam with his tongue. His gentle exploration immediately deepened into a passionate plunder as his mouth widened, demanding, hungry. My own need became equally as urgent as I sought to kiss him deeper and harder. His lips were firm and warm, salty and sweet, and I lost myself in the taste and flavor uniquely Luka.

Desperate for a breath, I threw back my head and gasped, tropical air filling my lungs. He licked a trail along my jaw and down my throat.

"I want to taste all of you." Using the buoyancy of the water, he shifted so one arm was under my knees, the other supporting my back. He carried me out of the ocean like a water god returning a rescued maiden to land.

Setting me on my feet, he pulled a beach blanket from the supplies he'd packed and laid it out under a palm tree. Turning, he unlaced the drawcord of his shorts and shoved them over his hips, kicking them away when they fell to the sand.

Completely unself-conscious, he stood and waited as I absorbed every detail of his body. Looking wasn't enough. I ran my fingertips over the sharp edge of his collarbone and curved my palms over his pecs. I dragged my fingers over the ripple of muscles along his ribs and stomach and traced the V-cut of his abs right down to the thick erection jutting proudly from a dark patch of hair. I wrapped my hand around the powerful length and stroked leisurely, flicking my gaze from the shifting expressions on his face—furrowed brows easing as anticipation became actuality—to the sexy hand job.

"Wait." He wrapped his fingers around my hand to stop the pumping motion, voice thick, like the word was hard to get out. "Bad timing, but I'm a...doctor. Protection, and all that."

"My annual exam came back clean, and I haven't been with anyone since. I have an IUD, but I brought condoms, too."

"Do you always pack condoms when you travel for work?" His words were terse—jealous, not suspicious.

"I had different expectations about this trip. I envisioned a resort with cabana boys who deliver tropical drinks with tiny umbrellas in them and singles looking for a vacation hookup.

Instead, I got a bungalow with a great view of the *Isla Tortuga Verde* cove, mango bellinis, and you." I wet a finger and spiraled the flat coin of his nipple. "Reality is so much better than fantasy."

"I haven't been with anyone in…years." The admission cost him. Male ego and all that. "When I applied for the temporary assignment that landed me here, I underwent a thorough medical screening. I can wear—"

I slipped my hands under his arms, ran them down his sides, and bracketed his hips as I sank to my knees. His hip bones pressed into the fleshy pads under my thumbs as I steadied him, opening my mouth around the head of his cock.

PIV sex—penis in vagina—is awesome, but oral sex is a different level of giving and receiving. There's also a greater differentiation in control—who's dominant, who's subservient, who's *really* calling the shots. Kneeling in front of Luka should have felt submissive, yet he was completely at my mercy.

I gathered saliva on my tongue, laving his cock until it glistened. Hollowing my cheeks, I sucked as I bobbed my head back and forth, lips dragging up and down his slick flesh. He tasted of sun and salt, clean and natural, having just swum in the sea. I closed my eyes to focus all my attention on the fullness in my mouth, the rhythm of my sucking, and learning what he liked best.

The crown plowed the ridged palate along the top of my mouth and then banged the back of my throat.

"Ah, Britt. Like that. Again." Deep guttural groans punctuated each bump.

I opened wider to keep from gagging, swirled my tongue around the warm pulsing length of him, and increased the tempo of my oral strokes.

My moans echoed his, filling the humid air. Noisy sex turned me on like crazy, and I felt myself getting wetter and hotter.

He wound his fingers in my tangled hair, holding on but not trying to control me. As if he understood sucking his cock gave me just as much enjoyment as it did him.

I didn't want our first sex act to end so quickly, but it had been years for Luka. His muscles tensed and shuddered as he fought to hold back his climax, but I wanted him to come. I wanted his body to go rock hard and then liquify as his pleasure hit a pinnacle and then drifted back to earth like a feather.

"I'm about to come," Luka shouted, his grip tightening and causing a pleasure-pain burn on my scalp. "Let me pull out."

My fingers clenched, digging into his hips. I slammed my mouth up and down his cock until I felt the surge of ejaculate against my throat.

He swayed, took a faltering step backwards, and then dropped onto his knees. Cradling my face in his hands, he kissed the corner of my mouth and then the other. His touch was reverent, grateful, enthralled.

Instinctively, I knew Luka didn't often reveal his vulnerabilities and needs. He was a protector, a healer. Strong, wise, dedicated. I felt honored that he'd entrusted me with his soft side... and a little frightened.

There would be no casual sex with Luka. He didn't do casual.

In my head, the sound of someone clearing his throat warned me Master Po was about to dispense with more indisputable advice.

Since when do you do no-strings-attached hookups, Grasshopper?

8
LUKA

"Move in with me, Britt. Until you leave." I traced patterns over the smooth skin of her hip as we spooned after another mind-blowing session. Since the trip to Shark Rock, we'd spent every minute together—working on the materials she needed for the advertising campaign and making love. She only had three more days on the island, and I wanted every second of that time.

"I thought we were going to keep business and pleasure separate." She snuggled closer, the warmth of her ass jump-starting another hard-on.

"It's a small town, babe. Everyone knows we're sleeping together." I slid my hand across her stomach, flat and toned and golden from hours in the sun. Murky morning sunshine cascaded through my bedroom window blinds, horizontal bands of light and shadow that reminded me of prison bars. It soured my mood, deflating my rising lust like a pinprick to a balloon.

A huge weather system was headed our way, and the gloom matched my mood.

"All of my stuff is at the bungalow."

I didn't know if that was an excuse or a logistical issue. "You can set up your laptop at the kitchen table."

"I don't know. The WiFi signal is better at my place because it's up that hill." She twisted to face me, stroking the scruff that left her inner thighs red and abraded after I went down on her but that she said was part of the pleasure. "Let me think about it."

"Sure. No pressure." Unable to say what I really wanted to, I resorted to the one thing I knew might convince her.

Flipping on my back, I urged her to straddle me, hands on either side of my head. I scooted down the bed, kicking the sheets out of the way, until her pussy was right above my mouth.

She splayed her legs, making it easier for me to lick and suck the pink folds covered in her juices.

"Unnnn, Luka. I can't think when you do that."

That was my intent.

Three days. To an exhausted medical resident, seventy-two hours tunneled to a tiny point on some distant horizon. To a man in love, it was a cruel time warp.

I filled my hands with tight, firm ass, holding her against my mouth so I could bury my face in the scent and taste of her. I nosed her clit as I darted and swirled and stroked. Her thighs pressed against my ears, blocking out everything except her.

Britt rocked against my face, a signal her climax was close. I found the tiny nub at the top of her cleft and caught it in my teeth.

She squealed in protest and squirmed, but I held fast. It interrupted her rhythm, forced her to rebuild the moment leading toward satisfaction.

"Lu-ka." She murmured my name in a seductive sing-song voice. "I love the way your mouth feels on me. Please let me come."

I released her and started licking her again with the flat of my tongue. Each time I swiped her clit, she gave a little jerk. I loved when she rolled her hips, gently humping my face, breath coming in short pants, lost in her own perfect world.

"Don't stop," she gasped. "Almost...there!" She crooned the last word, raised up on her arms, spine arching, as the orgasm surged through her body.

My cock stood rigid, and I longed to buck up into her heat and tightness for my own release. Instead, I reached down, fisted my hand around the base and stroked the turgid length as I languidly circled my tongue around her clit while she came down from her high. I clenched my ass cheeks, felt my balls tighten, and came, hot semen spilling over my hand.

"That's hot. I love watching you touch yourself."

With my mouth full of Britt, I could only grunt in agreement. She wiggled her way down my torso, rubbing her slit against my sticky cock. She lay across my chest, and a sense of rightness settled over me.

Same thing happened when Doc offered me the position on *Isla Tortuga Verde*. We'd met when I was working a locum tenens assignment at St. John's Hospital on Montserrat. He was looking for a physician to take over the clinic so he could retire to nearby Belle Isle where his daughter and grandchildren lived. I had no interest in returning to Boston and wasn't sure what was next. I needed to make a difference, but Doc recognized I also need a sense of purpose and a place to belong. The island, the clinic, and the people there provided everything I needed...until I met Britt.

"Martina is going to come looking for us if we don't get a move on." Britt rolled off me and sat on the side of the bed.

"Go ahead and grab a shower. I'll put on a pot of coffee." I needed some space. It was getting harder and harder not to ask Britt to stay. As much as I cared about her and believed we could make a relationship work, it wasn't fair to ask her to move 2,500 miles away from her family and forfeit her career. Especially when I wasn't willing to do the same.

"We can have coffee at the clinic." She posed in the doorway to the small bathroom. "I need someone to wash my back."

"Go. You put the fear of God in me now, picturing Martina marching down the street and pounding on the door while I'm doing you doggie-style."

She laughed, and a second later, I heard the shower.

Three days wasn't nearly enough, but it was all I had.

"How far along are you, Ana?" Britt set the digital recorder on a small metal stand next to the exam table.

"Thirty-four weeks." My patient reclined on the table as I took her vitals and listened to the baby's heartbeat with a fetal doppler. The fetus sounded good, but I was worried about Momma.

Over the cacophony of whipping wind and torrential rain, thunder boomed. A second later, there was the sharp cracking sound of a tree trunk splitting. We all waited, listening for the telltale sound of metal screeching or walls crashing that would indicate the tree had landed on a building, but nothing followed except the reverberating thud of the tree hitting the ground.

"I'm glad you made it before the storm hit." I pulled Ana's flowered shirt down. "I didn't think it would be this bad. The winds are really causing problems, but you're safe here."

Eljon Mendoza, Ana's husband, stood near the doorway, running the brim of his hat through his fingers. Ana had lost her first two pregnancies around fifteen weeks, so they were understandably anxious. Over the past two days, Ana had begun experiencing symptoms that alarmed me—severe headaches, blurred vision, vomiting, and edema in her face and hands.

"Do you know if it's a boy or girl?" Britt was doing a great job keeping Ana distracted as I ran through my assessment.

"No. We'll find out when the baby gets here." Ana's smile wavered, her face pale against her long brown hair. "Eljon wants a boy. I'm hoping for a girl."

"That doesn't matter, *mi amor*. As long as the baby is healthy." Eljon's tense expression relaxed as he offered his wife reassurance.

"Thank you for allowing me to talk to you and take some pictures for the advertising campaign I'm working on with Dr. Stanic. It's very important that people understand the challenges faced by small clinics like *Isla Tortuga Verde Clinica Medica* and how they can help."

"Anything for the doctor. He's takes good care of us." Ana gave a tiny sob and covered her pregnant belly protectively. "Especially our baby. Every day brings us closer to holding our precious bundle in our arms."

Guilty frustration rose in the back of my throat, the taste bitter. I hadn't been able to prevent Ana's miscarriages, and now this pregnancy was in jeopardy. Her blood pressure was through the roof. I was waiting for Martina to check in with the results of her urine test. If protein was present, my diagnosis would be preeclampsia, a complication that could be fatal for Ana and her baby.

A quiet knock signaled Martina.

I poked my head out of the exam room.

"Da results not good, Doctor Man." She held up the test strip.

"Damn it."

Treating severe preeclampsia required a fully outfitted medical center. Ana needed monitoring, medications I didn't have, and if her condition worsened, the baby might need to be delivered early. A pre-term baby needed NICU support. Thirty-four weeks was early, but with the right care, most infants developed normally.

On a tropical island in a clinic with two treatment rooms, one physician, and limited equipment and meds, the odds of a positive outcome for Mom and baby were zero.

Icy fear washed over me. I couldn't feel my hands and feet. I couldn't breathe. A gray fog crept into my peripheral vision.

"Doctor Man." Martina's fingers bit into my shoulder as she hissed at me. "Ana and da baby need you. Dey don't got nobody else. You do da best you can."

My best wouldn't be enough. Not in this situation.

"Call the hospital on Montserrat. Ask how soon they can get an air ambulance here." I lowered my voice. "Tell them it's critical."

She nodded and scurried down the hall. I closed the door and drew in a slow breath.

"Is everything okay?" Eljon's eyes were wide.

"Ana, your blood pressure is very high. Sometimes this causes preeclampsia in pregnant women. It can be a serious complication." I braced myself. "I don't have the medicine needed to stop this from getting worse. For now, I want you and Eljon to remain at the clinic so I can monitor you."

Britt blinked as the implications of the situation registered. Her gaze skittered from me to Eljon to Ana and back to me.

Do something.

She didn't speak the words out loud, but I heard her loud and clear.

I dropped my head, staring at the scuffed beige tile floor.

"Thank you, Doctor." Ana reached out for her husband, who grasped her hand in a white-knuckled grip, sad resignation on her face. "Can we be alone for a few minutes?"

Britt scooped up the recorder and followed me out of the room. Before the door shut, Ana began sobbing while Eljon murmured what sounded like a prayer. Wind and rain lashed the clinic, adding its fury to mine.

Doc warned me there would be times like this. People with injuries or medical conditions too severe for what we could do with our limited resources. He'd lost patients because of that and still carried the grief physicians felt when they failed their patients. I did not want Ana and her baby to be my first.

"What are our options?" Britt leaned against the hallway wall, shoulders hunched, arms folded.

Our. As if she were part of *Isla Tortuga Verde*. If I wasn't so worried about Ana, I'd smile.

"Martina is calling the closest hospital to have Ana airlifted out."

"How close?"

"It's an hour flight."

Thunder boomed again, and dread rode the fear careening up my spine. I jogged to my office to see what Martina had found out.

"How long is da delay?" A thunderous look rivaling the storm outside darkened Martina's usually placid countenance. She covered the phone with her hand. "Da 'copter can't fly because of da storm. I told dem a baby and momma need help."

I plucked the phone out of her hand. "This is Dr. Stanic. Who am I talking to?" I inhaled to gain control of my anger.

"Hey, Luka. This is Virgil Bridges. We worked together a couple of times when you were on temp duty here."

Bridges was one of the medevac pilots. He was a good guy. If he said the air ambulance was grounded, it was with good reason.

"Did Martina give you all the details? I have a thirty-year-old female, thirty-four weeks, gravida three, para zero. Diagnosis, severe preeclampsia."

"We're grounded." Bridges's declaration was grim. "One of

our choppers almost went down on an earlier run. We're waiting for the all-clear. As soon as we get it, I'll send the team out."

"We don't have time." I curled my fist around the phone. "She lives on one of the other islands we support and didn't come in until her symptoms were bad."

"My wife had preeclampsia during her last pregnancy. I know the risks." Bridges blew a heavy sigh. "Do what you can. You'll be my first run as soon as the weather clears. Good luck."

I wanted to throw the phone across the room. One of the first things I learned about island life was the threat tropical storms and hurricanes posed—flooding, landslides, wind damage, erosion. We followed the weather reports like sports addicts watched ESPN.

The storm battering *Isla Tortuga Verde* was part of a massive system sitting over the Caribbean that wasn't forecast to clear until sometime late tomorrow. Ana couldn't wait that long.

"Martina, stay with Ana. I need to know if anything changes. Vomiting. Seizures. Chest or belly pain." I ticked off the symptoms as I grabbed my slicker out of the closet.

"Where are you going?" Britt grabbed my arm. "Is there anything I can do?"

There was nothing anyone could do, but I had to try. "Oz has a fishing boat. For charters. It's the sturdiest vessel on the island. I'm going to ask him to take Ana and me to Montserrat."

9
BRITT

Luka had forgotten all about me.

He was completely focused on Ana. In the last hour, her condition had worsened. As I helped prepare supplies for the dangerous journey to Monserrat, Martina explained the risks. Stroke, heart failure, liver damage, placental abruption. I didn't understand all of it, but it was scary as hell. As soon as I was home, I was going to educate Mona all about preeclampsia. I didn't want to lose her or my niece-or-nephew.

My heart ached for Eljon. He stayed next to Ana, praying with her, smoothing her forehead, keeping her calm, but those were trite efforts when her life and that of their unborn child hung in the balance.

I'd never felt so useless or so privileged. Allergies? Get a shot. In a car wreck? Call the ambulance. Having a baby? Check into a labor and delivery room with all the amenities of a five-star hotel and a whole team of medical professionals just for you.

Luka was taking care of fifteen hundred people with little more than aspirin and duct tape. Now, he was risking his life for his patients. Montserrat, Martina told me, was four hours by boat in good weather. No telling how long the trip would take in the middle of a storm.

I was catching it all on video. Since I didn't know what kind of footage I'd need for the campaign, I'd been recording everything. Luka's house calls to those on the mountain, the patients who came to his clinic, Martina, Shark Rock, the town, the ocean. Everything. Last night as Luka and I reviewed the day's footage, I realized I was capturing memories for myself as well.

Watching Luka through the lens of the video camera gave me a degree of objectivity. Anyone could see the danger in the undertaking. Blue-black clouds hung low over the ocean, rain coming down so heavy I couldn't see Fred and Ginger's bars at the far end of the harbor. Wind gusts shredded palm fronds, and several upended trees evidenced the storm's fury. Oz's fifty-foot boat rocked and rolled against the dock as five-foot swells pummeled the cove. Luka and Eljon stood on either side of Ana, steadying her bulky profile as they timed the waves and movement of the boat to get her onboard safely.

When I lifted my head and watched Luka, there was no objectivity. There was only emotion—fear lodged in my throat, trepidation in the pit of my stomach, and love in my heart.

"Ana and da baby, dey be alright." Martina stood next to me at the shore-end of the dock, holding the hood of her raincoat tight beneath her chin. She yelled because of the wind, but I heard the certainty in her voice.

"I hope so," I hollered back, raising the video camera to keep recording.

"Doctor Man make it be so."

How I wished I shared Martina's faith in Luka. He was incredible, for sure. Dedicated and resourceful when it came to treating his patients. Loyal and thoughtful when it came to his friends. Idealistic and principled when it came to the CFA campaign. Eager and generous and passionate and vulnerable when it came to me.

But he was just a man.

One man who gave everything to the people he cared about. What would it be like to be loved by such a man?

Tears blurred the image.

I would never know. Luka's life was here on the island. He would never be happy returning to a big city hospital. More than that, the people here needed him. It would be pure selfishness to ask him for something more than a temporary fling.

Doctor Man doesn't do flings, and neither do you.

I snorted a snotty sob-laugh. Now my inner guide was a cross between Master Po and Martina.

"Dry da tears, *paadi*." Martina rubbed my back. "Doctor Man come back to ya."

He might come back, but then I would leave. The storm could delay my travel, but only for a day or two. My life—my family, my career—was in Denver. Loss and grief sat heavy in my chest. It felt like my heart had been chained to an anchor and thrown into the tumultuous sea.

Luka strode back down the dock toward us, bent against the wind. Ana and Eljon were secured inside the boat's cabin. Oz was above, in the cockpit area. The man's willingness to take Luka and his patients out into the storm was more proof of how much the islanders respected him.

"Call Doc Rodriguez and fill him in. Ask him to cover until I get back. If anyone needs a doctor, they'll have to go to Belle Isle. Stay in touch with Bridges at the hospital. Let him know we're on our way. I'll try to make radio contact with him if I can." He crouched so he was eye to eye with her and gripped her shoulders. "Martina, I—"

"Not da time for farewells, Doctor Man." She patted his check. "I see ya in a day or two."

"I love you, Martina." He pressed a loud smack to Martina's cheek.

"I know dat, Doctor Man."

When it was my turn, Luka looked over his shoulder at the rocking boat and then back at me.

"Go." I blinked away the tears mixing with the rain on my cheeks. I couldn't distract Luka with desperate confessions of falling for him or wanting more. Not now. Not when Ana and her baby needed him more than I did. "I'll be here when you get back."

He tunneled his fingers through my hair and kissed me hard and long and deep.

Then he turned and ran back to the boat.

I thought I heard him shout, "I love you, Britt," as Oz steered away from the dock, but it was just the cruel wind and my imagination.

10

LUKA

I returned to the island once Ana and the baby were out of danger. When I got back three days later, Britt was gone. I missed her by a few hours. Martina told me she'd taken the last ferry of the day but couldn't wait any longer or she'd have missed her flight back to Denver.

I used a lot of four-letter words. Martina didn't chide me once.

I think she knew.

I gave myself twelve hours to act like an ass. I walked down to Ginger's and got drunk on mango bellinis. At midnight, Oz found me passed out at the end of the dock. The next morning, he asked me about the song I'd been singing as he threw me into bed.

"Something about rocks and mountains," he said the next day.

Behind the Oakleys I wore to cut the glare of the sun and hide my hangover, I'd archly informed Oz the tune was "Rocky Mountain High" by the one and only John Denver.

Life on *Isla Tortuga Verde* continued as it had before Britt Connolly arrived and changed everything. I made rounds on my mountain bike, ate conch fritters at Fred's since it was his turn, swam out to Shark Rock, and cared for my patients. Everything on the island was the same, except for me.

Ten days later, Martina burst into the exam room where I was stitching up a gash one of the tourists had sustained on a nearby coral reef. "Doctor Man, hurry up. Britt on da phone."

My heart started thudding.

"Ow! Hey, be careful, dude." The tourist, a young surfer type on spring break, jerked away when I accidentally poked him.

"Dat be Doctor Dude to ya, young man!" Martina glowered at the guy. "Go. Dis one can wait."

"I'm done. See your family doctor when you get home. Keep it dry and stay off the reefs." I tied off the last stitch. "Martina, collect the payment from Mr. Galway, please."

I ran to my office and snatched the phone from the desk.

"Hello?"

"Luka!" Britt's sweet, familiar voice reached out from 2,500 miles away. "I've been trying to reach you all week. How are you?"

"I'm good." I lowered myself into the desk chair. "The island is still cleaning up from the storm. We just got WiFi back last night, and phone service has been spotty. How are things there?"

Why didn't you wait?

Do you miss me?

Does your heart ache like mine?

That's what I wanted to ask her.

"Have you seen the baby yet? I called Ana at the hospital, and they set up a video chat for us. He's so tiny!"

"Not yet. I came back to the island with Oz the next day. The doctors at St. John's got Ana stabilized, but she started having kidney problems. They ended up doing a C-section. Eljon said it will be a few weeks before the baby is ready to leave the NICU, but he's doing well for a preemie."

"I got Care For All to cover an apartment for them in Montserrat so they can stay there and get over to the hospital to see the baby. What does it feel like to have a namesake?"

I heard the smile in her voice. It made me feel marginally less miserable. "Luka Eljon Mendoza. It's quite an honor."

"A well-deserved honor. My God, babe. You risked your life for them."

Babe.

I decided to go for it. We didn't stand a chance at forever, but maybe now and then would do. Britt had to go on vacation somewhere so why not *Isla Tortuga Verde*? Seeing her once or twice a year was better than nothing.

"I miss you." I pressed the phone to my ear.

"I miss you, too." Her voice went husky. "I waited as long as I could, but I had to catch my connecting flight in Miami."

"We got back a few hours after you left."

"Oh."

Just *oh*. The disappointment hit like a ton of bricks.

"How's the campaign coming?" I stood and began pacing.

"Seymour, my boss, loves the footage. We've been through the video and stills, and a transcriptionist is typing up the interviews. I have a bunch of meetings scheduled with folks at Care For All. Their PR people, Finance, the board of directors, and reps from some of the other projects they fund. And guess what!"

"Tell me."

"CFA hired Drummond to handle all of their marketing and advertising. Seymour said this will be huge. He wants me to get a better perspective on the scope of their operations, so he set up a three-week junket with stops in Thailand, South Africa, Kenya, India, Greece, and France."

I wondered if she was packing condoms but then castigated myself for the thought.

"Congratulations, Britt." I surprised myself at how genuinely enthused I sounded. "That sounds like a great opportunity."

"Your clinic showed me the consequences when medical care isn't readily available. This is a project that really matters. I can't go back to making up cheesy slogans for dating apps after my experience on *Isla Tortuga Verde*."

"I'm glad you don't have to."

"Seymour asked me to have something mocked up for the CFA board by the end of May." She paused. "Would you consider coming up for the presentation? I thought it would be nice to include Martina and Doctor Rodriguez, too."

"May?" I stalled to cover my disappointment that her invite wasn't exclusively for me.

"Does that give you enough time to find someone to cover for you?"

The hopeful lilt was all I needed to hear.

"We'll be there."

Though Britt hadn't been there when I got back from the emergency trip to Montserrat, nothing would keep me from making the trip to Denver in May.

11
BRITT

I twisted the silver bangle on my wrist and watched the second hand sweep the face of the clock in the conference room. This was it. My big moment. I'd been working night and day for the past two months to launch a campaign that would save people like Ana Mendoza and her baby. And provide the necessary equipment and meds doctors needed so they didn't have to risk their lives like Luka had.

The eight hours Martina and I had waited for word of their safe arrival were the longest of my life. We drank coffee and played dominoes and Martina taught me Creole swear words. I told her about Mona and Nick and my friends and my parents and how I felt like I no longer fit in, and she gave me Master Po-worthy advice.

"Maybe it be dem dat no longer fit."

It gave me something to think about while I was banking airline and hotel points on my three-week junket for CFA.

"Ready, Britt?" Seymour rambled into the conference room, slicked up for the meeting; he'd swapped out his usual flannel shirt for a forest-green sports coat. "I'm looking forward to seeing what you put together. I don't usually let the junior account executives develop campaigns on their own, but most of them aren't emotionally invested in their subject matter."

"This wasn't just another assignment," I admitted. "If I hadn't gone to *Isla Tortuga Verde* and seen their struggle firsthand, I'm not sure I would have had enough depth or insight to create a truly compelling campaign."

"How's that li'l fella you told me about?" Seymour took his seat at the head of the long glass-topped table.

For a second, I thought he meant Luka. "He's—"

"That baby who almost didn't make it."

He meant Ana's baby.

"He's doing great. He went home a few weeks ago. His mom emails a new picture every week."

The most recent photo was part of my presentation.

Louella cleared her throat from the open door. "Your guests have arrived, Mr. Drummond."

"Thanks, Lou." Seymour caught my eye and mouthed, "Good luck."

I knotted my fingers behind my back to hide their trembling. I wasn't worried about the presentation. It was still far from finished, but the core was solid. Successful storytelling marketing required a story worth sharing, and Luka had provided that in spades. Seeing Luka after two and a half months and awaiting his reaction to the presentation was what had me shaking in my Louboutins.

"Hello, Britt." Alistair Deacons, a public health official with the state of Colorado, was the first through the door. He bent to kiss my cheek.

We'd become well-acquainted during the collaboration between CFA and Drummond, especially after I learned he was expecting his first grandchild. His son and daughter-in-law were due around the same time as Mona and Nick.

"I'd like to introduce you to my father, Stanford Deacons."

The elder Deacons bore a striking resemblance to his son. Both were tall and rail-thin with kind blue eyes and curly dark hair, Alistair's significantly less gray that his father's.

Stanford was deep in conversation with Doc Rodriguez. It was easy to tell the two were good friends who hadn't seen each other in a long time by the way their heads tilted in and the fact that Stanford hadn't heard his son's introduction.

"Dad." Alistair laid a hand on his father's shoulder. "You and Dr. Rodriguez can continue your visit after the meeting. He's here through the weekend, and I invited him to stay at the house with us. This is the young woman I've been telling you about."

Stanford and Doc swung their attention to me, and I smiled politely, but like them, my attention was elsewhere. Beyond them, in the hallway and at the back of the group, was Luka.

"Where is dat gal? I need a hug and a squeeze." Martina shouldered her way into the conference room, a wide smile lighting up her brown eyes. "What is dis? Where is my island girl? Dis Miz Business Lady."

"Let me read your T-shirt, and then hugs." I straightened the hem so I could read the tie-dyed fabric. "It's better at the beach."

I agreed one hundred percent.

"Everyone on da island miss ya." She threw her arms around me and mashed me into her huge bosom, whispering, "Doctor Man most of all."

"That's your place over there." I pointed to a chair with a large giftbag on the seat. "I wanted your collection to be complete, so you've got T-shirts from all of the Denver sports teams and tourist attractions. I think your favorite will be the one from a local vegan restaurant."

Seymour and I exchanged a look and grinned.

My introductions to Stanford and Doc were perfunctory. They moved to the end of the table and started a chat with Seymour while Alistair moved the line along. Two other board members, the head of public relations, and the chief financial officer. Luka was last.

He looked amazing. Hot and successful and confident. He'd made the transition from tropical island doctor to corporate spokesman effortlessly. He'd gotten a haircut that emphasized his angular cheekbones, now smooth but with a hint of a five o'clock shadow. In his navy suit, white shirt, and red tie, with a hint of something wild and rugged beneath, he could have posed for *GQ*.

"Hello, Britt." He didn't extend his hand or lean in for a hug. "It's good to see you again."

"I'm glad you could be here, Doctor Stanic." I held my smile, the tight false stretch taking me back to Mona and Nick's wedding. I straightened my spine and squared my shoulders. Our reunion was *not* going down like this. Master Po and I had been having a lot of discussions lately. Convos that sounded like:

Speak your truth.

Love finds a way.

No risk, no reward.

Okay, maybe I saw that on one of Martina's T-shirts.

Tell the guy you're in love with him.

That nugget came from Mona.

"If you aren't busy after the meeting, I thought we could... catch up." I pictured our tryst on Shark Rock and used my psychic powers to share the memories with him.

It must have worked because the shuttered expression on his face cracked, and I saw a glimmer of *my* Luka. The man who cared enough to slather my boobs with sunscreen before he fondled them. The guy who drank frou-frou cocktails like mango bellinis with nary a care that some might question his manhood. The doctor who dedicated his life to his patients, and his heart to—

That's what I intended to find out.

"Hurry. Up." He spoke so quietly I wasn't sure I heard him, but there was no missing the heated look he gave me.

It was the first time I gave a presentation with soaked panties.

12

LUKA

I stood outside the glass office building where Britt worked. The Drummond Agency had a suite of offices on the twentieth floor with a stunning panorama of the Rocky Mountains west of downtown Denver. It didn't compare to the view from Corcova Mountain, though.

My head was spinning. From the fact that Britt was close enough to touch, from the campaign presentation, but mostly from Alistair Deacons's invitation to come work at the Care For All Denver headquarters. I felt like I'd killed a case of Red Stripe at high noon in August. Heat and alcohol don't mix. It's a crappy buzz followed by a hangover that's the equivalent of lying in a puddle of puke with flies buzzing up your nose.

Don't ask how I know. Just trust me on this one.

"Isn't Friday game night with your family?" I stood next to Britt, waiting to see what happened next.

"I told my family I had other plans." She unbuttoned the top two buttons of her blouse. "Whew. I'm glad that's over. Are you hungry? There's a microbrewery down the block that has a great IPA. If you want steak, I'd recommend Guard and Grace."

I didn't know this Britt. This woman in high heels and a

fitted silk suit, hair elaborately coiled, nails manicured, and artfully applied makeup asking me about IPAs and steakhouses was a Stepford version of the playful, uninhibited woman who'd whipped off her bikini top and pranced into the Caribbean Sea and then got on her knees and sucked my cock.

Maybe I'd misinterpreted her signals. I thought "catch up" was code for make love. I thought the intense eye contact between us as she narrated the presentation was an indicator of where her attention lay. I thought the diamond sheen in her eyes was happiness when I was the second person to give her a standing ovation after viewing the TV commercial she'd created to promote public donations to CFA—the first person being Martina, of course.

"I don't have much of an appetite." I shoved my hands in my pants pockets.

"Hmm, I'm sorry to hear that."

"I think I'll head back to my room."

The Drummond Agency had reserved rooms for Martina and me at the Ritz-Carlton. "On the concierge level," pointed out Martina to six or seven other guests when we first arrived.

"I was hoping you'd say that." Britt tucked her arm through mine.

I was stunned—a little confused and a lot hopeful—as we walked the three blocks to the hotel. She kept hold of me the entire way, burrowing closer when a group of young women, one wearing a pink sash that read "Bride," crammed into the elevator. Neither of us said a thing as we walked the length of the hall to my room.

Once inside, Britt slipped out of her shoes and did something that sent her hair spilling over her shoulders. I relaxed in response to the change in her appearance and toed off my own footwear. It had been years since I wore leather dress shoes and a suit.

"How are your sister and brother-in-law? Did you find out if they're having a girl or boy?" I sat on the edge of the bed, sweat trickling down my back despite the air conditioning.

I didn't know where to start. The lines I'd rehearsed were nothing more than a word salad in my cranium. It would be so much easier to have this conversation with a plate of fish tacos and round of bellinis.

"Oh, Luka. I don't want to talk about my family or the clinic or the campaign or anything else right now." She stood at the window, backlit by the setting sun, hands loose at her sides, eyes dark with longing. "I want to talk about us."

"Is there an *us*?" I so wanted to create something with Britt—an *us*, a home, a life together, a baby.

"There could be." She crossed the room and knelt between my legs.

God, she was so much braver than I was. If she was willing to start the conversation, I'd better find the balls to keep it going. The problem was that so much was riding on this discussion. If she didn't feel the same or if she wasn't willing to meet me halfway, there was no way we could make a relationship work. Hoping was safer than failing.

But hoping wouldn't get me Britt.

Just do it.

Martina had been wearing that T-shirt a lot lately. It suddenly made sense.

I bolted off the bed, sending Britt onto her ass. She landed on her elbows, skirt hiked, knees wide, giving me a splendid view of her pink thong. I forced my gaze away.

"I love you. I want to spend my life with you, but hell if I know how to make that work when you're a Denver city girl and I'm a doctor on a small tropical island." I realized I was shouting and toned it down. "Alistair Deacons offered me a position here in Denver. If you're serious about us, I'll take the job."

"He what?" Britt's eyes widened.

"He didn't get into specifics. Just said they'd love to add me to the team at headquarters."

She started laughing. Not a snicker or chuckle but all-out can't talk, can't breathe, can't stop belly laughs.

Right then, I wanted her more than I ever had.

Levered up on her elbows, head tossed back, wine-red hair brushing the floor, throat arched, knees spread, she was everything bold and vibrant and glorious. I didn't know why she was laughing but it didn't matter.

"Alistair...he..." She started giggling again. "He...offered me...a job, too." Britt looked at me, and I realized she was crying. "He offered me a job on *Isla Tortuga Verde*. Care For All wants to open a series of regional offices. It's part of the new campaign. A boots-on-the-ground sort of thing."

"Fuck. Does everyone know we're in love except us?" I liked Alistair Deacons a whole lot more now than I had earlier when I saw him kiss Britt hello.

"I know I love you. And you said you love me." She sat up, expression sobering. "We'd have to make some big decisions, but we have options."

I offered Britt my hand and helped her up, circling my arms around her waist. "There's only one thing I need right now. That's you. Naked. On the bed. Over the back of the chair. In the shower. Tits pressed against the window while I take you from behind. Take your pick."

"You know I like it when you talk like that." She unbuttoned her blouse, slow and deliberate, teasing me.

I spun her around and unbuttoned her skirt, shoving it over her hips. I helped her out of her jacket like a gentleman would, but my patience ran out. Hand between her shoulder blades, I bent her over the bed, so she was leaning on her palms. I shoved her thong out of the way so I could slide two fingers inside her as I fumbled with my belt and zipper.

The succulent sound of her wet juices made me harder. I pulled my cock free and guided it into her, sinking as deep as I could. It wasn't enough. I gripped her hips and pulled her closer until I felt my balls nestled in the heat of her slit. She contracted the muscles in her vagina, holding onto me, tightening around me until it felt like the only thing tethering me to the world was this intimate, erotic connection.

I began pumping in and out of her, slow and shallow at first, rubbing the sensitive crown against the rim of her opening. When my balls tightened, I curved an arm under her hips and pounded into her. Again. Again. Again.

"More, Luka." Braced on one arm, she began fingering her clit. She spread her legs wider so I could go deeper. "Harder."

Her command gave me permission to not hold back.

I closed my eyes, insatiable lust and expansive love insistently demanding release.

"I *love* you. I *love* you. I *love* you." Each *love* came with a powerful thrust of my hips that made her ass and tits jiggle. "I *love* you...ahhhh!"

Her scream followed my shout as we came together. Her walls spasmed against my cock, our hearts a crazy duet of *ba-bum, ba-bum, ba-bum*. My legs gave out, and we tumbled onto the bed. She wiggled her backside against my groin so my still-hard cock remained inside her.

"I didn't plan our reunion sex to be like that." I smoothed her hair away from her face and kissed her earlobe. "I wanted it to be slow and romantic."

"Fucking can be romantic." She reached behind and tugged at my dress pants, which rode just below my hips. "A guy who wants you so bad he doesn't even wait to get his clothes off? And who tells you over and over again how much he loves you while hitting just the right spot as you play with your clit for a whole-body orgasm? I'll take that over flowers and chocolates any day."

I kissed her neck and inhaled the scent of perfume, perspiration, and sex. It made me want her again, this time straddling my lap and riding my cock as I stared into her eyes and watched her expression shift from joy to wonder to bliss.

Then a thought came to me. "There's still time to make game night with your family."

Her breathing stilled for a moment, then resumed. "You'd trade more awesome sex for Cards Against Humanity?"

"No. I'd *delay* more awesome sex for the opportunity to meet your parents, sister, and brother-in-law."

"We have a little bit of time," she drawled, dragging my fingers to her mons. "I really, *really* missed your mouth."

"All you have to do is ask, Britt."

I waited until she mounded the pillows behind her and opened her legs in invitation.

One taste of her sweet juices, and I knew we were going to be late.

Didn't matter.

We had all the time in the world.

MANGO BELLINI

1 cup fresh diced mango
   3 tbsp fresh squeezed lime juice
   1 bottle Prosecco

Put the mango into a blender with the lime juice. Blend until it is a smooth purée. If it is having trouble blending, add 2-4 tablespoons of the Prosecco or of water. Note that some blenders will never get rid of some of the bigger pieces. You can put a bowl under a colander with big holes and strain your purée through there to remove larger chunks. Chill the puree if you so desire.

Stir the mango puree. Measure about 2 tablespoons into each of 6 wine flutes. Carefully top each glass with Prosecco.

Proportions: One part mango puree to two parts Prosecco.

Serves 6

ABOUT THE AUTHOR

EmKay Connor is the author of #sexysassy contemporary romantic fiction infused with quirky humor and engaging characters. Her bright and breezy instalove romances are set in tropical locations and glamorous destinations where her heroes and heroines discover passion and fall in love.

Her manuscripts have finaled and won numerous contests, including RWA's prestigious Golden Heart.

She lives, writes, and drinks coffee in northeastern Florida. Visit her at http://sexysassyromance.com/, and subscribe to her newsletter here: https://www.subscribepage.com/EmKayConnor.

HER PERFECT GUY

Lyz Kelley

1

Devon Gaines plastered a smile on her face, because best friends supported each other, even if one was hurting inside.

Her life was about to forever change, and the pending reality made the emptiness inside her expand.

Kayla Lewis, Devon's bestie, danced out of the five-star hotel lobby, down the steps, and over the bridge toward the pool that wove through the sprawling beach complex. Reaching out her arms, Kayla twirled. "I can't believe it's finally happening. We're in Jamaica, and I'm getting married!"

Devon managed to keep up with Kayla's skipping steps as they made a beeline for the Caribbean blue-tiled swimming pool and nearest vacant table, which happened to be complete with a white umbrella sitting at the perfect angle to protect them from the intense summer sun.

A cute server wearing white shorts and an untucked polo shirt appeared to take their drink order and was back in minutes with two cucumber and mint detox smoothies.

While the server set the filled-to-the-brim glasses on the hotel's signature pink flamingo cardboard coasters, Kayla chatted about the adorableness of the yellow-and-orange paper parasol toothpicks holding the flower-shaped melon balls.

Kayla had every reason to be excited. In Devon's opinion, Kayla was marrying her dream guy—her perfect soul mate—and the only person Kayla's heart had ever throbbed for. If only Devon could experience a tenth of Kayla's joy.

Kayla grabbed her phone to scroll through her social media feed for a picture of the rainbow bouquet she'd been describing when her chatter rolled to a stop. The sudden silence yanked Devon out of her brooding thoughts. She looked up to see her friend blinking hard, her breath hitching in almost a sob.

"Kayla? What's wrong?"

"This place. The wedding. I must be having pre-wedding jitters." Kayla pushed her drink to the side and clenched her hand into a fist. "I keep worrying that Brandon might change his mind. Last night, out of the blue, he was talking about developing this gamer app. He has all these big life plans. What if at the last minute he decides this marriage isn't what he wants?"

"Take a deep breath, Kayla...and another. There, that's better," Devon said as soon as Kayla's grip loosened a bit. "Brandon Myers is more than lucky to be marrying you. Don't you ever forget that important fact."

"You think so?" Kayla's sighed response was almost inaudible.

"I *know* so. Who wouldn't want a beautiful, sweet, sexy and—not forgetting—super-smart, financially independent woman for his wife?"

"Oh, Devon." Kayla's worried expression changed to one of relief.

"My point is," Devon continued, "you have nothing to fear. You're going to walk down that aisle with your head held high because you are Kayla Lewis, the woman who is adored by all who meet her."

Chapter 1

"You are the sweetest."

"I know." Devon shrugged with a bit of a smirk and then took the first sip of her drink, letting the zingy cucumber and mint flavors solidify her resolve to be the best friend she could be. She sat back against the cushioned seat and let the sun warm her freshly pedicured toes.

"I mean it, silly." Kayla smacked the table, her solemn expression transforming into a fit of the giggles.

Devon couldn't resist joining her.

As hiccups replaced Kayla's chuckles, Devon glanced at her iPad. "So where are we? What's the next thing to check off the list?"

"I think my next appointment is..." Kayla paused when voices overlapped each other and interrupted her.

"Who's making all that noise?" Devon glanced around the pool area, searching for the commotion, until she spotted Mike Lewis, Kayla's older brother.

He was on the far side of the pool, surrounded by a crowd of glamorous, scantily clad women vying for his attention. Some were tugging at his sleeve, while others wrapped their arms around his waist to pose with him while the paparazzi cameras click-click-clicked. Devon was sure she wasn't imagining poor Mike's frustration and annoyance as he tried, with little or no success, to break free of the swarm.

Her heart did that fluttering thing it always did when Mike showed up.

If one googled Mike Lewis, the definition of demigod—luscious, smart, talented, and uber rich—would appear under his name. His deliciously smooth voice alone was enough to sweep any woman off her feet and into his bed.

Devon couldn't help but stare at him while her mind took her down memory lane to the day heaven blessed her life with her perfect guy, although the mortifying events that followed were forever stamped in her memory.

It had been a typical Friday night, her freshman year at Yale.

DEVON WAS WEARING her R2-D2 pajamas, sitting on the hard dorm room bed, leaning back against the headboard with a neck pillow keeping her comfy.

A bowl of pasta was cradled in her palm, a fork in her other hand, and Mirjana Pavlovic's *Bioengineering: A Conceptual Approach* rested on her lap.

"Devy!" Kayla staggered into the room, her hair in an unusual tangle, and her blurry-eyed expression suggesting she'd had one or three too many drinks. It was week two, and Kayla had yet to find time to crack open a book.

Kayla, an English Literature major, was out doing "humanity research," the term she used when she wanted to avoid studying. Even though they were opposites in every way, Devon and Kayla hit it off on day one, when Kayla rolled into the 140-square-foot room with her thirty boxes of must-haves. Devon laughed at Kayla's horrified expression when she saw how small the dorm room was and then assured Kayla there would be enough space for all her precious things.

Devon finished swallowing her mouthful of pasta. "What's up, Kay-K?"

Kayla teetered her way to the desk chair and flopped down. "I brought you someone."

"Who?" Devon twisted her fork, rolling up another wad of pasta as she did her best to feign interest. Kayla always brought people back to the dorm, her goal being to prolong the party for as long as possible.

Kayla pointed toward the door instead of giving a reply.

Chapter 1

Devon tilted her head back, a pasta noodle still hanging from her mouth, to behold a gift from heaven. She choked out a cough as the noodle got stuck from slurping too quickly. He was wearing a hoodie and khaki chinos, plus the latest in sports shoes that must have set him back a few bucks. He had thick eyebrows, high cheekbones, and full, symmetrical lips...and best of all, at five feet eleven, he was, as Goldilocks said, just right.

"Meet my super-annoying workaholic brother and big-time pain in the ass." Kayla's statement was delivered with a mix of sarcasm and excitement.

Devon pounded her chest to recover from the cough. "Mike. Right?" She glanced at her pajamas and fuzzy slippers, thanking every deity in the universe she hadn't done an herbal facial that evening.

Kayla had always bragged about her brother, Mikey, being a dreamboat. Not one to be attracted to guys easily, Devon dismissed it as girl talk and was expecting nothing more than a typical guy. But the senior standing in the doorway was a heart-throb. So much so, her brain shut down, refusing to cooperate by creating a proper sentence.

Kayla laughed and slapped at Devon's Yoda-slippered foot. "I kinda only have one brother, and yes, this is Mike." Kayla weaved toward her brother, paused to hold onto the closet handle, and pasted a sloppy grin on her face. "Mikey, bro, meet my college roomie, my new best friend and heart-sister, Devon Gaines.

Devon set her half-eaten bowl of pasta aside and slapped her textbook shut.

"Hey," Mr. Hottie said, his baritone voice caressing Devon's ears—and skin—as he pushed away from the door.

Mike sauntered into the room, his gaze sweeping over the matching pink-and-purple flower-power comforters, corkboards crammed with pictures, and Kayla's bed piled high with pillows.

When he was close enough for Devon to touch, her throat tightened. Then she sighed. *He's perfect,* she thought, and her heart added, *mine.*

Kayla climbed onto Devon's bed and settled in next to her. "This is the point where you say, 'the pleasure is all mine,'" Kayla whispered, not so quietly, in Devon's ear.

Yes, all mine, Devon almost whimpered.

"Told you he's a dreamboat," Kayla said with a soft chuckle.

"It's nice having you in our room... I mean here. Meeting you in our room." *Oh, God. I need to shut up now.*

Devon elbowed Kayla when her bestie snickered and thrust her hand out for a shake because she just had to touch him, feel his skin against hers, feel his heat. When he took her hand into his big, strong one, her entire body sighed, and then a rush of electricity zipped through her when his gaze fixed on hers.

"Intros over with," Kayla said, interrupting the chemistry sizzling between them—or, to be more honest, exploding in Devon. "The three of us should go to dinner. I'm starved."

"Make that dinner for two," he said.

Yes, just the two of us. Devon's heart pounded and her toes curled and wiggled as she sighed. *Oh, what a magnificent man.*

"C'mon, Mikey. You never make time for me anymore." Kayla's expression changed to that pouty little frown Devon had already seen too often.

"I got you back safe, and now it's time for me to cram. I have a test tomorrow," Mike said, his tone so calm Devon wondered if he had ever shouted at anyone in his lifetime.

"But you just got here. You didn't even sit down."

"I'm sorry, gumdrop. I need high scores if I'm going to get into graduate school." He pulled Kayla into a brotherly embrace.

Devon gazed at them, her insides eaten up with jealousy. She so, so, *so* wanted to be the one in Mike Lewis's arms.

Chapter 1

FROM THAT DAY FORWARD, that soul-level craving for Mike Lewis had never diminished.

Now here he was, in Jamaica, on the other side of the pool, with a white sand beach as his backdrop. He was still a heartthrob, and still a "hands-off" option.

Devon picked up her drink and let the dreamy reminisce slip away while she took a long swallow and wondered how Mike Lewis kept getting better looking year after year. She let out a heavy sigh.

"What the F?" Kayla skidded her chair back an inch as she leaped to her feet.

Devon was familiar with that determined look and reached for Kayla's arm to prevent another outburst. "Where do you think you're going?"

"To help my brother, of course. I can't just let those paparazzi embarrass him like that." She took a step away.

Devon was quick to nab Kayla's arm again. "Yo, Kay-K, I understand you want to protect Mike, but don't forget about the wedding reception menu—which needs reviewing—plus you haven't delivered a final guest count to the hotel caterers." Devon reached for any other excuses she could dig up to make Kayla see reason.

"But what about Mike?" Kayla pointed over her shoulder with a grimace. "I don't want those women and camera jerks ruining my wedding."

"I'll take care of it. You need to complete the checklist. You made me promise to keep you on track, and the rest of your family should arrive soon, so you need to be available to welcome them. Don't forget. Once everyone arrives, you won't be able to check on things for yourself. Your mom will insist on taking over."

"You're right. You always think these things through. I don't know what I would have done without you all these years."

"The feeling is mutual, believe me."

Tremors of fear cascaded through Devon as visions of Kayla slipping further away choked off her air. At the end of this weekend Kayla would be married, and then she would have a house to set up, babies to raise, soccer practice, or dance recitals. Where would that leave Devon? She shook off the panic.

No self-pity. Not now or ever.

"Oh, no!" Kayla pulled away, reaching for her room key. "I'm already ten minutes late. Good luck with whatever you have planned. I can't wait to hear how you solve this one. You've always been one for clever solutions." Kayla sprinted up the path leading to the hotel's lobby.

As Devon walked over to rescue Mike—whether he wanted it or not—her heart did that little pitter-patter it always did when he was around. But it didn't distract her from assessing the scene while she worked on a solution for Mike's dilemma.

Promising to rescue Mike might not have been such a good idea, but backing out now wasn't an option. Kayla certainly didn't want to have Mike distracted by hordes of women trailing in his wake. And he'd be annoyed if photographers kept springing out of bushes to take his picture. She sucked in a deep breath for courage.

"What's going on here?" she demanded as she got close enough for the others to hear.

No one paid any heed.

Raising her voice, she repeated, "I said, what's going on here?"

Mike seemed surprised by her sudden appearance, and the women surrounding him appeared more confused than anything.

"Babe." Devon used the tone she'd perfected when giving

presentations to large audiences, even though her nerves made her legs a little wobbly. "Why are you not checked in yet? I've been searching everywhere for you." She pushed aside the woman who stubbornly held onto Mike's arm.

"Excuse me." The half-dressed woman with the designer sunglasses—and more diamonds around her neck, wrists, and fingers than in the gift shop's window—gave her some heavy shade.

"Who are you?" A man in khaki shorts, a navy-blue T-shirt, and a beer gut demanded. He gave Devon the impression he enjoyed watching sports and drinking on Sundays and did very little else besides making a nuisance of himself taking unwanted pictures of people who didn't want to be disturbed. "More to the point, who are you to Mike Lewis?"

Devon turned around to face the crowd. "My name is Devon Gaines, and I'm engaged to this man. I am Mike Lewis's fiancée." Her fears paused for a second as she held onto her serious expression. Thankfully, she'd managed to speak the lie without a stutter.

"What?" The tall woman who looked like she only ate salad greens sneered at her.

The clicking of cameras started up again.

Mike placed an arm around her waist and pulled her closer. "Smile," he whispered in her ear.

Goosebumps swept a chill across her skin as she did her best to pose for the camera.

"Mike, can you please confirm what this lady said? Is she really your fiancée?" the football fan's buddy demanded. "When did you start dating? Why haven't we seen you together before?"

Mike eased the pressure of his hand around her waist but kept her by his side.

Devon hiked up her chin and gathered her courage. "We came here for Mike's sister's wedding. I ask you not to interfere or ruin her special day. The world will hear about us soon enough, but for now, Mike and I must maintain a low profile for his sister's sake."

"If you have any more questions," Mike said, calm for a man who'd just had a family friend claim she was his fiancée, "I suggest having your respective media houses send a request for information to my personal representative. That's all I want to say for now." He pointed to the path up to the hotel and raised an inquisitive brow. "Shall we?"

With a barely polite "If you'll excuse us," Devon allowed herself to be guided away from the scene.

Neither said a word while they navigated a small bridge through the lower garden toward the hotel restaurant area, but just before they entered through the door leading them to the resort bar, Mike interlaced his fingers with hers and leaned in. "They're still following us, but we should be safe once we're inside."

Devon's heart raced faster and faster as the impact of what she'd just done ballooned in her head. For years she'd hidden her feelings for Mike so they wouldn't affect her relationship with her best friend and the Lewis family as a whole. Especially since Kayla's parents were always so good to her.

2

Mike replayed the unbelievable scene in his head as he walked into the restaurant bar area, still too stunned to speak.

Devon—his sister's best friend, who he'd recognized right away in spite of the confusion surrounding them—had called him her fiancée.

That was weird, not to mention awkward. Yet Mike couldn't help wondering why she was so angry.

Wearing a white tank top with a lace bra strap peeking out on her right shoulder, she looked gorgeous in her fury. Her high-waist linen pants fit her just right, and the low-heeled sandals weren't quite as sexy as three-inchers might have been, but he liked her pink painted toenails, which matched her sun-kissed cheeks. Her brown hair was tied in a rough ponytail with loose strands floating around her head.

But what was up with her calling him babe?

Mike's brain was still having trouble working out what was going on. He didn't need a soothsayer to tell him Devon was trying to pull off a prank again. She had sounded and looked so confident, with that smile lighting up her vibrant, virtually makeup-free face.

Over the years he'd become aware of Devon's mischievous side.

The first time was when Kayla came up with a scheme to travel to Denver for the holidays. The details of the moment were so vivid that they could have happened yesterday.

HIS MOM WAS SITTING beside Kayla on the ugly couch she had someone reupholster the year before, but the bright pink-and-yellow pattern did nothing to improve the room's decor. It was November, and he'd taken a vacation from his management trainee job. Kayla was home for the school break.

"Why do you need to be in Denver for Thanksgiving?" his mom had asked.

"I already told you," Kayla said with the little pout that worked on his parents like a charm. "It's for a school project. You can ask Devon."

Kayla's whiny tone was like listening to a constantly crying baby. The drama continued to unfold while he pretended to work on his laptop, doing his best to stay out of the fray.

"Hey, everyone." Devon walked into the living room, set her backpack on the floor, and took a seat across from Kayla.

"Good evening, dear," his mom replied with warm welcome. "Tell me about this project you and my daughter are working on."

"You know, Dev. The project in Denver."

Kayla kept her tone so cotton-candy sweet it almost made Mike gag.

Devon's confusion disappeared in a flash. The conspiracy was so obvious, but his mom seemed to miss it.

Chapter 2

"Oh...yes, the project. The school's newspaper is adding a special vacation column, and"—Devon's brows were almost up to her hairline at that point—"Kayla wants to become the editor for the newspaper. If they select her article for this new column, she'll get the open paid position. Having firsthand experience of Denver's landscape and cultural scene will be a big help and make her column stand out."

Mike had to cover his mouth so his mother wouldn't see him smirking.

He had to admit, Devon was quick to come up with a mighty persuasive argument.

His mother turned back to his sister. "You are over eighteen and a grown woman, Kayla. You must make your own choices, but I will worry if your studies slide. I'll pay for your travel this weekend, but you'll need to fund your spring break. Deal?"

"Deal!" Kayla launched herself at their mom, giving her a giant hug. "Love you."

The sappy endearments and the devious plan were not what interested Mike. It was Devon's reaction that won his affections. First was the satisfaction of winning the trip for Kayla, which slid into something that almost looked like envy. His dad had mentioned something about Devon's unfortunate family situation once, but looking at the confident woman sitting in the chair across the room, no one would guess she had family problems.

"Love you too, honey." Mom picked up the television remote and was quickly immersed in her program again.

Kayla and Devon nudged each other and giggled as they walked toward the kitchen. Mike resisted the urge to follow them...for all of two seconds. Their cooked-up story didn't add up.

"Have you called him yet?" Devon asked Kayla as Mike neared the kitchen doorway.

"Not yet, but I will soon. This trip to Denver is going to be special. You'll see." Kayla's voice vibrated with gleeful anticipation. "Thanks for always having my back."

"No problem. Promise me you'll be safe."

"When have I not been careful?" Kayla's attempt to sound innocent sounded more sarcastic than anything.

"When you forced your way into the football team captain's room."

"I needed to ask the quarterback an important question," Kayla replied.

"Really? He was naked!"

The suppressed laughter in Devon's tone was almost identical to his sister's. He imagined his sister busting into some dude's room and finding his nakedness funny. She'd done it enough times to him.

"And, what about the time you almost got yourself removed from the school's paper because you published your story about a girl cheating on her boyfriend without hiding her identity?"

"That story was my best one yet. It was real, and she had no right to cheat. Her boyfriend was a good guy," Kayla replied.

"You have no right to invade people's personal lives," Devon said.

"Yeah, but you helped me figure a way out of the trouble. You are the best problem-solver. It's what makes us perfect friends. I create the problems and you solve them."

"And what fresh trouble is brewing in Denver?" Mike asked, stepping into the kitchen and hoping he wasn't going to end up being pulled into another of his sister's schemes.

"Why would you ask that?" Kayla protested louder than she should have if she were innocent of scheming.

"You should tell him, Kay-K. You've always trusted your brother. Mike won't snitch on us."

Devon's words held such conviction, Mike almost believed them himself.

Kayla elbow-bumped him. "Please don't tell Mom, but Brandon and I plan to spend the holiday together. He's already booked tickets for Denver, but I assumed all along that he'd back out. It's why this is all last minute. I'm guessing he might be planning to ask me to marry him."

Mike had checked Brandon out when he first started dating his sister in high school. The computer geek was a good dude and treated his sister well, but that didn't mean he liked her lying to their parents. "I hope this doesn't blow up in your face. And you, do *not* end up pregnant." He gave Kayla a stern stare.

"Mike!" Kayla glared.

"Don't worry. Kayla will be texting me every ten minutes," Devon said. "I'll know if something goes wrong."

AFTER THE DENVER DEBACLE, Mike began to notice Devon during summer and winter family get-togethers. The round face with a radiant smile, hazel eyes, arched eyebrows, and a small nose—along with her five-six height—made her appear naïve, cute, and pure. But those innocent features were deceptive and challenged him to stay on his toes around her.

His sister had always spoken highly of Devon, never sparing Mike's ears a moment of silence as she went on and on about how perfect her roommate was. Devon never seemed to fall short. Kayla attributed her success in school to Devon's constant reminders to study rather than party. Little wonder his parents were so relaxed about the friendship between the beauty and Kayla. After college, Devon remained Kayla's true best friend.

Even Mike was jealous of their closeness.

Friendship of their kind was rare. He'd never found a friend as loyal as Devon—not even close. Then again, he always had far more important things to do. He had plans. Big plans. He was going to change lives. He didn't have time to date. Plus, after his two failed attempts at a serious relationship, he decided it was time to focus a hundred percent on his business. Period. When his company made it onto the top one thousand stocks list, *maybe* he'd search for a wife and give his parents the grandkids they hoped for.

And for that goal-defining reason, Mike played along with Devon's scheme. Her little charade seemed innocent and logical enough to get him out of the already-suffocating crowd, and it seemed to work like magic. Paparazzi no longer followed him, and women wouldn't be wrapping their arms around him or hailing him from across the room or even from outside the reception area windows. He was free. Free to enjoy being with his sister and family for once.

He stopped beside a lounge area and pointed to an oversized stuffed leather chair. Devon sank into the brown leather.

"Thanks for what you did back there." Mike took the chair opposite her, with a table in between. "It was an interesting solution. Over the top, but it worked."

"It was the only thing I could come up with. I'm thankful you played along. The plan could have backfired."

"I mean it, Devon. I truly appreciate it. It's been a tough week at work, and the last thing I need is to be hassled by clingy, nosy strangers. I was hoping this week would be devoted to catching up with family, plus a few hours of relaxation and rejuvenation."

She grinned, revealing that lively set of dimples on both cheeks and giving him a warm sense of satisfaction. A sensation he hadn't experienced in a very long time.

She leaned closer. "How's your newest intra-operative digital imaging device coming?"

His gut tightened as he looked at her. "That information isn't public yet. How did you hear about it?"

"Kayla told me."

"That loudmouth sister of mine. The project isn't going well. We've already been forced to push back the launch schedule once." He skipped the details since most women he knew found business-related topics boring.

"When Kayla told me what you were doing, I wondered why you would create another device that performs the same function as its counterparts. I mean, you already have several devices patented in the same functional range. Why make another one?"

For a second his breathing stopped. The question was insightful and strategic. Normally he wouldn't have answered, but since she clearly was interested, he wanted to indulge her. "I'm assuming you're aware of robotic surgical devices."

"I am."

"Good. What I'm working on will help robot-assisted surgeons perform many types of complex procedures with more precision, flexibility, and control than is possible with conventional techniques. But my guess is you already know this."

"I do."

"I'm working on a minimally invasive surgery device, one that's compatible with our other line of products. The new associated device supports a procedure requiring two to three tiny incisions, making the healing process much faster. This technology is already available, but my device is an improvement over what's already on the market. Am I making sense?"

"You are."

A soft melody oozed from the bar speakers, but he barely heard the song, he was so mesmerized by her interest in his work.

"Sounds amazing, Mike. If I understand you correctly, the

imaging and robotic systems combine surgical planning, simulation, training, and navigation platforms."

The excitement in her voice triggered an explosion of energy shooting to his fingers and toes. He nodded as a deeply satisfying feeling of accomplishment surged through him.

An olive-skinned server approached and gestured with his free hand to the half coconuts on his tray, each with a skewer of fresh fruit and an orchid. "Hello, sir and madam. May I interest you in today's cocktail special? It's a Jamaican Planter's Punch, made with light rum, a squeeze of fresh lemon, and a splash of orange juice, served in a freshly halved coconut."

"Yes, please." Devon waited for the server to set down the drink before retrieving the freshly-picked orchid and tucking it behind her ear. She then picked up the long toothpick of fresh sliced fruit from the halved coconut and tugged the strawberry off with her teeth while slipping off her shoes. From her pants pocket, she reached for a five-dollar bill and handed it to the man. "For your troubles."

"Thank you, ma'am." He bowed his head an inch. "And you, sir?"

"Oh, no. No thank you."

The server nodded and walked away.

"I'm surprised you know so much about digital imaging and robotic surgery," Mike said to Devon.

She eased back into the chair again, a spark of laughter brightening her eyes. Obviously she was finding what he said funny. He didn't like being laughed at, but right now he was too curious about Devon to take offense.

"Okay, I should fess up. I work as a design engineer for a company that produces prosthetic implants. While we aren't in exactly the same field, it's similar enough that I run across articles you've written from time to time. It's interesting stuff. You work on the surgical side of things, and I work to develop the artificial devices to replace missing body parts."

"A design engineer. Interesting." He mentally erased his built-in "design engineer" bias.

His design engineers wore glasses, ate pizza every day for lunch, and forgot to shave—or shower—most of the time. No one on his staff looked like Devon. And although he would have loved to have a few more women on board, he hadn't found a qualified candidate yet.

"Why is my background interesting?" She lifted her brow as she sipped the "hotel special" from the coconut-half-shaped glass. "Can't picture me as an engineer?"

"For some reason, all this time I've assumed you were an English literature or journalism major.

"Kayla's the English major."

Heat brushed up his cheek. "I know she is, but seeing as you two are best friends and all, I just assumed. Plus, you were always studying together."

"I was trying to *get* Kayla to study. There's a difference. She always had trouble with math."

"Tell me about it. Mom used to make me sit at the kitchen table and run through flash cards with Kayla. Twenty minutes every night. She drove me crazy. She'd remember the answer one night and forget it the next." He shook his head. "Bioengineering requires lots of math skills and is a fascinating field. There are so many job options."

"Agreed, but I always knew I wanted to work with those who had lost limbs." She shrugged. "I love seeing the videos my marketing department puts together of real-life recipients using our new products. It's nice to see the joy on their faces when they can move freely again."

"Exactly." His gaze was still locked on her.

"You've been busy over the past few years." Devon slid a piece of pineapple off the skewer from her drink. "I saw that you hit the 'ones to watch under forty' list. Seeing your face and name with all those other distinguished people must have felt good."

"It was pretty cool, I must admit."

There was that spark in her eye, the one that implied that no one would ever stop Devon Gaines from getting what she wanted. Nothing. "Maybe you'll be on the list someday."

"That's my goal."

He enjoyed her outward confidence. She wore it well. It was feminine but not soft. He got the sense she would accomplish whatever she set her mind to. She was like him—focused—and he liked that.

"I'd better go find Kayla," she said abruptly.

"Why?" Mike asked, not yet willing to let her get away. "Knowing Kayla, I'm sure she's arguing with the florist over the arrangements."

"That's why I must go," she replied with a fun, quirky smile. "Besides, she'll want to know she doesn't have to worry about you anymore."

"Me? Why would she worry about me?" Confusion ramped up his stress, tightening his shoulders and pinching his neck muscles.

"Gee...let me think... You were the one out by the pool with a gazillion women hanging on you. Those women looked like they wanted to have you for an afternoon snack." Her gaze locked onto him, as if she dared him to deny it.

A light energy floated up from his chest and forced a smile into place. This Devon, the one standing in front of him, was different from his sister's college roommate. Having a wedding partner for the weekend who wasn't boring or irritating might be the perfect solution. Her beauty was a bonus.

But he wondered if she'd had time at the pool to fully think through her solution. "You do realize those camera guys will have splashed your face all over the Internet by now. They probably already have your name and address and are trying to figure out where you work and how we know each other. I wouldn't be surprised if they've pulled your college transcripts already."

Her eyes widened.

Apparently she was a brilliant engineer, but she hadn't considered the effect this game of hers might have on Kayla and the rest of the family. He doubted she would want to be seen as a gold-digger, but that's what the media would spin. They would upload a story suggesting Devon came from some small town in Iowa, and how she'd befriended his sister just to weasel her way into his family. None of it would be true, but the public would digest every word as fact. His company lawyers would have a field day with this, bitching when he asked them to file another liability suit.

"Here's the deal," he said. "I'll clear the air with Kayla, but we'll have to act like we're engaged for the duration of the wedding."

"For the entire wedding?" She shifted in the chair. "Maybe I should go tell Kayla what happened."

"Kayla is most likely up to her eyeballs in wedding details and doesn't need one more thing on her plate. I'm sure you agree." He drove his point home and eased the way for him to legitimately spend time with her. He wanted to get acquainted... and discover why she'd decided to pose as his fiancée when, just off the top of his head, he could think of a dozen alternatives.

"Of course I don't want to upset anyone. But what will your mom and dad have to say?"

"I'll let my family in on the ruse, but no one else needs to hear about this. The press is not an issue that needs to be addressed right now."

Devon released a deep sigh and bit her lip, riveting his attention. He was mesmerized by her unconscious expression and wondered what kissing the sexy, smart, playful Devon would be like.

Whoa. Where did that come from?

Devon was his sister's best friend. He'd promised gumdrop he'd never date one of her friends. And he hadn't. But he made that promise a long time ago, so it was possible Kayla had changed her mind by now. Besides, now that he'd seen her in this new light, he had to wonder how any man could possibly keep his hands off a beauty like Devon.

Sure, she'd always hung around the house, but inevitably he'd end up in his room working most of the time he was home. He'd missed those sensual curves she developed, forever hidden under her endless collection of baggy college sweat suits.

"What if they don't support this idea?" Her angelic voice floated the question toward him.

"I'll handle my family. What you need to do is play along. This was your idea, remember?"

A frown deepened the creases on Devon's forehead. "I wish there were a better option."

"There *are* other options, but this one is the only option you have that's going to save you from future embarrassment. After the wedding, I'll call off the engagement. The press will find it believable since I'm already seen as a coldhearted workaholic." He maintained eye contact to drive his point further and deeper.

"Okay. I'll pretend to be your girlfriend till after the wedding."

"Not girlfriend," he emphasized, not giving her any wiggle room. "Fiancée."

"Whatever you choose to call this, the game ends as soon as Kayla tosses the bouquet."

"What are you so worried about? Think of it this way. You'll at least have a dinner and dance partner for the weekend."

"True." She nibbled on her lip again.

"If you truly don't like the idea"—he stood—"I can tell the press now and risk them ruining Kayla's wedding."

"No! Please don't." She held out her hands to stop him. "Kayla doesn't deserve to pay for my mistake," she begged.

"Okay, then," he replied, his body already anticipating the events of the weekend he was dreading...until Devon made her big announcement in front of the gold-diggers and paparazzi.

3

The hotel was getting rowdy, with children from another wedding party thundering back and forth across the reception area. The four little kids looked adorable in their matching suits and dresses.

A long line of people stood in front of the check-in clerk, who kept her warm, friendly welcoming conversation with the guests as brief as possible. Hotel stewards came to help with the luggage. Cool air from the open-air veranda drifted through the lobby, bringing with it the scent of sea air. In the middle of the large room was an ornate table with a three-foot-tall vase of tropical flowers in several shapes and sizes, including some green ones with burgundy centers that Devon couldn't name.

She was about to make her way toward the beach when one of the galloping children bumped into her legs, yanking her out of her analysis of the Mike dilemma.

She looked down at the young boy, who reminded her of a child she'd often seen playing in the park by her apartment in Connecticut. But this boy backed away and stared at the toy car lying at Devon's feet.

Chapter 3

"Whoa there, little man." Devon lowered herself to the boy's eye level. "Are you okay?"

"I'm sorry, miss." A mother trotted over to apologize and grabbed the young boy by the hand, pulling him to her side.

Brown eyes peered at Devon from behind the woman as little hands clenched on his mother's bright red cotton skirt.

"Ma'am, it's okay." Devon picked up the metal car and placed it into the boy's shaking hands. She offered a smile to the boy with the chocolate-drop brown eyes and got a bashful expression in return.

"And what will you say to the kind lady?" The mother tugged on the boy's hand.

"Thank you, ma'am," he replied.

"I used to have a racer like yours when I was little, only mine was red. Tile makes the cars go lots faster." She turned to the mother. "You have a wonderful boy. He'll be successful when he grows up. He's got a creative mind."

His mother's eyes softened. "Creative is one way to describe him."

Devon appreciated that motherhood was challenging, but she'd give anything to have a child of her own. At twenty-eight, she was hyper aware that her maternal clock was beginning to clang more and more loudly with every passing year.

Devon backed away and continued toward the beach. Unconsciously, her hand found its way to her belly while she yearned for the day she would have her own child. Michael Lewis would be the perfect name, a name she'd doodled repeatedly in her college notebooks when she faced a problem not readily solved. And Mike Lewis was a problem. He'd never shown any interest in her. Even now, this fake engagement was a game—a dangerous game for her heart.

What if she showed him how their relationship could be?

Maybe this wedding was a once-in-a-lifetime opportunity to see if her Mike Lewis fantasy could be turned into reality.

The only problem was getting and keeping Mike's attention. He never put his phone down to see what was in front of him. He'd never noticed her flirtations on the rare occasions she summoned enough nerve. Or he hadn't taken her advances seriously.

During her and Kayla's graduation from college, Devon adopted the belief that Mike didn't go for a woman who stocked her closet with black-and-white clothes because designer outfits were beyond her budget. But deep down she knew he didn't care about material things. He had his sights on improving the way surgery was performed. That was all.

Reaching the white sand beach, she removed her shoes and scrunched her toes in the soft, warm sand, the tension in her shoulders easing as she made her way toward the water. The ocean tides washed over her feet. The wind caressed and kissed her skin, and she fantasized about what it would feel like to kiss Mike.

The consequences of telling the entire world she was Mike Lewis's fiancée chose this moment to finally sink in.

What had she been thinking? Ugh. What a mess.

She gazed out over the ocean. The sun danced on the waves while the summer breeze whipped her hair about her head and across her face. She breathed in the fresh air as she turned and walked toward the rocks on the other end of the beach, letting the memory of Mike's reaction to her announcement replay in her mind. The silent meaningful looks, his off-balance fidgeting, and the way he leaned in to hear her explanation—all of his reactions were delicious.

"Devon."

A hand touched her, and she jumped.

"Jesus, Kayla. You scared the crap out of me."

"I've been calling your name for the past two minutes, but you just kept walking. What's got you so distracted?" Kayla turned around and walked backwards.

"I...uh..." Should she tell Kayla what happened? Probably not. Knowing Kayla, she'd worry, and more worry was not something she needed right now. "Just work stuff."

"Work stuff." Kayla nodded. "And that's what you're sticking with?"

I'm in love with your brother, Devon wanted to say, but she kept her expression blank. "I'm fine, Kay-K. You can stop being an annoying pain in the ass."

Devon found a clear spot to sit on the beach. Kayla sank down beside her.

"I'm not annoying," Kayla said. "A little pesky, but never annoying."

"Okay, Miss English lit major, even I know annoying and pesky are synonyms."

"Well, you may have a point. I'm a teeny-weeny bit annoying sometimes, but it's because I love you."

And it was love in the form of late-night chats, spur-of-the-moment cocktails, and last-minute movie nights that Devon coveted. She was going to miss those girl-power moments. Just the thought of it doused her with a melancholy she tried desperately to hide.

"Don't be sad."

"I'm not." Devon forced a laugh and refused to let her friend see the tears stinging her eyes. Time to change the subject. "Why were you looking for me?"

"I want to ask your opinion about the flowers. The florist chose white roses, and I'm worried there should be some color added, but I can't decide what flowers would work. The bridesmaids' dresses are blue, but I always think blue flowers are weird-looking." Kayla drew spiraling circles in the sand.

Time to distract Kayla, and give her a more appropriate task to focus on. "Have you checked on the menu? What about the caterers? Did you talk with them? How did it go?"

"Yes, and yes. The good news is the menu is as I requested. The bad news is my dad got a call from his sister. My aunt and uncle are flying in tonight, so I've alerted the caterers to add an extra two plates." She rubbed her eyes. "I hope there aren't any more last-minute surprises."

Like hearing your brother and I are engaged.

"Kayla," Devon began, doing her best to find a way to tell her friend about the Mike situation, yet not freak her out. Words failed her. There were times she wished she'd been an English major.

"Hey, you know what I need?" Kayla grabbed Devon's arm.

"A massage?" Devon suggested.

"Oh...that does sound good." Kayla closed her eyes briefly. "But no."

"You sure? Cuz I can picture you on the beach, a handsome man rubbing your back with lavender oil."

"Mmm, don't tempt me. But no. Right now I need to go greet the family members coming in today." She gave Devon an elbow bump. "Come with me."

"Your family is huge. Making sure everyone gets settled will take hours." Devon played up the whine, hoping it would get her out of meet-and-greet duties. Kayla was the extrovert. Not her, although she could make do in a pinch.

"Tell me about it. A massage would be more fun." Kayla pushed up off the ground and held out a helping hand to Devon. "Brandon and I are planning to have a couple's massage after the wedding. I'll need it after all this is over. This morning I was thinking I should have accepted Brandon's offer to elope, but my mom would have killed me."

"Yes, she would have." Devon nodded. "Keep a positive attitude. Nothing bad is going to happen. It's your wedding, and it will be the most perfect one ever. Besides, no one could be more beautiful than you."

"Aw. You're going to make me cry. I can't wait to tell you the same thing on your wedding day. That is, if you ever allow a guy into your life," Kayla teased. "No one is ever good enough for you."

Except for Mike, Devon thought.

"What can I say? I haven't found the perfect guy yet." When the lightning didn't strike Devon for that whopper, she felt a slight relief.

"Speaking of guys, I forgot to ask about Mike. Were you able to get him away from the paparazzi?" Kayla asked.

"Mike? Mike is fine. He's more worried about making sure your wedding day is perfect." Guilt for keeping secrets sneaked in, and Devon had a hard time swallowing. "Kay, I need to tell you something."

Kayla stopped. "What?"

"It's just that..." Devon weighed her options. "Well, it seems... You see... Mike and I are sort of engaged."

"Engaged!"

Devon waved her hands to make Kayla suspend judgment for a second. "No. No. No. I'm only pretending to be his fiancée. It's not a real engagement."

"Okay." Kayla looked at Devon, her eyes narrowing. "What happened?"

"I made up this fake engagement excuse so women will leave Mike alone." Devon blurted out the story and finished with, "and Mike wants me to act the part of his fiancée until after your wedding is over."

Kayla's eyes got really, really big. Then she snorted and laughed. "That's outstanding. No, really."

"Um...I don't follow. You're happy about this?"

"I am. There's a hiccup in the accommodations, and we're a room short. The hotel is fully booked, but my uncle and aunt need a place to stay. The hotel is saying there truly are no extra rooms. My mom is dealing with it," Kayla explained in her typical rapid-fire manner as they walked toward the hotel lobby.

"What do your uncle and aunt have to do with Mike's and my dilemma?"

"You, my dear friend, have again solved my problem."

Devon's skin started to itch when Kayla's expression turned devious. She was all too familiar with that expression. Kayla was up to something.

"Why do I get the feeling I won't like what you're about to tell me?"

"Stop worrying. It's going to be perfect. You'll share Mike's suite with him, and my uncle and aunt can take your room." Kayla waved her hands in the air like the Good Fairy scattering around fairy dust to make everything perfect.

"Kay-K, I don't think your brother will go for this."

"My workaholic brother won't even notice another human sharing his room. He'll be too busy. As long as you remain quiet, it'll be fine."

A wave of sadness crashed over Devon. Mike's family had never seen him for the authentic hero he was, then or now. "This isn't a good idea."

"I wouldn't suggest the move if there were another option. Please, Devy, I need that extra room."

Devon didn't have much choice. Kayla's parents were paying for this luxury trip, a vacation Devon couldn't afford on her own. The all-inclusive resort boasted five restaurants, three pools, a workout center, a five-star spa, and more. The place even had a juice and ice cream bar. "Okay, fine. You win. Whatever will help."

"You're the best friend ever." Kayla skipped up the steps to the lobby. "Let's go find my mom and tell her we found an extra room. She'll be too distracted to ask where you're sleeping, so we won't need to tell her about you and Mike."

"What if Mike refuses to let me stay in his room?"

"I'll just tell him he doesn't have a choice. I already have two cousins staying with me."

Devon supposed she could always sleep on the floor or in the bathtub. The whirlpool in Kayla's room was large enough.

What had she gotten herself into?

4

Mike stood in front of his suite window, gazing out past the palms and white sand beach toward the teal blue ocean and the sun shimmering on the surface...but the memory of Devon with her sun-kissed cheeks pushed the scenic image aside.

The changing expressions on her freckled face were more fun to think about. The woman was a pure study in contrasts. Smart yet innocent. Bold yet restricted. She was a superpower waiting to be unleashed, and he wanted to peel back her layers to find out what lay beneath.

He imagined running his fingers through Devon's hair, kissing her neck—the daydream ignited a passion he'd believed dormant.

The chime of his cellphone pulled him out of his reverie. With a swipe right, he pressed the phone to his ear. "Mike Lewis."

"Mike, it's Greg. We've got a problem."

He tried holding onto the sizzling daydream, but it faded with the panic in his chief operations officer's voice. The man sounded shaken, which was odd, and maybe a little alarming, for a man so rarely fazed.

Mike took a deep breath. "What's up?"

"We have parts stuck in customs. I've been working to resolve the issue, but it looks like we'll have to delay the launch of the new product line again. There's no way around it, Mike. I'm sorry."

Shit. Mike cupped a hand over his mouth and started pacing. He squeezed his jaw, forcing his teeth apart, so he didn't crack a crown. "Pull the team together. I want options. Today. Greg, figure out a way to replace those parts. Don't worry about cost. I need the product line launched on time."

"Understood. I'll do my best."

He hated the doubt permeating Greg's voice. Mike considered for a moment stepping in to problem-solve, but his father's wisdom taught him you don't have a dog and wag its tail yourself. He tossed his phone on the brown-and-teal fabric chair just as he caught movement out of the corner of his eye.

He turned—and blinked. Devon was standing in his room, surrounded by luggage. She looked adorable, her hands fidgeting like she didn't know whether to stand there or leave.

"Devon? How did you get into my room?" He stared at her and did his best to appear calm.

"Kayla was supposed to call you." Devon took a step forward, even though she looked like she wanted to turn around and leave. "It turns out your uncle and aunt's arrival was unanticipated, and the hotel is a room short."

"And?" He crossed the room, wanting to be near her. Her sweet scent of suntan coconut oil hit first, and then the smell of her light perfume.

"Kayla thought that, since you have a suite, you wouldn't mind sharing your room. I told her about the fake fiancée thing, and she decided this would solve her problem...and yours."

"My problem?" He chuckled at his sister's audacity. "You were the one who announced our engagement." He stopped far enough away to avoid touching her or pulling her into his arms. Peeling back those layers was getting more and more tempting.

He released a breath of pent-up frustration. "This seems like a solution Kayla would come up with to please my parents and avoid my aunt's complaints. My father's sister is demanding, and knowing her the way I do, I guarantee she'd complain nonstop if she had the inconvenience of staying at another hotel, even though it's her fault for not being organized enough to avoid last-minute plans."

"Don't blame Kayla." Devon softened her tone. "Appeasing everyone is her way of showing she cares."

Kayla was a pain in his ass, always badgering him to take a break, have some fun, and stop working so much. When she started sounding like a video meme on a constant rewind loop, he stopped taking her calls, but then she'd just discover fresh ways to get him to stop working, like sending him tickets to his favorite sports events and the new release of his favorite role-playing video game. He appreciated that she cared, but he wished she were more supportive of his dreams.

Personally, he didn't blame his sister for her show of concern. They might have their differences, but he adored Kayla. Besides, she just wanted him to be happy and to stop hiding. She'd witnessed two of his very public and messy breakups after neither woman would sign his prenuptial agreement. Both had wanted his wealth and status, not him. Kayla swore there were women in the world who were not like that, but he had yet to find one.

Then again, it could be that one of those rare women was standing in front of him right now, but he'd never know, because his heart couldn't go there. Not again.

However, the vulnerable Devon looked even more luscious

than she had this morning. His head was saying don't touch, but his heart was sending different signals.

What the hell am I doing?

He had a new product to get launched. If past relationships were any indication, women wanted his time—time he didn't have to give. He needed to stay focused, and focusing on Devon wasn't where he needed to spend his time right now.

"I should go. I told Kayla this wasn't a good idea. I'll see myself out." Devon bent to retrieve her backpack.

"And where will you go?" he asked, just to make sure she'd thought her decision through. "You said so yourself. The hotel is fully booked. Staying with me is the only option."

"There must be a couch or a rollaway somewhere. Like you said, I'm the one who created this problem. I'll solve it."

He liked the way her chin lifted a little. "I'm sure you will."

She crossed her arms and bristled. "What is that supposed to mean?"

"Just that. You're a problem-solver." And he would have liked nothing better than to have her solve his problems, but his business issues would have to wait. "Don't make me look like the bad older brother who doesn't support his kid sister during her wedding preparations. The best solution would be for you to stay here."

"So you want me to stay?" Her brows hitched to their highest level.

"Yeah. I do." He walked to the door and closed it.

Devon slung her backpack over her shoulder. "I promise to stay out of your way. I won't be a distraction. You can work or do whatever it is you do. You won't even know I'm here."

"Oh, I'll know you're here, Devon. There is no doubt about that." Mike walked back to her slowly, taking in her long legs, narrow waist, and ample breasts—breasts he'd like to cup in the palm of his hand, feel their weight, and play with until the nipples tightened. "You are a beautiful woman. You'd be very hard to miss."

"You don't need to be patronizing."

"I might be a lot of things, but I'm not blind, Devon."

A blush caressed her skin from neck to cheek.

"Make yourself comfortable," he offered. "I'll call down for an extra set of towels."

"I don't want to be a bother."

"You already are, in the nicest kind of way." He couldn't help the tingling anticipation when he imagined exploring Devon's layers.

Devon rolled her carry-on suitcase over to the couch and pressed on the cushions. "Sleeping on the pullout won't be too bad."

"You'll take the bed," Mike stated in his normal executive tone, expecting there to be no argument. When her mouth opened, he added, "Kayla would flick my ear for not being a gentleman. Please, take the bed. Don't make me beg."

Devon laughed, actually laughed at him. "Somehow I can't see you begging a woman for anything."

She might be surprised.

"Fine, I'll take the bed, but only if we share. It's a king, I'm sure we can get extra pillows or something to make this arrangement work so neither of us has a sore back in the morning."

"Fine, whatever you want." He didn't sleep much anyway. Thoughts of work always kept his mind whirling to the point he rarely went to bed before two.

"Fine." She pulled her iPad and earbuds from her backpack.

He checked his phone to see if Greg had left a message, but there was nothing. He took a seat at the small desk in the corner of the room and tried to review the latest project status report, but he couldn't seem to focus on the screen.

Devon was like a magnet.

Chapter 4

He was drawn to the way she played with her hair, the way she nibbled her lip while reading, and the way she flopped on the couch. It almost seemed like she was tempting him, punishing him with her chaste looks. She was doing her best to ignore him, and that made her even more desirable. He wanted to touch her. Feel her beneath him. Hear her call his name.

Oh, shit. He thrust his fingers through his hair and yanked. He should send her away now. If for no other reason than she was his sister's best friend.

Moving away from the bed, he walked toward Devon, who was so focused on her iPad's screen that she didn't seem to notice him approach.

"Tell me something." He settled on the couch arm.

Devon pulled out an earbud to listen and adjusted away from him, grabbing her water bottle, twisting off the lid, and taking a sip.

"It seems we are doing our best to ignore each other, when the fact is, we're actually attracted to each other."

Devon choked on the water.

"Devon? Tell me it isn't true."

"At the risk of repeating myself, don't patronize me, Mike. My feelings are not something to be toyed with."

"I'm not toying. I've been attracted to you for a long time, but you're Kayla's friend, so hands off."

She narrowed her eyes. "And you're Kayla's brother, so hands off."

Mike crossed his arms. "It seems we both have a problem. We're smart, single, unencumbered adults. What do you propose as a solution?"

She liked to play games, and he was bent on showing her he was the better player.

"I suppose you are thinking casual sex is the answer, but it isn't," Devon replied.

He suppressed a cough and rubbed his chest. "Why not?"

"Because it might surprise you, Mike, but not all women are robots. We have feelings, and it just so happens I've had a crush on you since the day we first met." Her mouth dropped open, and she froze. "Oh, shit." She went into double-time motion, jamming her iPad and earbuds in her bag, shoving her feet into her sandals, and moving away from him as quickly as possible. "I should go."

"Wait." He grabbed her arm.

Her forward movement stopped. "Just ignore me. I shouldn't have said anything," she whispered.

He slowly turned her around. "Why didn't you tell me?"

"You're Kayla's brother."

"Hands off," he said, looking into her eyes.

There was hurt and confusion there, and he wanted to ease both away. He lowered his mouth to hers, intending to soothe away the sting, but when his lips touched hers, his mind quieted, and his soul sighed. Devon opened to his touch, and he pressed his mouth against hers, accepting what she offered.

This beauty was certainly an interesting woman, and apparently she had a crush on him. The annoying brother. The workaholic professional. The weirdest thing was she might be the only woman he could possibly bring home who would positively fit in with his wacky family. Mike lifted his head. Devon seemed frozen in place, her eyes closed.

"As I expected." Devon opened her eyes slowly and looked at him.

"What was expected?"

"That Mike Lewis does nothing unless it's perfect." She softened in his arms just as his phone rang.

He lowered his head again.

Devon pulled out of his arms. "Aren't you going to get that?"

"Actually, I'd rather let it ring and go to voicemail."

Chapter 4

"Didn't I overhear you have a problem at work? Something about parts and figuring out a way to replace them?"

Well, shit. She was right. He ran to retrieve his phone. "Mike Lewis." Irritation warred with his need to remain calm.

He heard only a little of what Greg said, because he turned to tell Devon he'd only be a minute, but she'd stepped into the bathroom. He was glad she hadn't left, because he had a lot more to learn about the beautiful Devon Gaines.

5

Devon sucked in a sharp breath as a shirtless Mike Lewis stepped out of the hotel bathroom in navy blue board shorts with an inch-wide white band that showed off his tan. Shock made her lower her iPad as she sat on the couch cross-legged, staring. She sat up, her muscles going rigid. His stomach muscles were droolworthy and sculpted to perfection, and his chiseled chest was as hairless and smooth as a baby's bottom. His biceps were lean, and his triceps were like a rare diamond—flawless.

Devon wanted to touch, to feel his hot skin beneath her hands, but she didn't want to give him another reason to kiss her. The first kiss had been perfect, and she wanted to remember it that way.

While she wasn't against having a fling, she didn't want to have sex with Mike. Temporary with Mike Lewis wasn't possible. Her heart couldn't handle his indifference or watching him walk away after the wedding, forgetting about her. She'd just have to ignore him.

"I'm going down to the pool. Want to come?"

Mike's question forced her to look up.

Yes, she wanted to come, just not in the way he was suggesting. "I have some work emails I need to catch up on." She forced her eyes back to the screen, not seeing a single word on the tablet.

"Finally, she speaks." Sarcasm added bite to Mike's words as he gave a slow, calculated, mocking applause. "Are you still angry that I kissed you?"

"No. Why?"

"You haven't spoken to me since."

"I promised you I'd stay out of your way and let you work."

If she kept to the facts, only the facts, he wouldn't be able to tell how she truly felt. His kiss had changed her. Forever. No longer was Mike Lewis a fantasy. While she was here, with him, he was real, and her body wanted him more than ever. She craved his touch. With his single kiss came an understanding that all those years of daydreaming about Mike were nothing compared to the real thing.

"But you're my fiancée. My protector. We need to be seen together if we're going to pull this game off. You promised we'd stay together until after the wedding was over."

"Mike, I don't want to play this game anymore. It's not fun. I was only trying help. If I had known claiming to be your fiancée to stop those women from clinging to you would create an even bigger problem, I would have minded my own business." She dropped her iPad beside her as he moved closer.

"Then you've finally figured it out."

"Figured out what, exactly?"

"That I'm a big boy. I don't need help."

She couldn't miss the aggravation in his tone...or the tension in his body.

"Everyone needs help sometimes. Even you, Mike Lewis." Devon sighed out her annoyance.

"So Kayla tells me every day. I don't need her best friend to start." He yanked on the ties of his swim shorts as he sank down on the couch.

She tucked her legs in closer while she tracked his every move, and he didn't stop until his lips were inches away from hers. She should back away—stop this insanity—but she couldn't stop wondering if this kiss would be devouring, or if he would take his time again. Either way was mouthwateringly tempting. Plus the tantalizing smell of his aftershave's rich notes of vanilla and cedar made matters worse. Much worse.

Why did Mike Lewis have to be so damn perfect? Everything about him was flawless. Well, except for the bit where he only wanted her for the weekend.

"Go change." Mike's eyes darkened. "It'll do us both good to get away from work for a while."

An awkward silence settled between them as he moved away.

"Fine, but I can only spare an hour. Kayla will have finished shopping with her aunt by then, and we have plans to meet for lunch." Devon pushed to her feet.

While they were still in Connecticut, Kayla made her pack a siren-red string bikini with more strings than fabric. Devon swore she would *never* wear the itty-bitty thing, but this situation called for just such a weapon. A naughty tingle of anticipation made her grin as she walked into the bathroom to get changed. She was going to teach Mike Lewis a lesson.

It took three minutes to pull on the tiny pieces of material and tug off her hairband, releasing the long strands to fluff and fall about her shoulders. Next she pursed her lips, applied lip gloss, and added waterproof mascara to her lashes. She pulled out the eyeliner, but decided not to overdo. Guys liked natural, and she would give him unadorned sensual.

If he wanted to play, she'd give him a good game.

She walked out of the bathroom and headed his way, making

sure he had a full view of what she offered. "Ready?" She kept her expression as blank as possible so he wouldn't recognize her real intentions.

He didn't take his eyes off her as he continued to listen to whoever was on the other end of the call, but his eyes darkened, and his tongue moved lazily over his lower lip. He was finally seeing her as a woman, not as Kayla's best friend.

Success. She sauntered past him, taking her time.

Mike eventually turned away, his phone in hand, black earbuds tucked in his ears. "Is everything under control?" he asked.

Devon leaned back on the couch and tucked her legs in to wait for his call to end.

"What do you mean, not exactly? I asked you to fix this. I don't need excuses." He paused, his head falling forward. "Look, I'm sorry. I know you're doing your best. But I need a solution, not more problems." He nodded. "Okay, so when can we get the parts?" He gazed at the floor, with a hand on one hip. "Two months? Are you fucking kidding me?" He cupped a hand at the base of his neck and squeezed. "Greg. Don't apologize. Just do your fucking job and fix this." He dropped his hand, gripping the phone so hard she thought he was going to break it.

"Is everything okay?"

"No." He stopped to let out a long breath, closing his eyes. "It seems the parts I need for one of the robotic units are stuck in customs, and my operations team is telling me it will be two months before we get them. But the marketing department has already set the schedule for the product to go live in less than five weeks. We won't have enough inventory. The launch is going to fail."

"What about 3D imaging? If you have the computer files, you might be able to get the parts faster."

"Yes. Yes. Yes." He paced away, waving her suggestion off.

"We already looked into that. No one has capacity to turn our job around fast enough."

"But you do have the loadable computer files."

"Yes." Mike continued to pace. "Imaged parts are what we are waiting on."

Devon flipped through the contacts on her phone and dialed. "Hey, Sarah, it's me, Dev. Got a minute? I have a favor to ask." Devon looked at Mike. Now she had his full attention.

"Sure. What can I help with?" Sarah's voice dragged a bit, like she'd worked one too many twelve-hour shifts.

"Last week you told me you had a major job cancel. Do you still have room in your schedule to fill another 3D print order? It's some type of robotic computer component."

"We still have capacity as long as it's not too big of a job. Why?"

"A friend's parts are stuck in customs. He needs a quick turnaround for a product launch. Do you think you can help him out?"

"What kind of part is it?"

"It's a robotic part. From what I've seen you do, I'm pretty sure you can handle it. How about I have the company's president get in touch. His name is Mike Lewis."

"Oh, my. You're kidding, right?"

"Nope. Why?"

"*The* Mike Lewis? *That* hottie?"

Devon giggled and turned away from Mike as her cheeks heated. "Yep, *the* Mike Lewis of Surgical Robotics."

"Man oh man. If I didn't have capacity, I'd find some. Kidding aside, we should be able to do a turnaround in two business days once we have the specs and complete the new vendor paperwork."

Devon cupped her hand over the phone. "Sarah says they can get a job up in two days if you can get them the files today."

Chapter 5

"I need an NDA," Mike said, taking a step closer.

Devon nodded. "Sarah, do you mind if I have Mike send over a non-disclosure agreement today? Once the agreement is signed, I believe he can release the files."

"Can you have him send along his private cell phone number too? Maybe his address? Heck, maybe just a picture. I'll hang it on my bulletin board. Better yet, just tell him I said he's hot."

"I can't tell him that. I'm hanging up now. Expect an email in a few minutes."

Devon giggled as she laid the phone on the coffee table. She turned to see Mike staring at her, his inquisitive brow lifted.

"3D Global Services is a vendor we use. Their parts are reliable. We haven't had any recalls. If they say they can deliver, they'll deliver."

Mike took a step around the end of the bed. "What can't you tell me?"

"Oh, that." Devon's face warmed this time. "Sarah thinks you're hot."

His gaze had again darkened and intensified. "I don't care what Sarah thinks. Only what you think."

"I think, Mr. Lewis, your problem has been solved. You will have your parts in time for your product launch."

"Devon"—he sat on the couch and moved in closer—"I'm not talking about my parts problem."

"You mean the problem I helped you solve. The problem you didn't need anyone's help with?" She leaned in toward his ear. "You're welcome, Mike."

He dropped his head, and his hot breath caressed her neck while he took the opportunity to nibble. "Thank you, Devon."

She pushed out of his arms and gave him a teasing smile. "You need to send off your NDA and give your operations team a heads-up. I'll send you the contact information."

She picked up her phone and typed in the cell phone number he gave her. She sent over the contact information and then met his gaze. "Meet you at the pool. Oh, and Mike? Thanks for letting me help. I know it's not your thing."

She didn't wait for his response, just sauntered out the door with an extra sway in her step.

Because waiting for Mike Lewis to accept her fully into his life would be like waiting for the *Titanic* to sink, and she wasn't willing to wait that long.

6

"Kay-K, what are you worried about now?" Devon sat with her friend on Kayla's king-sized bed in her luxurious hotel suite. "Tonight is going to be special, and tomorrow even more magical."

"Brandon's cousin informed me an hour ago that she's allergic to fish, and his aunt left a message on my cell that she's gluten-free. Ugh. Why didn't Brandon tell me Jessica and his aunt had food allergies before I finalized the rehearsal dinner menu?" Kayla flopped over to her side.

"It'll be okay. You'll see. Let's run through our checklist to see if we missed anything. That should calm your nerves." Devon reached into her backpack and pulled out her iPad.

"You're right. I need a distraction." Kayla took a deep breath and reached for her computer.

Devon opened the rehearsal dinner menu file. "Let's see what we have here. For the salad, we have mixed greens with carrot, shaved red onions, cucumber, shredded cheese, and croutons served with a choice of house vinaigrette or ranch." Devon pursed her lips. "The salad should work, minus the croutons. We can ask the caterer to put them on the side, and see what salad dressing options might work."

"True."

"What's next?" Devon scrolled down. "What if we substituted the fish dish for the fettuccini tossed with house-made alfredo for your cousin? It's already on the hotel menu and shouldn't be hard to switch out."

"That should work too." Kayla's shoulders relaxed. "Do you think there are any other changes we should make? What about the floral arrangements and chalkboard signs?"

"The chalkboard signs are ready to be put in place first thing in the morning. The artist did a magnificent job. You're gonna love them." Devon did a quick check of her email to make sure there were no new messages from the hotel staff. "Your wedding is going to be spectacular. Have some faith."

"You sure? What about the reception table centerpieces?" Kayla bit her lip.

"Brandon wanted candles and promised he'd take care of the arrangements, remember?"

"That's right, he did." Kayla rubbed her head. "He showed me what he was planning, and the candles with the tied lavender were perfect. Who knew he was so creative?"

A little surge of satisfaction seeped into Devon. She'd kept Brandon's secret hidden from Kayla. Brandon didn't have the first clue what to do about the centerpieces and had called to ask for help.

"And I sampled the sangria." Devon placed her iPad on the bed. "It's yum, and I made sure the help is prepared to serve the guests as they take their seats. It's supposed to be hot. The drinks will keep the family refreshed. I've also confirmed your hair, makeup, and photography appointments tomorrow. You're all set."

"Thank you," Kayla said, her voice almost choked with tears.

Gail Lewis ambled into the room. "No tears, baby girl."

Kayla looked up. "Hey Mom."

"Hey, Mrs. L." Devon moved over to allow Kayla's beautiful mother to take a seat between them as Kayla rolled to a sitting position.

Mrs. L had a classic style. Her hair was cropped short in a bob, and she wore a flowing peach dress with stylish gold earrings that showed off her long, slender neck. She always looked fresh, like she'd just walked out of a spa or salon.

Gail patted Devon's knee. "Thank you, darling, for everything you've done for my daughter."

"No thanks needed. Kayla would do the same for me if the tables were turned."

"I'm not sure about that," Kayla said. "You're the organized one. Not me. I wouldn't make it on time to my own wedding if not for you. You both know it's true."

Devon and Gail looked at each other and erupted into laughter.

"You girls should get changed for the rehearsal dinner." Gail stood.

"Yes, Mom." Kayla wandered into the bathroom.

"I'd better go get dressed as well." Devon rose from the bed. "I don't want to be late."

"And make sure Mike arrives on time, will you?" Gail said.

Devon froze as panic cut off her breath. "Mrs. L, I can explain."

Gail waved her off. "No need to explain, dear. Both Kayla and Mike already have. Although Mike had a little harder time coming up with an explanation. I think it's a good thing my sister-in-law came with her wretched husband at the last minute. A marvelous thing indeed." Gail patted Devon on the cheek. "Hurry along, dear, you don't want to be late. Oh, and I hope you wear your blue dress, the one with the shimmers. You look so lovely in that gown."

Kayla had insisted Devon pack the three-quarter-length gown with spaghetti straps—the skimpy dress she didn't dare wear with underwear because the lines would show—in the same travel pack as the string bikini. The dress showed off every body feature to its fullest.

What was Mrs. L suggesting? Was she okay about Mike and her being together—like really together?

Devon pondered the idea while she made her way to Mike's suite and was halfway down the long walkway with rooms on one side and tropical plants on the other before she realized she'd missed it. She retraced a few steps and inserted the plastic card into the electronic keyhole.

"Mike?" she called, pushing the door open, and paused to wait for a response. Apparently he wasn't back from the guys' bachelor lunch yet.

She dropped her backpack on the couch and went to the bathroom for a cooling shower before shimmying into the cobalt blue cocktail dress and three-inch heels. A quick application of makeup and blow dry of her hair and she was ready. She looked up as the door to the room opened.

"Bathroom's all yours." She ignored Mike as she went to pick up her purse and toss in breath mints and a tube of lipstick. She froze when he approached her from behind.

"You look stunning." Mike's voice had a sensual, husky tone.

"Thank you." Devon continued securing her dangle earrings. She didn't dare turn around. She wasn't sure what she would see on Mike's face when she did.

"We have time before the reception dinner. Why don't you stay awhile?"

Mike's suggestion compelled her to turn and look at him.

He cupped her jaw with a warm hand while he smoothed his thumb over her lips, his eyes conveying a dark, sensual spark. A rush of electricity surged through Devon, and her knees weakened as she fought for balance.

"I...uh...need to go help Kayla get ready."

He lowered his mouth until it hovered just above hers. "Are you sure?"

Her heart wanted to say no, but the practical, list-keeping brain of hers refused to allow her to deviate from the scheduled plan. "Rehearsal dinner." She backed away. "Your mom asked me to make sure you get there on time."

"My mom?" He raised his eyebrows.

"Yes. I saw her in..." Her mind went blank.

"Kayla's room," he provided.

She snapped her fingers. "Yes, your sister's room. And I'm scheduled to be with Kayla now."

"Or"—Mike unbuttoned the top button of his shirt, and then the next, and the next, letting the folds of cotton fall open—"you might help me dress. Make sure I make it to the reception on time. Of course, you would have to undress me first, though."

Oh, my God. Her body parts tingled, and she had to swallow the drool swirling in her mouth. He was teasing her, of course, but she didn't care. Seeing Mike Lewis stripped down to his birthday suit was definitely on her bucket list. In fact, it was at the very top.

His six-pack winked at her, tempting her to come play, but she couldn't. Kayla would kill her for falling for her brother.

"No. *No.* I must go." She backed toward the door. "Kayla is waiting for me. She needs my...my help." Devon reached past him and grabbed the purse she had dropped when his body heat made thinking too difficult.

"If you change your mind, you have a key."

His naughty-boy expression warmed more than one body part. Damn those smoldering eyes. When he caught her staring, a slight, knowing smile curved his lips.

She was so screwed.

He liked playing the game. She should have expected as much. You didn't get to the top in business without knowing how to outmaneuver your opponents. Playing for money was one thing. Playing for the heart was on a different level. She would need to play smarter.

"See you at the reception. Don't be late." Devon closed the door and didn't look back.

She raced down the corridor and made it to safety in two minutes flat. Her heart raced as she opened Kayla's door.

"I'm back." She walked down the narrow hallway, which opened up into the larger room, and then let out a gasp. "Why isn't everyone dressed? The rehearsal starts in forty minutes, and Kayla is supposed to arrive early!"

The other three women in the room were busy holding up mirrors and applying makeup in their underwear.

"We couldn't decide whether to put our hair up or keep it down," Brandon's oldest cousin, a cute, petite blonde, said as she opened the double-door closet to retrieve Kayla's lavender chiffon dress.

"Okay, fine. Let's focus on getting the bride dressed. Then let's worry about hair." Devon accepted the dress from Jessica, while Nicole and Lauren, Kayla's cousins, continued fussing with their hair.

It wasn't until this afternoon, when Kayla gave Devon the final guest list, that Devon realized she was the only person at the reception who wasn't related to either the bride or the groom. There were cousins, aunts, uncles, siblings, parents, and significant others, but no outsiders like her. She had tried devising a way to still help Kayla but let the Lewis and Myers families celebrate this important time together, but the list of ideas fell flat. Kayla would see right through every excuse.

Why was she so good at solving other people's problems but not her own?

7

What's up with Devon?

Mike had observed her throughout the rehearsal and dinner. With every passing minute, she'd become more distant, at this point almost reserved. Restrained wasn't her style. Not the Devon he was acquainted with. He strolled toward the outdoor pool, now lit with a soft blue glow.

"Shouldn't you be celebrating with Kayla?"

"Jesus! Mike." Devon turned so fast she had to grab the bridge's railing to keep from falling on her butt. She clapped a hand over her heaving chest. "You scared me. Don't you know it's rude to sneak up on people like that?"

"I didn't mean to frighten you, but I'm curious. Why are you out here alone? You should be inside, having fun." He handed his empty tumbler to a passing server walking in the opposite direction.

She turned and pointed. "I'm listening to the waves roll in."

He leaned his hip against the railing, the buzz of alcohol weakening his resistance. "Not that I'm calling you a liar, but why don't I believe you?"

"Mike, please just go back inside with your family. I'm fine."

She wasn't fine. She'd been crying. He could see the glisten of a tear in the moonlight. For her to show her emotions in public was alarming and so unlike the tough woman he knew. She was fierce. Smart. And she managed his ditzy, scatterbrained sister better than anyone else could.

He leaned in to peek at her face. "Devon, talk to me. Tell me why you aren't with the rest of the family?"

Devon rubbed her forehead and let out a long sigh. "To be honest, I'm torn. I should be happy for Kayla, but I know when she marries Brandon I'll lose a part of her to him. It sounds selfish, and I get that, but I need to acknowledge my feelings for what they are in order to deal with them. And then there's you."

"What about me?" Mike leaned back against the railing so he could watch her face.

"I envy what you have. You have a sister who adores you and parents who support you. Plus a successful business, and..."

"And?" Mike prompted.

"A large, loving family." She closed her eyes, but even the look of regret couldn't spoil her beauty. She huffed out a sigh before looking at him again. "Pretty soon you'll have nieces or nephews to play with, and I want you to promise me you won't take them for granted. Babies grow up fast. Please don't miss those precious moments."

She was jealous of his family. Not of his social standing or wealth. That was an unexpected change from most other women he'd been with.

"I wouldn't envy my family. They can be annoying sometimes."

Fury sparked in her eyes. "That's because you don't appreciate what you have. Every one of those people inside set aside time to fly hours to be here for Kayla's wedding. If today was my wedding day, not even my dad would show up. Your family is special, Mike. Truly special. You might overlook the benefits of a loving family because you have them, but a family like yours is everything I've ever wished for."

Her sad voice tugged at Mike's heart.

He should say something reassuring. Anything. But he never was good at expressing his feelings. He worked with robots for a reason. They were predictable, and they didn't slap him when he said the wrong things.

"Come here. Let me give you a hug," Mike offered.

"What? No. I'm okay. Besides, someone might see."

"No one will mind." He swallowed the urge to laugh. He didn't give a damn who saw them, but to her the concern was real, and he'd respect her. "Besides, we're supposed to be engaged." He stood and held his arms out wide.

He half-expected her to refuse, but when she turned and walked into his arms, it was better than winning a global distribution contract. He breathed in her sweet-smelling floral perfume while her body heat soaked into him. Tightening his arms around her, he gave her an extra squeeze when she rested her head on his shoulder. They stood for a moment before she pulled away.

He let her go, for no reason other than he wanted her to trust him. He wanted her to understand that this, right now, was no longer a game. Not to him. Other than his family, she was the first person who'd ever helped him simply because she could, and she wanted to. She helped out of kindness and loyalty, never expecting a bonus, a contract, or any other type of reward.

He wanted to show her his gratitude and respect, but she made it damn hard.

Right now, though, he toyed with the idea of backing her up against the railing to show her what belonging meant.

He put his hands in his pockets as she gazed out to the horizon. "I hear what you're saying. Family is important to me, and I should carve out more time to be with them."

"Most people don't understand what they have until it's gone. I lost my brother to a roadside bomb in Afghanistan. Less than a year later, my mom was diagnosed with stage-four breast cancer, and eventually I lost her too. My dad left when I was three. As for my relatives, I have pictures, but that's all. I wouldn't recognize them if they walked by me on the street. If it wasn't for your family, I wouldn't have anywhere to go for Christmas. I would be alone." She shivered, rubbing her bare arms as goosebumps raced across them.

He took off his jacket and tucked the coat around her shoulders. "I can't imagine what that feels like."

"Every time I see you and Kayla having a sibling moment, I can't stop my mind from traveling back to high school." She stifled a short laugh. "My brother and I fought over the littlest things. The last cookie, folding laundry, what TV show to watch. I would give anything to have him here with me. Just when I thought I'd be alone forever, I met the most extroverted, carefree soul to ever walk the earth my freshman year at Yale. Kayla's my heart sister. She's one of the best things to ever happen to me. She was my saving miracle. And your family has been so kind and generous to me. For that, I am forever grateful." Tears glittered in her eyes and she swiped them away.

His gut clenched. "Kayla never told me about your brother or your mom." He cuddled her closer.

"No, she wouldn't. She knows I don't like talking about the past." Devon swiped again at the tears threatening to roll down her cheeks. "My brother's the reason I studied bioengineering and worked hard to get an academic scholarship to Yale. I want to help wounded soldiers."

"You wanted to turn your hurt into passion," Mike said.

"Exactly. It turns out I'm a pretty good engineer." There was the feisty attitude he had come to adore. "But I, unlike you, have a work-life balance."

"You're beginning to sound like Kayla."

"Good. Maybe with both of us saying the same things, you'll listen."

Mike liked how the wind whipped tendrils of hair around her face in circles. He was glad he got to glimpse this intimate, tender layer Devon kept so well hidden, and even more pleased because she let him in. But something told him that, while Devon was a complex puzzle he'd like to solve, there were no surprises, and he could take his time, like a lifetime, to put all the pieces in place. "May I ask you a personal question?"

"Sure."

"Why aren't you married yet? Or at a minimum have a serious boyfriend?" He shrugged. "I'm not asking to be rude. I just want to know why."

"I'm holding out for my ideal guy."

Curiosity got the better of him. "What's he like?"

"Well, I want a guy who is smart, caring, business-minded, passionate, handsome, and a splendid cook, possibly one who specializes in Indian curries."

Wait. Had she read the last article printed about him that mentioned his love for Indian food? Her beguiling expression hinted at the answer.

"Hmmm. I didn't hear you say drives fast cars, owns a boat, or has won the lottery."

"You must have missed it, because in my mind a passionate, business-minded guy who knows what he wants in life has the potential to be anything he sets his mind to. I'd rather marry a guy who's focused on solving the world's problems than someone who's comfortable just spending his father's money."

"Is that right?" He leaned in again to get a whiff of her sensual fragrance. This woman was addictive. He glanced over his shoulder. "Kayla and Brandon will be opening presents for hours. How about we take a short walk? If we go back in there, Kayla might see you've been crying and assume I had something to do with it." He grinned to make sure she understood he was teasing.

"A protective Mike Lewis. Who knew?"

"Shhh." He leaned in closer. "Don't tell anyone. It's a secret."

And he hoped she wouldn't tell anyone, because he'd never lent women his suit jacket, or soothed them when they were upset, or taken them for walks on the beach so their friends wouldn't find out they were upset.

His lifestyle didn't normally allow the time, but he would make the time for Devon.

Always.

8

"Get some rest, Kayla." Devon hugged Kayla and then handed her the key to her hotel suite, the one Kayla had sworn she would lose if Devon didn't keep it for her. "You've got a big day tomorrow."

"Hey." Kayla tugged on her arm before she could leave. "Where did you go tonight? I looked for you, but you disappeared."

"You know I'm not one for big parties."

"Jessica said she thought she saw you with Mike. Is everything okay between you two? Maybe I shouldn't have forced you to share a room, but you've had a crush on Mike forever, and if you don't take action now, you might miss your chance and always wonder 'what if?'"

"Wait." She swallowed air too quickly and choked. "You already knew about my crush on Mike?"

"Well, duh. I wouldn't be a very good friend if I didn't know. I've had this secret dream that you would marry Mike and then we could be real sisters, but I never wanted to put an expectation like that on you. It wouldn't be fair. Besides, my brother can be an idiot sometimes."

Chapter 8

That he can, Devon thought. But, wow, she'd never seen Kayla as a matchmaker. That was a new one.

"Let me know if staying with Mike becomes a problem. I'll figure out something else," Kayla assured her. "If Nicole and Lauren weren't sleeping on my pull-out and I didn't sprawl, I'd have you stay with me. I could ask Jessica if you could stay with her."

"Jessica, the one who has her own room because she snores? No, thanks." Devon shuddered off the bad suggestion. "Stop your worrying. You're getting married tomorrow."

"I love you, Devy. Let me know about Mike, and thanks for making tonight a success," Kayla reached for the door handle. "See you bright and early in the morning."

"Whatever you need, Kay-K. I'll be here for you."

The door to Kayla's room closed with a click as Devon made her way to Mike's suite. It was a good thing the rooms weren't too far apart, because she'd be running back and forth a lot the next day. Three women getting ready in one bathroom was bad enough. Four was impossible.

As she neared Mike's room, the door opened. "I was just coming to look for you."

"I wanted to make sure Kayla got back to her room okay."

"And what about you?" He guided her into the room. "Do you want me to run you a bath? You look tired."

"Exhausted, you mean. No, I took a shower earlier. I think I'll just crash."

She dropped her clutch next to her computer bag and slid out of her shoes. If she'd been staying alone she might have left them there, but this was Mike's room, and he was Mr. Neat. She dug out her pajamas and toothbrush and staggered toward the bathroom, completing her before-bed routine in record time to allow Mike access to the bathroom.

When she got to the couch, the thought of removing all the

cushions and unfolding the bed was just too overwhelming. But she did lie down for a quick rest, though, promising herself she'd get up in a few minutes and make the bed properly.

She awoke sometime later to see Mike draping a blanket over her.

"I didn't mean to wake you. You should sleep on the bed. It'll be more comfortable."

Waking up to find Mike in nothing but boxer shorts was a not-to-miss fantasy. She wanted to catch every second of the feature. "I'm fine." She curled her legs up to her chest, making room for him to sit down if he wanted.

"Why aren't you asleep?" she asked as he made himself comfortable. She hesitated before throwing the end of the extra blanket over him. She'd been enjoying the view, but as soon as she saw the goosebumps on his arms, practicality won the day. Kayla would never forgive her if Mike got sick and missed her wedding.

"My mind keeps coming up with things I should check on before my project launch." He pulled her left foot into his lap and started rubbing the aching muscles. "You've got knots in your feet."

"You try wearing three-inch heels for hours, and we'll see if your feet don't get knots."

"No, thanks."

She looked up to find Mike staring at her. For the first time since she met him, he seemed to be seeing her, not looking around or over or through her. Her stomach fluttered.

"I was list-building in my sleep as well. My mind is busy trying to think of potential disasters that I should take care of before Kayla's wedding. What's really keeping you up?" she asked, just to break the growing silence.

"Guilt."

She sat up straighter. "Guilt? What kind of guilt?"

"There's a king-sized bed over there, with nice fluffy blankets, and you're over here, freezing and half-falling off the couch. You would be more comfortable on the bed."

"Meaning you'd feel less guilty if I slept over there."

"Okay, yes, problem-solver. I would feel less guilty if you were to sleep over there. So are you going to solve my problem?"

"Ask me nicely," she teased. "C'mon, you can do it. You can ask for help. Just this once. I won't tell anyone. Repeat after me... Devon..."

He glared at her.

"Let's try again. Devon..." She beckoned with her hands.

"Devon," he said.

"...would you please..." She circled her hand again.

"...would you please?" He stood and looked down at her.

"Share my bed with me."

He never responded, because he reached down and picked her up, blanket and all.

She squealed with laughter. "What are you doing?"

"What does it look like I'm doing? I'm helping you solve a problem."

"Mike. Put me down." She wiggled and pushed, but his grip was too strong. After a few seconds, she relaxed against his shoulder. "You are one stubborn-ass man, you know that?"

"You call me stubborn, but isn't that like the yam calling the sweet potato starchy?" He gave her the what-for look. "You will be more comfortable here. Happy?"

"Very." She pushed back against the headboard. "Now tell me about why you can't sleep."

"I'm worried about the *next* project launch. My offshore investors are threatening to pull out of the project if it doesn't go well."

"Can they do that? I mean, aren't there some sort of contracts in place?" Devon moved over an inch or two to let Mike settle in next to her.

"There are contracts, but that won't stop them. They know a lawsuit can get tied up in court for years."

"This sounds bad."

"Funding for the project is running out, and my lines of credit are about maxed."

"What about your dad?" Devon asked.

"I can't ask dad for money again. He's already a silent investor."

"If it were me, I'd focus on figuring out why the investors are uncomfortable and ease their fears. Something must be giving them heartburn. Find out what it is, and you might save the relationship."

"You're right. Having a successful launch will be the first step, and thanks to you solving my parts problem, I think we just might make the launch date."

Before she could respond, he leaned in to kiss her. She considered pushing him away, but his urgency indicated he needed this, and he seemed to want her.

She opened her mouth and let his tongue caress hers. He moaned, and pressed in. Mike slid his hand up her side and found her already erect nipple. He pinched and teased, rolling the nipple between his fingertips. His kisses became more urgent—almost desperate.

"Devon?" he pleaded.

"Yes, Mike." She eased back and let his hand slide beneath the waistband of her pajama bottoms.

He caressed her skin. She savored his lips.

"Mike," she moaned, as he worked his hand between her thighs.

"Tell me what you want," he urged.

"You," she panted. "I want you. I've wanted you for so long."

She lifted her butt as he slid her pajama bottoms down, and as soon as they were off she pulled her cotton tank over her head and tugged on the elastic band of his boxers.

"Here, let me help."

He rolled onto his back, and as soon as his boxers were gone she pampered his already-erect cock and then kissed the head.

"Devon." Mike let out a soft moan.

The urgency in his tone sent a thrill down her spine. She continued licking and sucking, giving him pleasure before tucking her knees underneath her. She spied a condom on the side table next to his wallet, reached for the foil packet, tore it open, and slid the plastic skin down his cock. His dark, sensual stare lured her forward. She covered his mouth with hers. She guided his cock into her, opening her legs wider to make room for him, and then rose so she could again bury him deep inside her.

Another moan escaped him. "Devon." Mike reached for her breast. "You are *so* beautiful."

She changed her tempo, easing up to go slower and then faster. He pressed his head into the pillow. She reached over and gently pinched one of his nipples, and as soon as she squeezed, his muscles bunched, just before he rolled her onto her back.

"My turn." He trailed his tongue up the side of her neck, linked his fingers with hers, and held her arms over her head. Excitement reverberated through her. His warm mouth claimed hers.

He kissed like he was the king of foreplay. Tongue, lips, teeth... He devoured. And there wasn't anything gentle about these new kisses—they were all wet heat and lust.

He released her hands and shoved his fingers into her hair. She ran her tongue along the straight white line of his teeth. He moaned and nipped at her lip.

His gaze wandered from her eyes, over her nose, to her chin, and slowly his gaze rolled back up to her eyes. He traced her collarbone with his forefinger and kissed that extra-sensitive notch in the middle. Cool air cascaded over her skin.

He inhaled. "I want you, Devon, like I've wanted nothing else in my life."

He lifted her knees higher so he could push farther into her. His abs flexed. She skimmed her fingertips over his hard chest, determined to trace each curve and mound. Better yet, she'd lick every inch of skin. Before she could fantasize further, he captured her mouth and pinched her nipple, rolling the swollen skin between his fingers as he continued to thrust into her. She gasped, more from surprise than his boldness.

Somewhere in between the kissing, licking and touching she'd found paradise. At the base of her neck, he sucked hard enough to leave a temporary mark, and she shivered as he claimed her. He pulled her closer. The beat of his heart underneath her palm synchronized with hers, awakened a boldness she'd never risked before.

She wanted this. She wanted to stop hiding her feelings. She wanted him to claim her. She arched to meet him.

"Devon," he breathed, nuzzling the side of her neck. "Come for me."

True bone-deep freedom was at her fingertips.

"Fuck me," she said softly, with a hint of I-dare-you thrown in.

Before she finished her command, his mouth descended, claiming her, and erotic sensations sizzled their way to her core. She arched her back, allowing him greater access, winding her fingers into his hair and tugging.

"Tell me you like this." He again reached for a leg and brought her knee up higher, so he could thrust deeper. She opened for him and looked down between their bodies to watch.

"Ohhh!" She breathed out as fireworks flared from her core

to the tips of her fingers and toes, over her scalp and cheeks. "Yes! There." She dropped her head back. "Oh my God. I'm coming!" She convulsed again and again, body, mind and emotions as one. Before she finished, another blaze of excitement rolled from the top of her head to her fingertips and toes.

He continued to pump. Sensing what he needed, she lifted her head and sank her teeth into his shoulder. He stiffened and threw his head back, grunting as his body spasmed before going limp.

He didn't move. She couldn't either. Minutes later he lifted his head.

"Holy shit, woman." He buried his face again in the pillow and rolled off her.

What did that mean? She wasn't sure. She waited for his breathing to even out and for him to say more. And she waited… and waited…and waited. "Mmmm. Mike?"

The only response was his heavy breathing. She peered into his sleeping face and then grabbed the covers and pulled the heavy cotton over them both.

The guy who claimed never to sleep now slept.

9

"I'm getting married today!" Kayla squealed and spun in a circle while Devon shot several pictures. "Let the honeymoon start."

Devon laughed. In some ways Kayla was already married. She'd been there the day Kayla crashed into Brandon while walking across campus. Kayla's face was beet red. Brandon couldn't connect two words together. Devon swore it was love at first sight. The serendipity moment was the universe bringing two precious souls together, each meant to complete the other.

Devon had thought she had found the same when she met Mike, but for ten years the stars never aligned.

"Congrats, Kay-K." Jessica gave her cousin a quick hug.

Kayla radiated pure happiness.

"Hold still." Devon fluffed the white lace of Kayla's veil, letting it fall to her friend's waist. "You probably sneaked into Brandon's room for a rendezvous already, so you need to put out the fire in your panties. You can ride your man later."

Bride and bridesmaids erupted with laughter.

"I did *not* sneak out last night." Kayla jutted her chin.

"That's a first," Devon teased, trying to distract her friend. Devon picked up her selfie stick, calling out, "Group photo!"

The cousins gathered around Kayla.

"Say sexy!" Devon snapped the picture.

"You girls need to hurry." Mrs. L rushed into the room. "The priest has arrived, and most everyone is in the garden area waiting to be seated."

Devon wondered if Mike had gotten up in time. She'd left him sleeping but set the alarm by the side of the bed just in case. She'd been very tempted to crawl back in bed and give him a morning glory but wasn't sure how he felt after last night. And besides, this morning she was doing her best to hide the just-got-laid grin that kept threatening to give her joy away.

"My little baby is grown up." Mrs. L cupped the sides of Kayla's face and gazed into her eyes. "I love you, honey. In less than an hour you will become Mrs. Myers."

Kayla's eyes watered.

"Oh, no, no, no." Devon raced for a pack of tissues.

"No tears." Mrs. L snatched the tissue out of Devon's hand and applied pressure to the corners of Kayla's eyes.

Devon folded Kayla's train over her arm as they had practiced back home. Kayla shuffled in her long, tight-fitting skirt out the door and then, side by side, they walked slowly down the corridor and over the bridge leading to the gardens overlooking the ocean.

The flowers bloomed and the birds sang for Kayla today. The late-morning breeze was perfect—not too much, but enough to keep everyone cool. The florist and photographer met them as they approached the garden gate, where a white carpet had been rolled out and flower petals scattered all along the carpet.

Devon paused next to Mr. Lewis and then released the pile of fabric in her arms to fluff Kayla's train. As Devon accepted her bouquet from Jessica, she caught sight of Mike. His eyes were intimately locked on hers, as if he wanted a repeat of their playtime together, right then.

Then his desire disappeared like a light switch being turned off.

Time sped by, and before she knew it, the bride was standing beside her groom. The wedding was almost over, and that meant so was her fake engagement to Mike. Devon tried to figure out what possible reasons Mike might have to avoid continuing their relationship after the wedding, and mentally listed solutions while she moved mechanically through the often-rehearsed stages and steps.

She held Kayla's bouquet while the bride and groom exchanged vows and cheered while Brandon kissed Kayla. Every few minutes she glanced over at Mike, who sat with a rod-straight back in the front row, left of his mother. Only once did she catch him glancing her way.

"Hello, Earth to Devon! Can I have my bouquet back?" Kayla's voice broke through her reverie as the seated guests jumped to their feet, cheering and applauding.

Devon's hands tingled as she held tight to her bouquet and followed Kayla down the garden path, reliving the memories of how Mike's skin felt, how he responded to her touch, how he smelled of lust and sex.

Mike wasn't her first partner, but he was the best one by far, and would be the one by which all other men were measured from now on. Was it the physical act making her giddy, or the fact that they firmly connected?

She had dreamed for years about the day they might be together, but last night surpassed them all. The entire night was magical. But she feared there might not be another when she saw Mike glance at her, study her for a moment, and then turn away.

An emptiness crowded in, and almost choked off her air. Pressing her hand against her chest, she struggled to breathe.

She didn't hear Kayla running down the path until her friend swung her around. "Time to party!" Kayla hauled her along the pathway leading to the reception hall, chattering away, oblivious to Devon's pain. Devon finally managed to find and don a mask of enthusiasm but would rather have found someplace quiet to have an ugly girl cry.

She tucked away the hurt the same way she had folded away the devastation of her brother's passing to be strong for her mom.

It seemed like an eternity passed—an eternity busy with food, small talk and wedding toasts—before Mike once again appeared. Kayla's dad pulled Devon onto the dance floor to hand her over to Mike. Three heartbeats passed before he took her hand, which set Devon's alarms blaring.

Devon refused to look him in the eye, instead focusing on a center shirt button. His arm tightened around her waist as the slow dance continued.

When the tension became too great, she raised her chin and pumped up her pride. "Why are you avoiding me?"

He wrinkled his forehead. "I'm not."

"Oh, really?"

"Really."

"If it's because we had sex—"

"Lower your voice. My parents are right there."

He turned a few degrees so she could see Mr. and Mrs. L swirling by as they swayed to the tune. They looked so lovely together. Another trickle of envy settled in.

"May I remind you, Mike Lewis, we are both adults, not teenagers sneaking under the high school bleachers to do the wild thing."

"You had sex under the high school bleachers?"

"No." She rolled her eyes. "I was using it as an example to make a point. Never mind. I can see this conversation is not getting us anywhere."

"And where exactly did you want this conversation to lead?"

That was a good question. What *did* she want? She'd have to figure out what she wanted later, because right now Kayla was signaling Devon that it was time to toss the wedding bouquet.

She reluctantly left Mike's arms. "Let's talk later." *Or not.*

10

Mike wandered through the grounds of the hotel. The pre-dawn hours were chilly, but he hardly noticed.

Devon hadn't returned to the room last night. He'd waited up past midnight to talk to her, but she never appeared.

In the far distance, the morning clouds settled into a shape reminding him of a jagged mountain ridge. He walked miles along the sandy beach while his mind churned and he tried to avoid circling images of Devon naked, her head thrown back against the pillow, her mouth open, unable to utter a sound. With each tenth step, another erotic vision returned. The last was of her riding him with her perky breasts bouncing up and down. When the memories of her continued to taunt him, he forced himself to get a grip and headed back to the hotel.

He found himself standing in front of Brandon's hotel room door. He considered asking Kayla if she might be willing to help him figure out what to do with the disjointed feelings he was having, but it was the day after her wedding, and he didn't dare. His mother would never forgive him.

Mike continued down a garden path toward his room. He

pulled out the plastic card and entered. Devon had been there. The smell of her sweet perfume settled and calmed his nerves. When he saw her already-packed luggage, he closed the door behind him and waited to hear the click.

"Devon?" he called, praying she was still there.

"Sorry to intrude." She peeked around the corner. "I was hoping to be out of your way before you got back. A room has come open. I wanted to make sure you got your room back." She leaned over and placed her makeup bag in her backpack.

"Why are you leaving?" Mike demanded.

"That was the arrangement. Our lie would end after the last dance."

"Was it a lie, Devon? Was this, what we shared, a lie?" He shoved his hands in his pockets to make sure he didn't touch her, because right then he wanted to pull her into his arms and prove to her there was something between them.

"From the very first day, you viewed this as a fake engagement, so of course it was a lie to you."

The hurt in her eyes almost gutted him, and he wanted to wipe the pain away.

"This wasn't a game to me, Mike. This was real. My feelings for you are real. And I don't want to play games anymore."

"I need you to stay." He clenched his fists, his mind racing to find the right words. "Please, Devon. Please stay."

"Why?" she asked, the edges of her mouth turning downward. "Because you need me to help you solve a problem at work?"

"No."

"Because you need me to fend off more newspaper reporters?"

"No."

"Then why, Mike? Why do you want me to stay?"

She gazed at him, but he couldn't figure out how to put it into words.

Devon was different. She made him a better person. A better man. She laughed at his flaws but never made him *feel* flawed. She supported him in his work but never demanded more than he could give. And when she lay beneath him, she completely made his mind explode and then go still and quiet in a way he'd never experienced. *She* was more than simple words could express.

"I don't know why. I just do." He shrugged, hoping his answer was enough.

"I came by a little after dawn this morning to talk to you, but you weren't here. Where did you go?"

"I've been walking." He took a few steps closer. "You didn't come back to the room last night."

"No. No one knew where you were. You'd disappeared. Everyone assumed you were working. Kayla went to Brandon's room last night. I used her bed so you wouldn't be disturbed."

"When you didn't come back, I..."

"What? You what, Mike?"

When he didn't answer, she grabbed the handle of her suitcase. "Never mind. Have a good life, Mike Lewis. I hope your product launch goes well."

"Wait, Devon." Mike reached for her arm to stop her. He closed his eyes and swallowed his fear. "Yes. I've been avoiding you, but not for the reasons you might think."

"Then why? I need to know." She clutched the suitcase handle and her knuckles turned white.

"Every time I've gone down this road, it hasn't turned out the way I planned."

"What road, Mike? You're not making any sense."

"I'm in love with you, Devon," he blurted out.

Her mouth fell open, but no sound came out. She pulled her arms inward. "And how is that a bad thing?"

He glanced at her and then sank down on the couch. "The last two times I've felt this way, it turned out my feelings were one-sided. You had a crush on me when you were in college, but you don't really know me. Sure, you've read articles about me, but that's not the true me either. You love the fantasy the media makes me out to be."

"You're wrong, Mike." Devon walked back into the sitting area. "I know you. The real you. When you weren't aware of me, I was watching you. You love to play video games, and you hate to lose. You hate wearing business clothes"—she held up her hand to stop him from speaking—"and I know this because in every press conference or interview you've ever given, you keep pulling at the collar of your shirt. Also, you'd like to have a dog, but you don't adopt one because you feel you wouldn't have time to walk or take care of it."

When he opened his mouth to ask something, she pointed at his phone. "You have a labradoodle as a screensaver." She sank down on the couch beside him. "And I know you're a good man because I've been able to see you through your mom's, dad's, and even Kayla's eyes. She adores you, even if she won't admit it."

He leaned in closer. "Maybe you do know me."

"Yet I still don't understand why me loving you scares you so."

"Because when I love someone, I feel consumed. I can't help it. After last night, I stayed away to get control of my emotions, but I can't. I tried."

"Loving someone doesn't have to be painful. Look at Kayla and Brandon. Look at your parents."

"That's the point. I want what they have. Twice I believed I'd found it. But it turned out the women didn't want me. They wanted my bank account."

Chapter 10

Devon pushed away from the couch and walked over to the desk in the room's corner to rummage through the drawers.

"What are you doing?"

She pulled out a pad of paper and a pen from the drawer. "Found it." She scribbled something on the pad of paper, tore off the top sheet, then walked back and handed it to him.

The precise handwriting had a slight right slant and feminine curls. The note was dated and read, "From this day forth, I will not accept any compensation, in any form, from Mike Lewis that he doesn't freely give. In return, I promise to do everything in my power to make him happy."

Mike choked and his eyes turned glassy.

"I love you, Mike, and I believe you can love me if you would just trust in us. If what's holding you back are fears about whether I love you and not your money, there's your answer." She took his hand in hers. "I'm a smart woman. I don't need your money, because I can—and do—make my own. What I do need is your love."

He squeezed her hand, holding on tight while a thousand different emotions dizzied him as he fought to breathe deeply.

"From the first day you showed up in our room at Yale I've had a crush on you," Devon said.

"And here I was, thinking you were indifferent to my charms." Mike's chuckle died after a few seconds and the room settled into an awkward silence.

"I've never been indifferent. I had a complete fantasy world built around you, but there was only one problem."

"Kayla," they said together.

Devon nudged him. "But now she's married, and I don't think she would mind. She even hinted as much. I know she wants us both to be happy."

"I did promise to never date one of my sister's friends...but that was a long time ago." He smiled. "You know what would make me happy right now?"

"What?"

"You naked in that bed. I want to show you how much I love you."

She pulled back. "Is that so?"

"Yep. Last night was amazing, but I think I can beat it."

She stood and backed away. "Really?" She took another step and kicked off her shoes. After another step she unbuttoned her jeans and rolled them over the curves of her hips. "Then get over here and prove it."

"Devon? I'm out of condoms."

"Your point?" She tugged her shirt over her head. "I love you, and you love me too, but you need time for me to prove I do really know and love you. I get that. I've always believed that if two people truly love each other, they can always work things out."

He expected fear to freeze his feet to the floor, but right now what he wanted was Devon in his bed. He stood and pulled off his shirt. "So you want kids?"

"I've always wanted at least two, maybe more."

11

A shiver rolled up the length of Devon's spine while Mike's warm, wet tongue tangled with hers. With her eyes half open, she splurged, eating up his attentions while he gripped her shoulders and plunged deep inside her. His eyes darkened with desire.

"I can feel you're almost ready to explode," he whispered against her lips before blanketing her face with kisses.

Mike ran a hand down her bare back, his tongue still dancing with hers. Devon's entire body was electrified, and she arched up to meet his touch.

His mouth came down hard on hers. And she grabbed his ass, pulling him deeper, deeper, while his grip tightened around her shoulders to hold her steady as he pumped hard. She curled her legs around his back and butt and pulled him even closer.

"Mike. I need you, right now," Devon groaned.

"Patience, my dove." He trailed kisses down her neckline, sucking and kissing each spot.

A soft moan escaped, signaling the swell of her orgasm.

He licked and fondled her nipples, attending each one as Devon threaded her fingers into his hair.

"Mike, please?" she begged and spread her legs wider to give him a hint.

Drunk with love, she clawed at his back with love and lust, throwing her head back, her eyes closed. She wanted this man.

"Fuck me," she demanded, as his hips continued to thrust and she fought to regain the breath he'd pounded out of her. Her heart hammered. He pulled out, reached between their sweaty bodies, and plucked at her sweet spot. She bucked against his touch while he kissed his way back down to capture her nipples again. With one hand dancing inside her and the other hand cradling her breast, he was driving her higher, and higher, until she could feel the scream rising from her belly. She was swamped, aware of nothing but him, as their bodies melded together.

Then he paused, trailed kisses from her breasts down to her belly, and then licked his way back up. Oh, he was such a tease.

"I enjoy seeing you squirm," he whispered. "I think you might be ready now."

Devon let out a moan, unable to articulate a response. He entered her again slowly, pushing even deeper.

"Do you like this?" he asked.

"Yes. Oh! Yes!" She blurted out each word between gasping breaths.

He slipped his fingers down to touch her clit, and she twitched, crying out in a half sob of pleasure as he touched delicate, aching flesh with fingers sifting between her golden curls. He changed the angle of his thrusts, and she gasped, a mindless utterance, then shook with orgasmic spasms. He continued rocking her world, taking her higher and higher until he reached his own peak with a groan and a final thrust.

He pulled her against him and rolled them to their sides, both still panting.

"Holy shit," she sighed.

"My thoughts exactly," he mumbled. "Let's take a shower." He patted her butt and rolled out of the bed, heading for the bathroom.

She enjoyed the backside view as her breathing leveled, and the sound of water hitting ceramic tiles echoed from the next room. Easing out of the bed, Devon forced her still-wobbly legs across the soft wool carpet and the tiled bathroom floor, finally swinging the glass door open and stepping into the steamy chamber. Mike gazed at her breasts as he lathered his hands with soap.

Without waiting for him to respond, she gave him a sloppy kiss while she wrapped her hands around his cock and massaged him, reveling in his already reawakening reaction. Breaking the kiss, she smiled at the sight of his erection pressed against her belly. She lowered to the tile bench and pulled his hips closer, tasting him.

A soft moan escaped him while she bobbed her head, driving his cock deeper into her mouth and throat. He turned the shower to a soft rain setting and let the water add to the sexy sensory assault while his moans echoed around the bathroom.

Mike tucked his hands under her arms and lifted her to her feet, turning her to face the wall. With one hand cupping one of her swinging breasts, he parted her thighs, bringing his hard cock to the entrance of her pussy and pushing inside her. She arched her hips back to give him unrestricted access.

"Come for me now, babe," he gritted out as he gave her one last, deep thrust, keeping his cock buried inside her while they both exploded. "I need you."

He kissed her on the neck and then the lips while he cuddled her against him. "Devon, you're *The One*. How could I have been so blind?"

"You're not blind, just absent. It's hard to see someone who lives in Hartford when you live in Philadelphia."

He turned her around to look in her eyes. "And that's going to be a challenge for you, isn't it?"

12

Mike awoke to find Devon still cradled in his arms, her hair spread across his pillow, her hand gripping his arm like she, too, wanted to hold tight and never let him go. He smoothed the hair off her beautiful face as she stirred from sleep.

"How is my morning dove?" He kissed her forehead.

"I think I'm in heaven." She stretched, her toes reaching for the end of the bed before she again snuggled up against him.

"I can relate to that." Mike drew circles on her shoulder with his finger while he thought some more. "I've been thinking."

"Oh, no. I don't like the sound of that. What have you been thinking?"

"I need someone like you, someone who can problem-solve and spot issues before they become problems." He rested his hand on her hip.

"Someone like me." She rolled onto her back.

"Come work with me, Devon." He took her hand and held it against his chest. "Let's put our efforts together and help others live a better life."

"Let me get this straight. You want me to quit my job, move to Philadelphia, and work for you?"

"Not *for* me, *with* me. There's a big difference."

She curled her arms into her chest and tucked her hands underneath her chin. "That is not a good idea."

"Why not?" He kissed her hair and pulled her closer.

She didn't pull away. "Because what if you change your mind about us?"

"I won't," he said.

She tensed under his hand. "If not for your sister's wedding and my fast problem-solving abilities, we might not even be together," she teased. "Admit it...just yesterday you had misgivings about this relationship."

"True, but now I realize we're just wasting time, and I don't want to waste any more. I want to be with you, Devon. Let's work together to build something amazing."

Her eyes sparked. "Does building something amazing include building a family?"

"If you're asking if I will support you and our child, the answer is yes." Excitement surged through him. "You're very important to me, Devon. I would love any child of ours."

She snuggled deeper into his arms, throwing a leg over his hip. "Do you think your parents are going to be okay with us being together?"

"Why wouldn't they be?"

"Being Kayla's friend is one thing. Becoming a family member is a completely different story."

He understood she might have insecurities stemming from her single-mother upbringing and his family's lavish lifestyle, but his parents wouldn't see Devon as anything else other than the kind, generous, smart, gorgeous woman she was. He wasn't worried about others' pettiness, and neither should she be.

"Plus, I don't know about you giving me a job." Her tone was calm, but that calm was what bothered him.

"Please don't talk yourself out of moving to Philadelphia. It's a nice place to live with plenty of museums, arts fairs, and it's just a train ride to New York. We can catch some shows."

"Maybe I should keep my job, earn my own way. I wouldn't want you to second-guess the reason I took a job at your company."

"But my company needs talented people like you," he added with a thrust of hope. If she decided to keep her Hartford job, he feared the distance between them might cause issues.

He needed to act fast.

"Tell you what. There's an innovation engineering role my vice president of operations just created. And trust me when I say it's a juicy offer. The person who gets the job will work with a team of engineers who will have access to all the latest technology and get to create the next best thing on the market. I won't have anything to do with the hiring. The VP of engineering is brilliant, and she only hires the best." He touched her nose to get her attention. "And you, my dove, are the best."

"Even if I got the job, there's another problem."

"What's that?"

"I have an unbreakable rule. I don't date people I work with. It just leads to problems."

"But you're a problem-solver. I'm sure we can come up with a compromise."

She buried her face against his chest, and he couldn't see her eyes. He tightened his grip around her shoulder.

"You are an intriguing woman. You know that, right?" He nudged her head closer with his arm so he could feel her lips on his skin.

"Intriguing? How?" She tilted her head back, her wide eyes glinting in the light.

"There are women who would jump at this offer. The position comes with status and a nice salary, but I get the impression you would turn the job down just so we can continue dating."

"I told you the truth when I admitted to loving you. I have secretly loved you for a very long time, Mike. You and your family are more important than any job." She looked away. "I'm tired of struggling alone. If two people are truly together, there's nothing they can't accomplish."

"You wouldn't be working for me directly. Managers dating direct-report employees is prohibited. I am not excluded from those rules."

She pushed out of his arms and sat up. "See? Even your human resource team agrees with me. Dating at work is not a good idea. I appreciate the intention, but the solution is flawed." She shrugged, and tears welled in her eyes.

"However."

She turned to look at him, waiting.

"There is one more option." He tugged her tighter against him.

"Which is?" She wiped her nose with the edge of the sheet.

"There's nothing that says a husband and wife can't work together."

Her hand flew to her chest. "Are you... Are you asking me to marry you?"

"There is one way we both can get what we want." He lifted a strand of her hair to wrap it around his finger. "Marry me. You already gave me what is essentially a signed prenup, but I have a feeling you and I won't need a legal agreement."

"When I signed that piece of paper, I meant every word. The only things I want from you, Mike Lewis, are your love and your children. Anything else is just a cherry on top." She leaned closer. "But don't play games."

"Who's playing? You're the perfect woman for me, Devon Gaines. Become my wife. Let's build a life together."

"Then if your offer is real, my answer is yes." She kissed him. "Yes. Yes. Yes."

"I love you, Devon." He rolled her onto her back to make sure she could see the love in his eyes. "You are the woman made for me, but I've been too blind to notice. You were right here all this time. Marry me, Devon. Complete me. Help me find balance in my life."

"I can't..." she whispered, as the tears streamed down her cheeks.

"Why not?" The hurt almost gutted him.

"You didn't let me finish." She giggled and threw her arms around his shoulders. "I can't believe you asked me to marry you. I couldn't love you any more right now if I tried. When do you want to get married?"

"How about tomorrow? Most of my family is here for another couple of days."

"Tomorrow? Really?" She kissed him hard.

"I don't see why not. And it'll happen so fast, even the paparazzi will be caught off guard. It will just be us and family."

"I like the sound of that." She slid a hand down the side of his face. "I love you, Mike Lewis. I hope you hear me this time, because I've been saying it for a long time. You just haven't noticed."

"You have?"

"Who do you think nominated your company for the World Tech Awards? Or sent your lead design engineer notes about how to solve a connectivity problem? I've been helping you solve problems for years. You just never knew it."

Mike's heart swelled with adoration and surprise. Could this woman be any more awesome? "What did I ever do to deserve your love?"

She shrugged. "You decided to change the world. Who couldn't love a man like that?"

JAMAICAN PLANTER'S PUNCH

2 ounces light rum
1 ounce fresh lemon juice
Splash of orange juice
Ice

Place all ingredients in a cocktail shaker. Shake well. Strain into a chilled glass and garnish with a lemon wedge, if desired.

ABOUT THE AUTHOR

A healing love is at the heart of all of award-winning author Lyz Kelley's books. She mixes a spoonful of heart, healing, humanity, happiness, hope and honor in these small-town stories written especially for you. Creating these wounded yet amazing characters—discovering what drives them, frightens them, heals them, makes them laugh—is what gives her joy.

She's a total disaster in the kitchen, a compulsive neat freak, a tea snob, adores her four-legged fur babies, and adores writing about and falling in love with everyday heroes

To keep tabs on Lyz's newest releases, connect with her by signing up for her newsletter at LyzKelley.com or by signing up at, https://geni.us/LyzKelleyFreeBook

CPSIA information can be obtained
at www.ICGtesting.com
Printed in the USA
JSHW022059160521
14835JS00001B/5